GREEN FEES

GREEN FEES

TEXAS LADY LAWYER VS BROWNO ZARS

MANNING WOLFE

STARPATH BOOKS, LLC

Starpath Books, LLC
Austin, TX
www.starpathbooks.com

Library of Congress Cataloging-in Publication Data:

Paperback: ISBN-13: 978-1-944225-08-7
Ebook: ISBN-13: 978-1-944225-09-4
LCN: 2018906469.

Manufactured in the United States of America
10 9 8 7 6 5 4 3 2 1

For Jean Springer

Golf is a good walk spoiled.

Mark Twain

Prologue

My name is Merit Bridges. I'm a lawyer in Austin, Texas, and I'm hanging on a meat hook.

I don't know who hoisted me up here, but I intend to find out. My eyes are covered with some type of fabric tied around my head and I'm in a place that smells like rotted wood and dried blood. I hope that's not my blood. I feel a cut or a gouge on the back of my head, but I don't feel anything dripping from it. It hurts. A lot.

I haven't heard a voice yet, as I was unconscious when I was brought here and hung up. So far, I haven't heard any people in the room. No doors or windows have opened or closed.

My legs and knees are weak, and my arms feel like they are pulling out of the sockets. I'm not wearing any shoes and my feet are touching something dirty and coarse.

I'm trying to stay calm and use my mind to hold off panic, but the headache is winning the battle. I've been mentally sorting through my legal cases since I came to and trying to figure out if there's a crazy client or adversary involved. I remember a case from last year when I went up against a huge billboard corporation. They sent a crazy landman named Boots King to clean my clock, but he's dead.

A client was recently murdered, but I have nothing left to do with that case. The mortgage company took the property in foreclosure. They'd have nothing further to gain and it's a reputable corporation as far as I know.

I'm also considering a new file I'm currently working on involving a Russian loan shark. He's shady, but I don't think he's after me. What would be his motive?

There's also a file I just completed against a nutso music producer, L.A. Baron. Baron's crazy enough to do this, but as far as I know, he's still in the Texas State Lunatic Asylum now know as Austin State Hospital.

I keep passing out and I can't think straight for extended periods of time. I have no way to do research or enlist the help of my staff. Surely they are looking for me by now. Betty will be worried when I don't show up for work, or maybe I already missed work and she's sent Ag, my friend and investigator or Chaplain, a detective at APD, to find me. I have no idea what day it is or whether it is morning or night.

I miss Tony, my husband. He could help me, but he's dead. Sat in our back yard in a lawn chair and shot himself in the head. I'll never forgive him, and I love him at the same time. Is that possible? Tears come when I remember it. I can't think about that right now.

I'm terrified for Ace, my son. He's in Houston in a boarding school for children with learning disabilities. I didn't want him to go, but he insisted. His reasoning was good, there's no school here in Austin with the expertise of that school when it comes to dyslexia. He has to live away, and I don't see him for weeks at a time. He's the light of my life. I hope he's safe. Please be safe. I hope that Betty or Ag or someone else in my office has sent a guard down to protect him. I have to assume they have or I couldn't bear this.

And dear Betty, is she safe?

Since I'm trapped here, I hope that whoever's behind this won't go after the people I love.

My mind is wandering, grabbing onto bits of my life, then blurring, then sleep.

My arms ache, my head burns, my whole body is trembling with the effort of standing for so long. I can hang by my arms for a few minutes, then I have to put weight back on my feet.

I think I hear footsteps. Am I imagining things? A door is opening. Oh God, give me strength.

Chapter 1

NINE MONTHS EARLIER...

Merit Lady Echo Bridges stood outside the Travis County Courthouse in Austin, Texas before a bevy of reporters. Once again Merit's high-profile client and real estate developer, Terrence Long was in the news and in trouble. Merit had just filed an injunction to stave off foreclosure of Mr. Long's Hill Country Homestead, his planned unit development in West Austin.

Merit had lost.

A dozen microphones were thrust into Merit's face. In front was a sexy redheaded reporter wearing a mini-skirt and tight sweater.

"Ms. Bridges, Red Thallon, KNEW 9. How does your client intend to pay his multi- million-dollar bill on this project?" Red asked.

"Ms. Thallon, I cannot reveal my client's confidential information, but I assure you a plan is in place and he will be able to refinance the loan on the project before foreclosure day," Merit said.

"Mr. Long," Red pivoted, "What is your plan to bail out your development?"

Long started to respond, then pursed his lips and held his tongue.

"That's all at this time," Merit said.

Merit pushed through the crowd with her client in tow who had been admonished not to say a word. They brushed past Red and Merit winked at her.

"Drinks. Thursday?" Red asked.

Merit nodded but kept a serious look on her face for the cameras and her client.

∞

Later that day, Merit sat at her desk in the Law Office of Merit Bridges reading legal cases from a book thick enough to be a door stop. She absentmindedly twirled her blond ponytail and tapped her foot in her designer pumps. Black and white photographs of bridges hung on two walls. Occasionally her eye wandered from the photographs to the view out the window of Lady Bird Lake and downtown Austin. A fourth wall held shelves of books with titles referring to finance and banking, Texas property rights, contracts, and corporations.

In front of her desk were two black leather guest chairs. Over the years, many clients had sat in those chairs sharing their secrets, fears and transgressions. Merit didn't have the power to pardon or forgive their sins, but she certainly had the burden of hearing about them. Sometimes it was an honor and more often lately it was a duty. She was restless, bored and tired of pushing paper. Merit yawned.

I need a challenge.

Betty, Merit's office manager, entered the door in an ill-fitting baby blue business suit. She had on chunky orthopedic heels and thick stockings. Her hair was teased and sprayed in an Ann Richards style gray football helmet.

When Merit had made the move from a large firm to a solo practice years ago, Betty had come along. Now, Betty managed the office and sometimes Merit's personal life, whether Merit liked it or not, although she usually liked it. Betty had hired most of the staff and kept them all on a short leash. It took a lot of pressure off Merit, giving her time for more billable hours, and a private life. They were a good team, like family.

"Hey. What's all that?" Merit asked.

Betty carried a stack of files that she put on top of Merit's already full *IN* basket.

"Client correspondence. Falling a little behind, aren't we?" Betty asked.

"I don't have to do mundane tasks, I'm a celebrity now. Didn't you see me on the news this morning?" Merit asked.

"Yes, I did, and we still have other clients. I'm heading home. Everyone else is already gone," Betty said as she tucked a stray hair back into her Aqua Net dome and gave it a bump.

"Party Pooper," Merit said.

"That's me. There's a letter in each of these files that needs to go out tomorrow. All routine. Sign them before you go, please."

"Yes, ma'am," Merit said.

"You have an appointment with Ag first thing in the morning. Don't be late," Betty said.

"Am I ever late?" Merit asked.

Ag Malone had been Merit's investigator for several years. They had a running joke about her being a Longhorn and him being an Aggie.

Betty looked at her. "I see you're bored. Don't start trouble just to make the drama junky happy."

"I'm not a drama junky. Besides, I have you to keep things on track," Merit said.

"I've been getting the sense that we're about to have some trouble again," Betty said.

"Of course we're not," Merit said. But then her armpits prickled, and she jerked from the electricity. Her eyes met Betty's.

"Oh no! Shit fire in a hurricane," Betty said as she took a step back.

Chapter Two

A faint coral glow signaled the sunrise as Mark Green sped along Interstate 35 in his Jeep Wrangler past the Austin City Limits sign. A sticker showed through the dirt on the bumper: TEXAS OR BUST. A small orange and white U-Haul trailed behind the Jeep.

The top of the Wrangler was open to the sweet morning air. Mark wore only a baseball cap and a pair of Levi's jeans. Not one hair grew on his tan chest. On his hat was printed *Ping*. His scarred and gnarled hands wrapped tightly around the steering wheel. On the radio, Willie Nelson sang "Whiskey River" as the ignition keys swung back and forth in time with the music. Attached to the key ring was a medallion engraved *golfboy*.

As Mark drove across the Colorado River, he saw the downtown skyline with the granite capitol anchoring the center of the city. He'd driven all night.

Mark's lopsided grin lit up his face. *Home of Ben Crenshaw!*

Mark exited on Martin Luther King Boulevard and noticed the University of Texas Tower lit burnt orange. He'd read about the lights being turned on when one of the school teams won an important game.

Must be football, Mark thought.

Mark's online search had revealed that there were over a hundred thousand students in Austin. He wondered how many of them played golf. He'd heard UT had a pretty good golf team. Maybe he could meet them. He'd need new friends. His mother had sent him an e-clipping ranking Austin as one of the top three places for young singles in the U.S. He might even meet a girl.

Mark cut across town on Loop 1 and over to the apartment he'd rented on his flight down a few weeks earlier. He'd been in Austin only that one time for the job interview that had landed him his new position at Austin Creek Country Club, or ACCC for short. He wondered if everyone would talk as twangy as his new boss, Bob Tom Jakes. Mark had actually been surprised at the job offer. He was sure that Bob Tom hadn't liked him during the interview. No matter, Mark had accepted the job, rented the apartment, and moved. All within three weeks. It was a big step and he hadn't done a lot of planning about what would happen next. He wasn't worried, though. Things always worked out in the end.

The family farm was so distant in his rear-view mirror he could scarcely feel it. The thread that held him to his family was connected to his mother, but not to Check, his father. It wasn't only Mark who had disappointed Check. The farm had fallen further and further behind each year, and age was limiting Check's ability to make headway toward course correction. The fact that Mark wanted to pursue his own interests was perceived by Check as a betrayal. Check became more brittle every year until he was so dry his bones popped when he stood up.

For Mark, that was all in the past. The terrible tournament was in the past and Check's disapproval was in the past. The excitement Mark felt as he drove across his new hometown flushed his cheeks. It was good to finally be on his own: a new job, a new state, a new life. With a fresh start, anything was possible.

He whistled along as he drove, Willie sang on, and the city drew nearer.

Chapter Three

Merit and her client Terrence Long sat in her conference room with laptop computers and boxes of files opened before them. A large plat map of Long's Hill Country Homestead was unrolled and anchored on the table with coffee cups on each corner. Long stood up, paced, and revealed his six feet and three-inch height beneath a full head of dark hair.

"We can reconfigure the loan with the bank, but you have to buy down the full interest. If you can do that, I think I can get them to wait on the principle until the next payment date. These bridge loans for construction are tricky," Merit said.

"I know. You warned me not to set up the financing this way. Too late. Exactly how much do I need?" Long asked.

"One hundred eighty-three thousand dollars and change," Merit said.

"Whew," Long whistled. "Talk about a bind. I just don't have it."

"There's nothing else in your portfolio of real estate that we can sell quickly enough to cover it. And, it's all been cross-collateralized, so the bank probably won't release it anyway," Merit said.

"Agree," Long said.

"Any other loose change in your piggy bank?" Merit asked.

"Not much. A few stocks and bonds. I put everything I had into the development," Long said.

"Think it over and let me know what you want to do. I can go to the bank again, but not without something to offer them in exchange for more time," Merit said. "If we can't pay something, they will foreclose."

"I'm pretty much tapped out. Borrowing money right now would cost me an arm and a leg," Long said.

Chapter Four

After her client left, Merit returned to her office, closed out the work files on her computer, and opened Facebook. She checked her timeline, liked a few posts from friends, and shared a picture of Jordan Spieth and Ben Crenshaw holding up a Hook 'em Horns sign.

She had just switched the clocks to standard time from daylight savings time. It was the season in Austin when crisp fall days gave relief from summer heat and golfers competed for tee times.

Merit wanted to get more serious about her golf game. She was also itching for a fling. Since becoming a widow, she'd been seeing only younger men and enjoying it immensely, but quietly. It wasn't the smartest thing to do, but it appealed to her, called to her. It didn't allow her to get too involved, and it provided a healthy sex life for which she had a profound appetite. Betty jokingly warned Merit that she needed therapy. Merit called it owning her sex life.

No therapy for me this week. Maybe some foibles are worth keeping.

She especially kept it quiet from clients, but Betty always seemed to catch onto her latest dalliance.

How does she do that? Merit thought.

Merit opened her favorite social media site and plugged in the key words: single, male, golf, Austin. Up popped Mark Green, a/k/a golfboy, wearing an Austin Creek Country Club golf cap, holding a driver and grinning like a kid on his birthday.

"Great smile!"

Merit sent him a friend request and continued her search. A message came through notifying her that Mark Green had accepted her invitation.

He must be online, Merit thought.

She checked his picture and a green dot by his face indicated he was active.

Merit sent him a personal message.

ladylawyer: Want to play a round of golf?

No response from golfboy. Merit tried again.

ladylawyer: Probably afraid to get beaten by a girl.

golfboy: Not hardly. Do I know you?

"Gotcha," Merit said to his picture on the screen.

ladylawyer: You might like to know me.

golfboy: Are you a member of the club?

Country club? Sex club? What club? Merit wondered.

ladylawyer: No, I just wanted to chat with a fellow golfer. Have a minute?

golfboy: Sure.

ladylawyer: Where do you play?

golfboy: Mostly ACCC, where I work.

ladylawyer: Do you work in the pro shop?

golfboy: Yes. I give lessons.

ladylawyer: A golf pro?

golfboy: Right. Just moved to Austin.

I hit the jackpot on this one.

ladylawyer: Want to give me some lessons, golfboy?

golfboy: Sure, where do you play?

ladylawyer: I'm not a member anywhere. I'm thinking of joining a club if I get better at the game.

golfboy: Before you decide, take a look at Austin Creek's website. We have a great round robin tournament for women.

ladylawyer: I'll check it out. Maybe I'll check you out.

golfboy: Are you flirting with me?

ladylawyer: Yes.

golfboy: Cool. What do you look like?

ladylawyer: Tall, blonde shoulder-length hair, green eyes, curvy, long legs.

golfboy: You sound nice.

ladylawyer: And you?

golfboy: Tall, short blond hair, brown eyes, athletic, long legs. lol

ladylawyer: Well, golfboy, you sound nice yourself.

ladylawyer: How old are you?

golfboy: 27

"*Oops*," Merit thought. Her boy toy history had included several younger men, but this one might be too young.

golfboy: Are you there?

ladylawyer: I'm here. I'm a bit old for you, or you're too young for me. lol

golfboy: How old?

ladylawyer: Let's just say thirty-something.

Knocking at forty, she thought.

golfboy: That's not so old. You're younger than my mother.

ladylawyer: Ouch!

They chatted on for a while, but the age difference tempered Merit's interest. Ace, her seventeen-year old son, was in Houston in his junior year of high school.

Yikes!

Merit chatted with golfboy anyway, thinking she'd make him smile and exercise her flirting chops. Maybe later she'd look for someone a bit older to talk to.

What was she doing cruising the Internet like this? Looking for a distraction? Merit had worked hard to get ahead. She was fit and healthy, had a brain in her blond head, and dressed like a Neiman Marcus model. She was written up in Austin's Business News over the years as one of the best attorneys in the city.

Lately, her attitude needed an adjustment. All of her hobbies had fallen away. She hadn't taken a photograph in months. She felt the need to find a new way of being, or thinking, or something. She felt claustrophobic, like a dog that had outgrown her kennel.

Betty stuck her head in the door. "Don't work too late, now. And, don't forget you have a meeting with Leonard Smith tomorrow."

"Who's that again?" Merit asked.

"The one with the mother who works with my fifth cousin twice removed." When Merit's face showed no recognition, Betty added, "You know, the one who cooks brisket at Black's BBQ and could start an argument in an empty house." Both of them grinned.

"Oh, that Leonard Smith. He's selling some land, right?" Merit asked.

Betty nodded and took her leave. Merit thought about following her out. But her condo was empty; Ace was at school and no one was waiting for her.

Something in golfboy's style made her decide to continue chatting with him. It brought back a nostalgia that reminded her of the days of her grandmother and Elvis songs and gardening and shopping on main streets. She had warmed to him immediately. It was like he was already an old friend.

Chapter Five

M ark entered the side door of Austin Creek Country Club and punched his time card. He waved to his co-worker Joe who manned the reception desk, then moved down the hall of offices to the staff locker room.

"Good morning, Bob Tom," Mark said to the course manager as he passed.

"Uh," Bob Tom grunted at him but kept his head in his paperwork. Bob Tom was a scruffy looking turkey with a big belly and slightly floppy neck. He said little, often made noises instead of verbal responses, and never gossiped.

Mark pulled his lesson assignments from a clipboard on the back wall behind a long row of damaged clubs waiting for repair. He checked the schedule, went outside and loaded his clubs on the cart, went back inside to the cafe and got a commercial-sized thermos of water and a stack of paper cups.

Browno Zars sat at the last booth in the cafe, his usual, sipping black sugary coffee and looking at the racing news while he kept tabs on the Golf Network playing on the wall-mounted TV. He occasionally took a nip from a flask he carried in his pocket. His bulk filled the entire booth and his knees almost touched the seat across from him under the table.

"Morning, Mark," Browno "Hello, Mr. Zars. Any luck?"

"*Neudacha*, the ponies have not been good to me," Browno gurgled in his deep Russian accent.

"Too bad," Mark said.

"Maybe I do better at golf today," Browno said.

"Have you been working on your swing like I showed you?" Mark asked.

"Sure. Getting better every game. Are you getting settled in?" Browno asked. With his Russian background, it sounded more like '*Ah ew gat ting set elled een*'.

"Pretty much," Mark said. He looked down at his shoes.

"What is problem? Your girlfriend smash your heart?"

"I wish. I don't have a girlfriend. What I have is a bag full of bills to pay. Moving down here was not as economical as I thought. Austin is an expensive place to live compared to the Midwest," Mark said.

"It sure is. But cheaper still than New York," Browno said.

"Is that where you're from?" Mark asked.

"Brighton Beach. Let's not talk about old days. I could loan you some money," Browno said.

"No, it's okay. I shouldn't have said anything. Just feeling sorry for myself. It'll turn around soon," Mark said.

"I see. I see. I've loaned money to lots of folks. It's part of my business. We should talk," Browno said.

"Nah. Thanks. I'll manage," Mark said, even though he didn't have a plan at all and the bills were mounting fast. He was behind on his Jeep note and his rent was coming due. He'd never had to worry about money before, but if he worked hard, he knew everything would turn out all right. It had to.

∞

Mark stopped at his favorite coffee shop on the way to work and settled into a booth. He opened several apps and skimmed a few of the sports stories while he drank his coffee. The season was shaping up about the way everyone thought it would. Jordan Spieth was holding near the top and Rory McIlroy was climbing the ranks. Tiger Woods was still trying to make a comeback.

Mark checked to see if Merit was online and was disappointed that her green dot wasn't lit.

"Shit," he swore under his breath as he looked up and noticed the clock; he'd been there a lot longer than he'd realized.

He scrambled to his feet and headed for the door just in time to see his Jeep being towed away.

"Aw, man."

It was the last straw. His resources were dwindling and now he had to bail out his ride.

He just couldn't seem to get ahead.

∞

The next day, Mark caught up to Browno at the driving range. Several golfers were lined up in a row, all with buckets of balls at their feet.

Browno whacked away at his allotment of balls like a baseball batter, pausing occasionally to curse in Russian.

"Dermo!"

"Straighten up your stance and try a few more. Don't bend your elbow," Mark said.

Browno hit a few more and paused for a drink from his flask.

"Better, but you're still swatting the ball." Mark said.

Browno offered Mark the silver container.

"No thanks. I'm driving," Mark said.

Browno stalled for a moment, as if translating the joke in his head, then laughed.

"I get it. You funny guy," Browno said.

After watching Browno whack a few more balls, Mark looked at his watch.

"Lesson's over. Try a few of the things I showed you on your own."

"Will do, big man."

Mark opened his mouth and then closed it. He considered Browno's offer of a loan. He couldn't believe he was so close to being broke. He'd never borrowed a dime in his life; he didn't have any credit or even a credit history. Mr. Zars was a successful businessman and a good tipper. And Mark only needed a small loan. Just this once. Just to tide him over.

"I was thinking. Do you still want to loan me some money?"

Browno showed all his teeth to Mark in a wide smile. "How much we talking about?"

Mark did some mental calculations. Better to ask for a bit more than he needed, just in case. "Just ten thousand. I'll pay you right back."

"Straight up business deal. No *budspok*," Browno said.

"What's *budspok*?" Mark asked.

"Means fooling around. Way Irish say shenanigans."

"Of course. Serious business," Mark said.

"Okay. Meet me in café on Friday at my regular booth. I have cash for you and ticket to sign."

"Like an IOU?"

"Right. Right. IOU."

"Okay. Try another shot. Follow through. See you Friday and thanks," Mark said, waving as he headed back to the clubhouse. Browno waited until Mark was out of sight and then hit the speed dial on his smartphone. "I just promise a little money to kid at country club. Name Mark Green. Check him out and give me report. He seems good for it."

Chapter Six

Merit parked in the garage at her office and gathered her briefcase and handbag from the back seat. She was late to work. She had a full day's schedule and should have gotten in earlier. Her mobile phone rang, and she saw Ace on the caller ID. She pushed the talk icon to take the call.

"Hey, Ace," she said. "You're up early."

"Hi, Mom," she heard him say into the phone.

"Peaches, what's the matter?"

"Mom, I'm having such a hard time with school. It's going so fast. I don't think I can keep up."

"Did you ask for modifications?" Merit asked as she leaned against the car. A car went by and squealed tires on the garage concrete. "Sorry, I'm in the garage."

"Yeah, the teacher gave me some extra time and I've got the books on tape, but the load is just so great. I think I'm going to have to drop a class."

"Oh," Merit said. "It's okay. It will be okay. Maybe a little time off would do you good. We'll go to Port Aransas to the beach house. Take a break. You can pick up an extra course in the Spring with the new semester."

"I think I'll have to," Ace said. "I need to take this class at another time when I have a lighter load."

"Okay, then that's what you'll do. It is okay. We expected some adjustments. We knew you would have to make judgment calls along the way."

"Mom, I feel like such a failure. It's so hard. Why does it have to be so hard?"

"I know, I'm sorry it's hard. Tom Cruise." Merit started their private game.

"Not now, Mom," Ace said.

"Yes, now, Henry Winkler."

"Whoopi Goldberg," Ace answered reluctantly.

"George Washington."

"Orlando Bloom."

"Salma Hayek."

"Robin Williams."

"Feel better?" Merit asked as she walked toward the elevator.

"Not yet," she heard Ace say into the phone.

"Albert Einstein," Merit said.

"Keanu Reeves."

"Jay Leno."

"Cher."

"Charles Schwab."

"Leonardo DaVinci."

"Nolan Ryan," Merit said.

"Okay, I'm good," Ace said.

"All dyslexic, all successful, all had to struggle," Merit said.

"Thanks, Mom."

"You're welcome, Peaches. I love you."

"I'm getting a little old for Peaches," Ace said.

"Never," Merit said.

"Love you, Mom. I'll let you know what the teachers say."

Merit's heart cracked a little more. Each time Ace felt hurt, she took it in and tried to hold it away from him. She knew it would never work, but she had done it so long it was habit.

Merit took off her symbolic Mom hat and put on her lawyer hat then charged into the elevator and on to the legal battle field.

Chapter Seven

Mark woke to the nagging sound of his alarm clock rooster crowing. He had a huge hard on. He liked to think it was huge anyway. He smiled at the thought of ladylawyer flirting with him in cyberspace. Something had changed, but nothing had happened, and yet, it had. He felt it.

He lay from corner to corner across his king-sized mattress on the floor of his apartment. He stretched, causing the fitted sheet to pop from the corner, exposing the bare ticking.

He groaned as he thought of another day with his boss. The job was good, but Bob Tom was a pain in the ass, giving him all kinds of chores unrelated to playing golf. Since he'd been at ACCC, he'd fixed clubs, folded clothes, cleaned golf balls, and a plethora of other tasks, trying to get into Bob Tom's good graces. Mark was hoping he'd get a raise, but not likely with Bob Tom in charge.

But, a day on the golf course pleased Mark like nothing else, and Austin was growing on him. In the short time he'd been in town, he'd started to enjoy the pace. Much more exciting than the farm. Still, he was alone.

Mark got out of bed, stepped over the clothes strewn across the floor, stumbled into a steamy shower, and ducked his head to fit under the nozzle. He scrubbed his hair with shampoo that smelled like grass. He'd received it in a swag bag at some charity golf tournament. He couldn't remember which one.

His apartment was littered with things he'd gotten for free or that were hand me downs. He owned almost nothing that was new.

Mark wiped the steam from a mirror he'd mounted on the shower wall, looked into his chocolate eyes, and shaved his few blond whiskers. Twice a week was about all it took to keep his face scraped clean.

The only comfy chair in his apartment was an overstuffed aqua number from the apartment dumpster, discarded when a UT student had left town after graduation. A dozen sets of golf clubs in various colored bags lined the back wall of his living room. Most of them had been awards from past wins.

He pulled up online news while he waited for the Folgers to brew. The headlines showed that The Enforcer had tortured and killed another victim.

"Why don't they catch this guy?" Mark said.

He sat down in the tiny dining alcove and ate Lucky Charms out of an orange plastic bowl with Longhorn logos on the sides.

I'll just check my email before I head to work. Mark justified his usual dawdling, although he knew he was thinking of ladylawyer and avoiding Bob Tom.

He typed in his password, and her name popped up.

golfboy: Morning, Sunshine. You're up early.

ladylawyer: Hi there. I'm at the office.

golfboy: Can you chat?

ladylawyer: For a minute.

golfboy: I thought of you this morning. I was trying to guess your name. BTW, I'm Mark Green.

ladylawyer: I'm Merit Bridges.

"Merit," Mark said into his coffee cup.

golfboy: How did you get from Merit to ladylawyer?

ladylawyer: Lady is my middle name. One of them. I'm a lawyer.

golfboy: How many names do you have?

ladylawyer: Merit Lady Echo Bridges. Both Grandmother's names.

golfboy: Wow. Lot to live up to.

ladylawyer: They passed away a long time ago. Mother and father too. You?

golfboy: My Mom and Dad are in Wisconsin.

ladylawyer: You're lucky to have them alive.

golfboy: Do you like your work?

ladylawyer: I like the people, and I like the building here. It's close to the courthouse.

golfboy: So, you are a court lawyer.

She sounds smart, how will I keep up with her? Mark thought.

ladylawyer: A little. I do mostly business law, but I have to go to the courthouse and the county offices a lot.

golfboy: That sounds interesting.

Mark pulled on his sneakers as he watched the screen.

ladylawyer: My staff needs me. Have to get to work.

golfboy: I better get to work, too. Will you be on later? Phone number? Text?

There was a long pause then her mobile number appeared on the screen.

"Tah tah for now," Mark said to the screen as he logged off, added the cereal bowl to the pile of dishes in the sink, and scooted out the door.

∞

Mark jumped into his Wrangler.

"Late again. Bob Tom is really going to get me." Mark said.

He drove off, mentally replaying his chat with Merit. *Hmm! It might be worth the ass chewing.*

He cranked up the music, self-talking all the way to work. "I have the best job in the world. I play golf and get paid for it. People would kill for my job. I'm the luckiest man alive." He repeated the mantra over and over.

By the time he arrived at the parking lot of ACCC, he was upbeat and ready to tackle the day.

Time to face the bear.

Chapter Eight

After a hard day's work, Merit got home late and tired. She got into bed and turned on the Longhorn Network to catch up on the latest scores. She propped up on pillows and took in the view of sparkling downtown lights. Surrounded by an aqua silk duvet, she looked like she was sitting in ocean foam surrounded by stars.

She sipped a nice dark red Malbec and stared at the screen. Just as the college scores were announced, the phone rang on the night stand. Merit grabbed it and spilled the wine.

"Hi, lady lawyer," Mark said.

Merit dabbed at the mess with a wad of tissues.

"Hi, there," Merit said. "How are you?"

"Nice voice," Mark said. "A real southern belle?"

"Somewhat," Merit laughed.

There was an awkward moment when neither spoke.

"How do we get to know each other?" Mark asked.

"Just ask a question."

"Okay. Ever been married?" Mark asked.

"Widowed. How about you?"

"No, I've never felt very secure around women. I'm sorry about your husband."

"Thanks. You seem secure to me."

"This is one step removed. If you were here, I might not be so talkative."

"Where did you go to school?"

"University of Wisconsin in River Falls. Was on the golf team there, but I'd been playing since I was five years old."

"Wow, that's a long time for a sport," Merit said.

"Game, not sport. How old is your son?" Mark asked.

"Seventeen. He lives in Houston part of the time at a boarding school for dyslexic students."

"You miss him?"

"Every day. What are you planning to do tomorrow?"

"Run errands, iron clothes. I always do the laundry on Tuesday since I work on Saturday. Saturday was always the day we did chores on the farm."

"A true Midwesterner if I ever heard one. How was work today?"

"Great, I played a good game. I took the afternoon group out for two-dollar Nassau. Won twenty-two dollars, but don't be too impressed."

"Winning's good."

"Golf pros always shoot low on their own course. It's the ones who can do it consistently on any course that make the grade."

Merit got out of bed and shoved her feet into slippers that matched her blue pajama pants. She paced as she talked, straightening a picture frame here, a book there.

"The grade?"

"The PGA tour. Professional Golfers Association."

"Right."

"Mr. Shasta cried like a baby when he lost today," Mark said.

"Took him to the cleaners did 'ya? A whole twenty-two dollars." Merit teased. She walked down the hall past a wall of black and white photos of her son at the beach. She ran her fingers over the frame of one checking for dust.

"What's that noise?" Mark asked.

"I just walked into the kitchen. It's water running in the sink," she said. "Is that better?" She turned off the water.

"No problem, just curious," he said.

"I came in here to peel a mango." She took the fruit from a bowl, put the phone on the counter, and pressed the tiny speaker icon.

Pepper, Ace's Cairn Terrier, woke and stretched, then walked around Merit's feet checking for dropped food.

"I've never had it. We didn't grow much mango in Wisconsin. What does it taste like?"

She began to peel the skin, and clear juice ran over the cutting board and onto the counter. "It's delicious. I always wondered what the explorers must have thought when they discovered mango. It's an ugly looking egg-shaped fruit, but bigger. Like an ostrich egg, only pink and orange."

"Maybe they thought it was an egg," Mark said.

"Maybe they thought they'd found heaven."

"They were probably growing mangos in their backyards at home and wished they'd found a banana," he laughed.

"Yes, but my story is better."

"Why aren't you dating anyone?" Mark said.

"Men my age have no sense of adventure, nor do they understand mangos."

And they leave. They die. They cause hurt.

Chapter Nine

Mark looked at the document before him. Mr. Zars sat across the table at his usual spot in the ACCC cafe. Browno looked confident and was smiling.

"This is a big IOU," Mark said.

"I got to protect myself, *nu?*" Browno said. "You don't 'spect me to just hand you so much *hrusty*, as we say in Russia. Ten thousand, this is a lot of dough-re-mi."

Mark nodded. It was a lot of money. Most of the language was straightforward; the principal, the interest rate. Words he'd heard before. He rifled through the pages again. Well, he guessed this was the way businessmen like Mr. Zars did things.

"Maybe I'll take this with me," Mark said finally.

Browno shrugged. "Maybe this rate won't be available later. This is special rate, friend rate."

The truth was that it felt wrong to sign this without his Dad seeing it first, Mark admitted to himself. It was the first time he'd done something like this without Check's oversight. But, he was older now and on his own. Besides, Check wasn't going to help him anymore. He'd made that clear. He had to start taking care of his own finances.

"I don't know how I will be able to pay you back. My salary and tips are all I have as income, and they won't be increasing any time soon," Mark said.

"We are friends, yes?" Browno said. He pushed a pen over to Mark. "I will promote you, get you some charity matches and exhibition games. You earn the money to pay me back. See, it says here I promote you. I do this all the time, is my business. Good, *nu?*"

It sounded good. Mark just wanted to play golf. So maybe it would be a good idea for Browno to bail him out then he'd have something invested in getting him some paying work, so he could pay him back. Still, Mark's gut said, "Don't sign it."

A club server deposited a double cheeseburger in front of Browno. He attacked it like he'd been trapped in Siberia for the last ten years.

Over Browno's left shoulder, a slight young man who looked like a rapper, wearing a Z-Ro ball cap lingered. He held a drink with clear liquid in his tattooed hand. When his gaze intersected Mark's, their eyes held. He shook his head and looked away.

Mark took the pen and signed.

Browno wiped his chin with a paper napkin and smiled.

Chapter Ten

Merit and Mark's conversations eventually led to sex chat and past experiences. They flirted increasingly, and after using her vibrator for three nights in a row, Merit decided to suggest a meeting. Mark called, and after the initial howdy, she popped the question.

"Do you think we should get together? See if we like each other? Maybe try some of these things we've been talking about?" Merit asked.

"Yes, I thought you'd never ask. Let's meet right away," Mark said.

Merit smiled at his boyishness. "Let's set some boundaries and talk about the age difference."

"We like each other, so what's the difference?" Mark said.

"We both have reputations in the community, and I'm not interested in explaining myself to my staff or my clients, so we'd have to keep it between us," Merit said.

"It can be our secret," Mark said. "Only thing is, you know I'm not very experienced. Golf I can do. Sex, I have the mechanics down, but I don't know about the rest."

"You have a great imagination. I'll teach you."

"You'll teach me sex?"

"Yes."

"Really?"

"Yes, but it will cost you a golf lesson."

"So, you'll teach me sex, and I'll teach you golf?"

"Yes," Merit said.

"Yes, yes, yes," Mark said.

"My favorite word," Merit said, grinning.

Neither one of them expressed whether sex or golf would come first. They made a date for later that week.

After saying goodnight, Merit began to think further about the differences in their ages and complicating her well-structured life. This was far beyond the age span she had experienced before with a man. She wondered how she'd feel if it were her son becoming involved with an older woman. She wondered what Mark's mother would think if she found out.

Merit came to the conclusion that it had been fun to entertain the idea, but that it was best for all involved if left as a fantasy. She wanted to play, but she also needed to be careful. She determined to tell Mark.

∞

First thing the next morning, Merit considered how she would break the news when the phone rang.

"Hi, I was thinking about our date and just had to call. I can't wait to meet you," Mark said.

"Mark, I need to talk to you," she said.

"I want to feel you against me. I can't wait to see what it's like to kiss you," Mark said.

"Mark, I've changed my mind."

"What?"

"I just don't think it's a good idea now that I've had some time to play it out in my head. It's so complicated with the age difference, and all," Merit said.

"You approached me. I am so damn lonely, and now this is gone, too."

Lonely? But, of course he was. New in town and working all the time.

"I'm sorry," Merit said, but he'd hung up.

Merit went into the bathroom and mumbled to herself as she looked into the mirror and brushed powder over her makeup.

Damn, you know you want him. Own "Don't be so provincial," Merit said to the mirror then flipped off the lights and went into her room to get dressed.

She thought about what Mark had said about being lonely, and the fact that she really wanted to explore with him. She thought about who could and would be harmed. No one, really.

Merit wanted to enjoy her life, not work herself into her grave. She needed some fun. A new man. That would be plenty relaxing.

She sat on the end of the bed and picked up her iPhone.

Mark answered.

"I will proceed under two conditions. First, no one will know, and second, when one of us decides to end it, we tell the other and remain friends. No anger in parting," Merit said.

"No problem."

"Listen. I really mean it. If we stop being lovers, we will talk, golf, invite each other to lunch, parties, all that, and remain friends."

"Okay, your rules," Mark said.

She looked at the phone after they'd hung up.

This is going to be an adventure. Oh hell, I said 'yes' was my favorite word. Time to prove it.

Chapter Eleven

B rowno sat at his favorite booth at the ACCC cafe. These days he was bitter about being ousted from Brighton Beach. He didn't like to think about it, but down deep, he burned to show them all. He had a lot to prove.

He had a good business going here in Austin, and solid associates who helped him when his clients couldn't pay the juice on the loans he gave them. Associates, that's what he liked to call his small army of disciplinarians.

Occasionally, Browno did his own wet work. He had plenty of muscle around him to take care of the day to day stuff, but he often enjoyed a session with a particularly beautiful woman or a cocky man who'd disrespected him.

The main thing he enjoyed was the head game. He liked how his clients became his, a little bit at a time, like pulling in a fish. He especially liked how they struggled on the line. His game was all about the mental cruelty. As much as he could inflict on another human being.

Maybe that's why they'd pushed him out of his home in Brighton Beach. They didn't like how much he enjoyed it all. Then, there was the littering of bodies around the area. It was bad for business, they said.

Browno adjusted his considerable bulk and looked at the pro tennis player sitting across from him. The young man occupied less than a quarter of the booth and he seemed to be trying to shrink even further. Browno especially liked this man. He'd almost forgotten his name, but that was all right. It was the look on his face he enjoyed, the sweat that dripped down his neck.

"I'll have the money next week, I swear," the tennis player burbled.

His face had turned a pleasant shade of red. Sometimes they passed out when they turned this color. The young man made a noise almost like a sob. But not quite. He was not quite upset enough to cry for him yet. So Browno ordered another beer and waited for the little man to cry.

They always did.

"If you no give me my money, we have to collect," Browno said.

"One more week. Please," he begged.

After the tennis player had left, Browno called his main muscle, Petrov. He didn't allow any of the henchmen to come into ACCC with him. He had to appear business like and above board around the club.

"Catch him in the parking lot. Show him we mean business," Browno said.

Chapter Twelve

The day finally arrived when Mark and Merit would meet. Mark stood in the closet, hair wet, with a blue towel around his waist and stared at a row of shirts. He pulled out a white one, looked at it and put it back, and then did the same thing with a pair of jeans. The week's clothes, usually strewn around the floor, were neatly hung on hangers, all starched and ironed.

He had thought about it all day at work, daydreaming during his lessons and pissing off Mr. Shasta with his distraction. Not much of a tip today, but he didn't care.

I'm worse than a girl, he grumbled. *What does a guy wear to a first date with a sophisticated woman?*

Finally, he picked out a pair of khaki pants and a light blue golf shirt. His mother always said, "When in doubt, wear khakis and a shirt with a collar."

Mark dropped the towel on the floor. He was tan to his waist, and on his legs. In between, he was white as milk. He slipped on a clean pair of boxers, beige with little blue golf tees, and put on a pair of tan socks. He went back into the bathroom and rubbed some styling paste into his hair, another freebie from some company wanting golfers to pump their products. He looked at himself in the mirror.

How does someone teach sex? Is it like golf, put your hands here, put your feet there? Is it like developing a good swing?

Since he'd been in Texas, he'd not had one date, much less sex. He took a last look in the mirror.

Done.

He took out a rather extensive manicure kit and began to work on his hands. He clipped and cleaned, pushed the cuticles back, and ended with a large squirt of lotion with shea butter from a bottle on the counter. After he'd rubbed the lotion clear, he stretched his hands out before him and took a look.

"It'll have to do." He hoped she'd like the looks of him before she noticed his hands. They were scarred and disfigured in a way that few hands ever were. Nothing about them looked normal or functional. They looked deformed but there was no way to hide one's hands.

He stared at his curled fingers and felt the heat of the fire on his skin from so many years before.

∞

As he felt the heat on his hands, Mark was mentally swept back to Wisconsin and on the farm. He could see himself and Check as if in a movie with a soundtrack.

Check watched two-year-old Mark scoot around the pasture. Check wore his Hardy Man overalls and Mark was his spitting-image miniature in OshKosh B'gosh bibs with a blue flannel shirt beneath. Mark scampered after butterflies, put his toes in the creek, and pulled the heads off of puffballs, all under the watchful eye of his father.

It was a workday for Check, but he and Mark made it play. They fed the chickens, watered the garden, and scooped fallen leaves into a big pile for composting. Check liked to burn the leaves in a big surround of chicken wire, mixing the ashes with the potato peels, apple cores, and various other organic material, making a rich fertilizer for the next season's garden.

Mark heaped huge handfuls of red and gold leaves toward the make-shift fence as his father tipped full wheel barrels in through an opening.

The sun was directly overhead, almost time for a lunch break. Check's wife, Martha, confirmed his sense of time by ringing a bell on the front porch of the farmhouse across the pasture. Check waved in acknowledgment and little Mark waved, too.

Check closed the makeshift gate and unrolled a band of chicken wire over the top to keep the leaves from flying out and setting the pasture on fire. He lit a branch with a match and waited for it to catch. Check cautioned Mark to stand back and tossed the branch into the leaf mound. The dried leaves burst into flames and began to crackle and pop. Mark watched in fascination as the big eruption settled down to a glowing bonfire.

Check busied himself by throwing in stray branches as he waited for the fire to burn down to a safe level. He was hungry for lunch and poked the fire to encourage the process.

Mark picked up a branch with dried leaves on the end. He tried to reach over the top of the fencing, but he was too short, so he put it through the holes in the wire just as a puff of wind caused the fire-mound to flare up. Fascinated by the display of leaping red and yellow flames, Mark froze. The fire ran up the dried leaves of the branch and scalded his hands. In his panic to get away from the heat, he pulled the branch out, rather than letting go, and the sleeves of his flannel shirt caught fire. Mark released the branch and shook his arms, trying to get away from the pain. The movement caused the flames to flare and run up his arms.

Check heard his son's scream and ran to him. He rolled Mark on the grass and put his body over his son's to smother the flames. Mark became absolutely silent as shock spun him to another world. Check ran through the pasture carrying his motionless son as he screamed for Martha to bring the truck. After what seemed an eternity, she pulled the truck into the pasture. As she ran from the truck, she saw Mark's bloody hands and smoking clothes, and began crying and screaming for Check to hurry.

The world stopped turning for a moment, then proceeded in slow motion. Check looked into the eyes of his wife as he placed Mark in the truck. Martha got behind the wheel as Check climbed in beside his son. Mark's hands were the same color as the rusty red pickup.

Chapter Thirteen

Across town, Merit finished dressing in a rush and picked up her purse. As she headed for the door, her mobile rang. It was her investigator, Albert "Ag" Malone, so she stopped in the foyer and answered it. They'd flirted around the edges of a relationship but had never crossed over from business to pleasure.

Does he have a sixth sense when I'm contemplating sex? Merit thought.

"Hello, Ag," Merit said.

"Merit, Chaplain at APD asked me to check with you about your client Terrence Long. His wife, Jessica, has reported him missing," Ag said.

"Oh, no. When?" Merit asked.

"It's been four days since she's seen him. She reported him on the first day and the cops have had an eye out for him but didn't really start to look hard until today," Ag said.

"We met for a strategy session in my office. We were trying to deal with the bankers." Merit said. "It's no secret he was looking around to borrow money."

"Do you know if he was successful?" Ag said.

"No. He hadn't reported back yet. He was under a lot of stress. I hope he didn't kill himself."

"Chaplain doesn't think so. There were signs of foul play in his truck. It was left parked in front of the construction trailer at Hill Country Homestead. One of the carpenters saw a black SUV leaving and the door to his truck was left open. There was some blood on the seat and the headrest," Ag said.

"How awful," Merit said. "What can I do to help?"

"I'll let Chaplain know about your last meeting. No calls since then?"

"None. I'll text you the name and number of his banker when we hang up. If I think of anything else, I'll let you know," Merit said.

"Okay," Ag said.

"I hope they find him," Merit said.

Chapter Fourteen

Merit drove her new red BMW SUV to the restaurant to meet Mark. She had totaled her last Bimmer when a crazy hacker took over the steering and plowed her into the Gulf of Mexico.

As she drove, "Mrs. Robinson" by Simon and Garfunkel began playing on satellite radio and she almost lost control of the car laughing.

She let the day flow out behind her, then pulled into Weird Pizza on South Congress. She had avoided the place since Tony had died. He had been a huge pizza fan. Mark had chosen the place. Her suspicion was that it was a place where he could afford the check in case it was part of the man's role to pick it up.

Merit found a parking place on Congress and aggravated the person behind her as she took three attempts to do reverse angle parking. She walked back to Weird Pizza through throngs of visitors exploring the various shops and restaurants of the area. She checked in with the hostess, walked through the restaurant to the outside deck, and spotted a tall slender young man with sun-bleached hair wearing a blue polo shirt. She wove through the tables toward him as she inhaled the scents of basil, oregano, and garlic.

Mark stood and smiled. He pulled out her green plastic chair beside a table covered in a red-checkered cloth. They bungled an awkward hug.

"Hi, sorry I'm late," Merit said.

Merit sized him up. He looked like a grown-up, except that his cheeks were pink like a child's. His voice was deep, and he towered over her. Merit watched him check her out. She had worn jeans and a Stevie Ray t-shirt with a denim vest, trying to be casual.

"I got a call about a client from my investigator on my way out the door." *Don't tell him about that. This is a date. Just keep it light.*

He looked at her. "How could such a cute person be a lawyer?" he blurted out, and then looked embarrassed.

"Oh, you know what they say about lawyers, can't live with 'em, can't shoot 'em." She smiled into his velvet brown eyes.

"I like your t-shirt," he said.

"Thanks, I got it at a fundraiser for Texas Reads. Got to meet Killer Delight."

"Sounds fun," Mark said, looking at her body in the shirt.

They sat on the deck in the cool evening air and ordered deep-dish pizza with beer for him and red wine for her. After a few sips she began to relax, and he seemed to as well.

"I wasn't sure you'd come," Mark said.

"Of course I came. I said I'd be here, didn't I?" Merit said.

"Yes, but after the other night, I wondered," Mark said.

"Well, it's a woman's prerogative to change her mind." Merit laughed.

The food was served. As Mark took a slice, she noticed his hands for the first time. They were scarred and curled. Some of the fingers had nails missing. She saw his eyes follow hers, but he didn't explain. She puzzled for a moment that he hadn't told her something so significant on the phone but decided to leave it for later.

"Smells good," Merit said, changing the unexpressed subject.

He sunk his teeth into the gooey cheese and pepperoni.

At her first bite, Merit said, "Wow."

"It's an aphrodisiac. I ordered it special for you," Mark said.

It was deep dish, glutenous, stuffed with spices that danced an explosion of flavors in her mouth.

They soon lapsed into a continuation of the conversations they'd had on the phone. Bantering away, they became friends. Friends with a secret no one in the world was allowed to know. It was delicious. They were going to be lovers and neither of them had to announce it.

As they finished eating, she observed his hands more closely when he wasn't looking. She gently inquired, not wanting to ignore the elephant in the middle of the room.

"Were you in a car accident?"

He responded with a grimace, "I walked into a leaf fire when I was two. I've had over a dozen surgeries since."

"Does it hurt?"

"Yes, almost all the time, but mostly it's like background noise."

"How can you play golf on such a high level with that challenge?"

"My father encouraged me in the game to give me a game I could master."

"I thought you weren't close to him?"

"I was when I was young, when he first introduced me to golf. When I got older and started thinking for myself, he decided I was being disrespectful. The more independent I became, the grouchier he got."

"How did you go for extended periods without using your hands during the surgeries?" Merit asked.

"My mother took care of feeding me and most of the medical things. Check couldn't take it. I think he felt guilty. He was with me when it happened."

"What do you like to do besides play golf?"

"I don't know a lot about what's here."

"Well, let me be your tour guide." Merit said.

Mark picked up the bill.

"Let's split it."

"No, I can't let you pay on the first date," Mark said.

"Okay then, I'll show you the night-lights. Tonight, we start your Austin education."

Merit led Mark to her condo and waited at the gate as he piggybacked through to the garage under the building. After he parked, she pulled up behind his car and he hopped in with her.

"Nice ride," Mark said.

Merit drove him to Lake Austin, down Scenic Drive along the water, then to the Capitol on Congress Avenue. She occasionally pointed out a structure with architectural interest or gave a bit of history on a statue or government building.

As she drove, she rested her free hand on his neck. He mimicked her advances and touched her gently and casually. Her arm, her hand, her knee.

They wound up at the scenic overlook of the downtown lights on Highway 360. They leaned against the limestone ledge of the cliff and watched the lights downtown in the distance. The night air was arousing. The taboo interaction was spicy.

Mark inhaled deeply.

"Your perfume is making me drunk," he whispered.

Their faces were close. Merit knew a kiss was coming, but it was so crucial. That kiss would make the final decision. Seal the deal. Either could turn back until that kiss.

Can he hear my heart beating?

They both leaned in and let it happen. The passion sparked, and it was right. Merit forgot where they were and who they were as their lips pressed, then opened.

Neither knew that the kiss bound them to something much more dangerous than sex.

Chapter Fifteen

Merit drove them to her high rise and parked in the garage. Once they entered the condo, a small brindled dog that looked like Toto ran over to greet them.

"This is Pepper. Ace's dog," Merit said.

"Hello, Pepper," Mark said and pet the dog.

"Water?"

"Please."

Mark took a big gulp, his Adam's apple bobbing up and down.

He followed her down the hall and grabbed her awkwardly from behind, catching her off guard. She stopped and let him caress her, stepping out of her shoes, then turned around and kissed him hard. They both melted into it. His groin pushed against her and she felt his arousal.

They sat on the side of the bed kissing and touching. They began to undress each other quickly. Mark hesitated.

"You can put your hands on me. I'm not afraid of the scars," she told him.

He slid his hands under her t-shirt, undid her bra, then found her breasts. She pulled his shirt over his head and touched his hairless chest and arms.

Mark fumbled.

Merit breathed in his exhaled breath.

"Suck gently."

He was trembling as she kissed his ear and rubbed her hand over his hardness.

"Does that feel good?" she asked.

"Yeah," he croaked like a teenager in puberty.

"Why don't you lie back and let me on top?"

A condom appeared in her hand like a magician's coin. She ripped it open with her teeth and placed it on the head of his penis, then rolled it down slowly.

Mark stretched out on the diagonal and she lifted one leg over him and settled onto him.

She took his hands and placed them on her breasts. His hands felt odd, they were hard where hands are normally soft, and curved where other hands did not. He began to explore her body above him, as she rocked slowly and sensuously.

She shifted her weight back a little and leaned down. She put her arms around his shoulders.

"Put your arms around my neck," Merit said.

He circled her neck and shoulders with his long arms and she sat up, pulling him with her. It caused his erection to shift deeply inside her. She limited her words and taught with her body language.

"I don't know how much longer I can hold back," Mark said.

She began to rock him. He held on, and when he felt her pulsating warmth, he released to the sensation. After they settled, she untangled herself and stretched out beside him.

Pepper looked up from her nap on the floor by the bed and yawned.

"So, does this mean we can play golf now?" Merit laughed.

"No, but I owe you a free lesson, not a game," Mark said.

"Are you serious? You won't play golf with me?"

"Don't be mad, Merit, I just don't golf with women."

"Well, now I'm sorry I gave you my super-duper woman-on-top lesson."

"Ah Merit, don't be that way."

"Why don't you play with women?"

"Because, so far, I haven't met a woman who could keep up with my game."

"Are you kidding? What a macho thing to say. How good are you anyway?"

"I shoot in the sixties pretty consistently."

"I guess you are good." She relaxed again, impressed. "I bet Sung Hyun Park could kick your ass."

"Yeah, there's a woman who could give me a game."

"Why don't you play the tour if you shoot so low?"

Mark hesitated. "I tried once at Whistling Straits near the farm. It was when I had just finished college."

"What happened?"

Mark looked up as if he was seeing the past. "Check was steering me through the golf system. He was helping me with the fees and being my caddie. I was playing a first step qualifier for the PGA tour."

"And then?"

"I couldn't do it. I froze. I just saw all those people watching, and the television cameras kept zooming in on my hands, and Check was cross, and I couldn't play. I shot a seventy-nine. The television commentator made me sound pitiful. He called me handicapped."

"That must have been awful," Merit s"Check blew a fuse. I just couldn't face the next round of the tour. Check and I had been fighting so long, it was a relief to quit."

"What made you choose Austin?" Merit asked.

"I found out about jobs through the PGA. There were three spots open. Austin was the furthest from Wisconsin, and the prettiest of the three. ACCC is a good course, good job. People would kill for my job."

"But?"

"No but," Mark said.

Are you sure? Merit thought.

∞

After they had sex again, they napped for a while, then woke up spooned together.

He rolled onto his back and doodled imaginary shapes around her belly button. "So, how did you first start playing?" Merit asked.

"It's a long story." He looked at the ceiling fan.

"I've got time," she said. "Tell all."

Mark hesitated then said, "I was about five or six years old when Check taught me to play golf."

"Why Check and not Dad?"

"He got the name Check from his poker buddies. Everyone called him that, even Mom, except when she was mad at him."

Merit laughed.

"He took me out to the pasture behind our farmhouse. We never went to the other pasture where the leaf fire burned my hands. We never mentioned it either," Mark said. "Check gave me an old set of his clubs that he'd modified by cutting down the sticks. He kept me practicing in the field for a long time so that my hands wouldn't be seen at a public course. I was really self-conscious. The first and most important surgeries were beginning to heal by that time, but the scars were pretty severe."

"Check placed my fingers around the clubs and pressed his hands on top to secure the grip. It didn't hurt, just felt strange to bend them like that. Somehow it worked. The grip, the swing, the mental game, all began to take shape in the middle of a Wisconsin cow pasture."

"Really? That simple?" Merit asked.,

"Yes and no. After the first year, Check took me to the driving range."

"Where did you play our first game?"

"It was a small municipal course a few miles out of town that looked more like the cow pasture than Colonial or Augusta, but it had holes and flags and that was enough to get the ball rolling, so to speak."

"Did you like it?" Merit asked.

"I think it was the only time Check and I ever got along. Maybe Check thought he was making up for letting me near a dangerous fire, maybe he was just trying to find something that we could do together. I don't know."

"That sounds sweet," Merit said.

"At first. Later, it got bad with him."

"How so?"

"My height increased to over six feet, and my swing became fluid and Check's never was. I passed him up at about age fourteen, and never lost a golf game to him again."

"That must have been tough for him, but it sounds like he wanted you to be a winner," Merit said.

"He did, and he didn't. We stopped playing together about the time I was sixteen. I wanted to play with my friends because it was a lot more fun. Besides, they admired my golf game and fed my ego. Mostly, Check wanted me to do it the way he would have if he'd had the chance, and I wanted to do things my way."

"Too bad," Merit said running her hand along his arm and holding his fingers in hers.

"Yeah, too bad. We still can't have a decent conversation," Mark said. "Then, of course, there was the game. The game of a lifetime that severed the last of our bond."

"What game?"

"Just a lousy golf tourney in Wisconsin. Check wanted me to win so badly. I choked, and he never forgave me," Mark said.

"That's unfortunate, for you and your Mother," Merit said.

"My mom never held Check responsible for my accident, or if she did, she never said so, but something old is there between them. He's cold to her, and drinks with his buddies a lot. The last few years he's soured the life of everyone around him."

"They're still together?" Merit asked.

"Thirty years and counting."

Sounds like a life sentence, Merit thought.

Chapter Sixteen

At the law office, Merit signed some paperwork while Betty hovered over her. She was distracted by flashbacks of her night with Mark. After a moment she realized Betty was saying something.

"What's that?" Merit asked.

"You look refreshed," Betty repeated, a twinkle in her eye. "Sort of like you've got some more snap in your garters."

Merit batted her eyes and said, "I don't know what you're referring to, Ma'am."

"Right," Betty said.

"Okay, so you know. It's not a crime to date a younger man these days," Merit said.

"No, but I wouldn't let it get around unless you think it's worth the trouble," Betty said.

"Not now. We'll see how it goes," Merit said.

Betty grinned at her, gave her hair a bump, and stopped talking as Ag sauntered in. He was tall and thin with long dark eyelashes that looked like they'd been curled with an eyelash curler. His uniform of maroon shirt and jeans worked for him.

"Hi, Ag. How are you doing?" Merit smiled at him. His handsome face looked tense and tired.

"Okay. You wanted to meet on some new files?" he asked.

"You look like you need coffee," Betty said.

Merit, Ag & Betty drank coffee and tea as they went through each of the files that Ag was investigating for Merit's clients.

"Any word on Terrence Long?" Betty asked.

"Nothing. Chaplain and his men are totally stumped," Ag said.

"The whole town is buzzing about it. Red Thallon is reporting by the hour on KNEW 9 ONLINE," Merit said.

"It's disturbing for sure," Ag said.

They set aside the drama and worked through three new client files that Merit wanted Ag to check out.

"Also, what if you did some checking on Terrence Long? Maybe see if there was something outside of his business dealings that we should know about," Merit asked.

"My thoughts exactly. Chaplain would probably be glad for the help," Ag said.

"Okay."

"I better get going. I've got another meeting. I'll keep you posted," Ag said.

Ag looked at Merit one last time as if she was the last slice of pie on the plate.

Betty saw the look.

"Please do," Betty said.

"See ya," Merit said.

After he'd left, Betty stayed in her chair.

"What?" Merit asked. "I know that look."

"He's still sweet on you," Betty said.

"I don't want to date anyone seriously right now. He's not a guy I can play around with and leave when we're done. Besides, he's important to our business," Merit said.

"I know, but you don't have to keep distracting yourself with these boy toys just because you won't date Ag, yet," Betty said. "There have to be men your age out there."

"I can make my own decisions about who I sleep with. I know you watch out for me, but there are some things that are private," Merit said.

"You have a son and a reputation in the community."

"I know. My son is not in my home when I entertain," Merit said.

"Be smart, Merit. Don't squat on your spurs," Betty said.

Chapter Seventeen

Merit met Mark the next day at the Austin Creek Country Club for a golf lesson. She parked in the lot and popped the hatch. Merit sported black linen slacks and a white long-sleeved polo shirt as it was a cool fall day. The teenager working the lot put her clubs on a golf cart.

"Great day for a golf lesson," she said.

"I'll have these for you out back." The attendant indicated the side of the building.

"Thanks." She gave him a tip and approached the clubhouse: a huge columned affair that looked like it was left over from the Civil War. The purple sage was blooming a soft violet. Water fell on the bushes from the intricate sprinkler system that kept the immaculate grounds green and lush. Behind the view of the golfers was an extensive gray water system established to conserve water and keep the bills down.

She skirted the main entrance connected to the restaurant and went down the sidewalk and opened the glass doors to the pro shop. Mark said goodbye to his client, a mover and shaker she recognized from the last legal seminar she'd attended.

Merit ducked behind a rack of clothes and avoided the lawyer. Mark saw her and played along, waiting until the man was out the door before coming over to her.

"Hello in there," he said.

"Hi," Merit said, coming out from her hiding place.

"Someone you know?" Mark asked.

"A little. It's my day off. No business."

Mark grabbed for her hand, but she pulled back as their fingers brushed.

They approached the reception counter. A tall thin man stood behind it with his foot resting on a chair. He was spraying WD-40 on his knee through a long straw attached to the nozzle on a can. As he pumped the oily liquid onto his skin, he flexed and extended his leg.

"Good for the joints," Joe said. "Arthritis."

Merit looked at Mark with wide eyes.

"Meet Merit," Mark said. Then to Merit, "This is Joe."

Mark and Joe had on matching uniforms, khaki slacks and Austin Creek polo shirts. Mark's was yellow, and Joe's was purple.

"Pleased to meet you," Joe said. His gray whiskers looked like snowflakes on his black skin. The phone rang.

"Pro Shop," Joe said into the phone in a deep raspy voice as he held up his finger for them to wait.

Mark looked at Merit and winked. She gave him a cautionary look. Merit saw Joe watching them.

"I've got you down for four at eight fifteen on Friday morning," Joe wrapped up the call.

He addressed Merit. "Well, little lady, are you going to let this young pup give you a golf lesson today?"

"Yes, sir, that's the plan."

"Watch out for him. He's a hustler. Don't make any deals with him."

"Too late," Merit said, smiling.

Merit and Mark went on as Joe stepped up the other leg and continued his medicinal treatment with the spray oil.

Mark pointed to an office in back.

"My boss Bob Tom works back there. He's out today. You'll meet him next time."

Merit saw a young man who looked a bit like Mark come out of Bob Tom's office, pull a Z-Ro cap down over his eyes, and slip out the back door. Mark and Merit continued past the cafe. Mark turned so he would not look at Browno and they continued outside.

They took the waiting cart with her clubs over to the driving range. She loved the new Callaway irons she'd bought for herself. They were beautiful, like jewelry. Mark pulled a club.

"Big Bertha. Good choice for starter clubs. Large head, forgiving nature," Mark said.

They approached the driving range manager.

"We'll take two large buckets, Dave," Mark held up two fingers.

"Hi," Merit said.

Dave carried the buckets over to an open spot on the driving range line and set them up.

"Here's a good spot," Dave said. "The ground is muddy from the rain. You'll have to use the artificial surface."

Mark put a ball down for her.

"Let's see your swing to start," Mark said.

Merit nodded.

Mark handed her a seven iron and she stepped up to the ball perched on the artificial tee. It looked like a chopped-off piece of surgical tubing stuck in Astroturf.

She separated her feet and gripped the green plastic grass with her spiky black and white saddle shoes. She lined her hands up on the shaft of the club, the way she'd been taught, and addressed the ball. She swung the head of the club up toward her right shoulder and then downward. At the last second, she pulled her head up and missed the ball completely.

How embarrassing.

"Not like that," Mark said, coming up behind her. He wrapped his arms around hers and moved her hands up the grip of the club a few inches. Merit tried not to get distracted.

"Here, now make sure the V of your right-hand lines up with the V of your left. Here, where your thumb and forefinger meet." He put two golf tees in the V's and pointed to the line they made.

"Okay", she replied and obediently adjusted her hand position. "Not Tigress Woods yet?"

"You'll get there."

She waggled her body a bit and pulled the club back over her right shoulder again. She paused at the top of the arc for a second and swoosh, pulled the club through to her left shoulder. She heard a crack as the face of the club impacted the ball with a golden sound that she had dreamed about so many times.

The sweet spot. Merit smiled.

"Good one," Mark said.

She hit a few more, holding her hands the way he'd shown her.

"Let's work on your distance. Try the driver," Mark said.

She did a test shot.

She wobbled at the end.

"There is a relationship between balance and swinging too hard. You want to stay in control but generate club head speed. Think of a ball swinging on the end of a string." Mark said.

She addressed the ball again, keeping her head down and thinking balance. She pulled the club into an arc and let her body unwind. Swoosh, crack, another good one.

The ball sailed high into the air, seemed suspended for a moment, plopped about a foot short of the one-hundred-yard marker, then rolled on a few yards past it.

"Look where you landed. Nice," Mark said.

She hit most of both buckets of balls while receiving bits of advice and encouragement from Mark. After she finished, Merit looked at his smile and smiled herself, catching the twinkle in his eye.

"I always give an etiquette tip at the end of every lesson," Mark said.

"Great, give me something useful," Merit said.

"Okay. When you're putting, after everyone is on the green, you know the person farthest from the hole puts first."

"Right."

"When you mark your ball, and again when you putt, it's considered bad manners to walk across the grass that someone will putt over. So, you walk a circle around the pin to get to your ball if you're on the other side. Understand?"

"Yes, I've seen players doing that, but why?"

"If you mash the grass with your feet, it may change the roll of the ball, and that's an unfair advantage."

"Coolio."

"If you want to read up, there's a book by Barbara Puett. She lives here in Austin. Harvey Penick wrote *The Little Red Golf Book*. Barbara, his student, wrote *Golf Etiquette*, same small size, but hers is green. They have them at BookPeople."

"I will," Merit said.

"How would you like to have a mashie-niblick?" Mark teased.

"What's that, Golfboy, another etiquette tip?"

"Come with me and I'll show you."

Mark loaded the clubs onto the cart and Merit walked behind a long line of men practicing their swings and returned the buckets to Dave.

Mark shot Merit a clandestine look as they jumped into the cart and headed toward the sixth hole, which ran along the creek in a secluded area next to the driving range.

"A mashie-niblick is an old Scottish term used for a steel seven iron," Mark said.

She put her hand on his groin, "I feel a bit of steel here."

"Mm," Mark responded. "Did you know that golf was invented in Scotland?"

"I believe I read that somewhere." She said, rubbing him harder.

"You'll love this, being the liberated woman that you are. Golf stands for Gentlemen Only Ladies Forbidden," Mark said.

"Well. It's a good thing we're not in Scotland then isn't it?" she said. Merit didn't take it personally; law was an old boys club too. She was accustomed to competing with the big boys.

"Old joke. Golf is an old Scottish word for club," Mark said.

"How old?" Merit asked.

"That will be my next research project."

"No, I'll be your next research project," Merit said.

"Yes, Ma'am." He grinned.

As they left the path and cut through the trees, avoiding the view of anyone who might be teeing off the seventh, Mark pulled her over in the seat and ran his hand up her leg along her thigh as he took the cart down and back up a rocky ravine.

As they bumped around, Mark said, "Did you hear about those guys who had hookers come out to the golf course near Houston to run around nude while they played golf?"

"They did not!"

"Yes, they rented the entire course for the afternoon and played golf with naked women running around. The girls would bend over at the flags and give special awards for the pars and birdies."

"How do you know this?" she asked suspiciously.

"It was on the news. A helicopter flew over and filmed the women jumping up and down naked."

"You're serious? No April fool?"

"I swear on my putter," Mark laughed. "No one got arrested, but I hear a lot of that was going on but now it's cooling down."

"I guess so. Maybe they should play with the men naked too," Merit said.

Mark drove the cart through a few dry creek beds and they came up to the back side of the tenth hole with no one around.

He motioned toward a bathroom that looked like a miniature of the clubhouse.

"What do you say?" Mark asked.

She wrinkled up her nose "Men are not always the cleanest in the toilet."

"Okay, Miss Priss, let's go au natural," Mark said.

He drove the cart to the edge of a thickly wooded area and pulled her from the seat. They entered between the trees and once concealed, began to fumble with each other's clothes.

Once they had their tops up and bottoms down, Merit leaned against a large oak tree, and Mark pressed in. She wrapped her legs around him and hoisted herself up. He got the idea quickly and moved inside her. It didn't take either of them long to find the sweet spot.

Just minutes later, they emerged from the trees flushed, but tidy, and managed to sweep away in the cart in time to avoid the course marshal and the next four coming up the fairway.

They didn't notice that they were being spied on.

Chapter Eighteen

Browno drove his cart up to the tenth hole just ahead of the others he had joined for an afternoon of play. He spotted a cart at the edge of the woods and saw a man and a woman get inside and drive off. He could not make out the woman but pulled his spotting binoculars just in time to catch Mark's profile and the cart number on the back, one hundred sixty-four. He noted the number on the top of his score card as he parked at the tee box.

Looks like a little hanky panky going on, Browno thought.

He took his phone out of his golf bag and speed dialed.

"Check out who comes into the club house in cart number one six four with Mark Green," Browno said.

∞

Merit and Mark took a short cut in the cart and drove up to the clubhouse to the Nineteenth Hole Bar and Grill.

It was a busy day and dozens of people were pulling in and out in golf carts. The young man with the Z-Ro cap whom they'd seen leaving Bob Tom's office leaned against a wall on the edge of the activity watching them drive up.

Merit's armpits prickled ever so slightly.

"Who's that?" Merit asked.

"Never saw him before," Mark said. "Security is right over there, so he must belong here."

As they entered the cafe, there was a strong smell of grilling onions coming from the kitchen. Canned music played from the speakers embedded in the ceiling.

Merit and Mark settled into a green vinyl booth and ordered Arnold Palmers from a college student wearing short shorts, a halter, and a country club visor.

"Would you like to add some vodka to that and have a John Daly?" the waitress asked.

"No, thanks. I'll stick to the iced tea and lemonade," Merit said.

"Same," Mark said.

A group of four men in Easter-egg-colored clothes settled into a booth. Merit saw Joe cruise through and grab a bag of corn chips off the rack by the cash register.

"Will you put this on my tab?" Joe asked.

"Sure," the waitress replied.

Joe winked at Merit and went back to the pro shop counter.

"How was your lesson?" one of the pros called over from another booth.

"Great, she's getting the hang of it," Mark yelled, then whispered toward Merit, "I'm getting the hang of it, too."

Merit nodded at the other pro as if she were pleased with her teacher.

They sat across from each other and minded their hands and body language as they sipped their drinks, talked golf, and looked respectable. Merit occasionally pointed to a scorecard for effect. Joe Ely crooned about *Twistin' in the Wind*, from the little speaker holes overhead.

Mark reached for Merit's hand but caught himself in mid-air as she gave him the look.

"It's amazing that your hands don't inhibit your game," Merit said.

"I know," Mark said, looking down at them. "It's almost worth the pain of all those operations. My parents were told I would not be able to use them, but then we found Dr. Hopkins."

"Is that a surgeon? Are you still under his care?"

"When I'm in Wisconsin I see him. I e-mail him now and then to let him know how things are going," Mark said. "He's a golfer, too."

"I bet he's really proud of you and all you've accomplished."

"What have I accomplished "Being a golf pro isn't okay with you?" she asked

"Sure, it is," Mark said, but didn't meet her eyes.

∞

Mark and Merit went out through the pro shop to unload her clubs. When they exited the building, a beautiful woman with an edgy black haircut walked in. She wore an expensive looking golf ensemble, huge sunglasses, and her olive skin was darkly tanned.

"Merit, this is Natalie. She plays in the women's group. You two would be good play partners. You're at about the same level."

"Hi," Merit said.

"Hello, I'd love to have a game," Natalie said.

They shook hands. Merit noticed a couple of nice sized diamonds on a ring on her right hand.

"Great. Do you have a business card?" Natalie asked.

Merit patted her pocket and pulled out a card with Law Office of Merit Bridges printed on it.

"Here you go," Merit said.

Natalie located a card in her purse.

"Here's mine. Email me and I'll write you back. I've got a tee time. I better go," Natalie said.

"She'll introduce you to the other women in the group. Very outgoing," Mark said.

"Coolio," Merit said.

She turned the card over. It was glossy and oversized. The purpose was obviously to stand out. Merit stuffed it into her pocket and followed Mark to her car.

Things are looking up.

Chapter Nineteen

"Our client Terrence Long has been murdered," Betty said to Merit as they entered the office from the garage and walked down the hallway.

"What? How?" Merit asked.

"Just saw it on TV this morning. Red didn't call you?" Betty asked.

"No, she must be caught up at the murder scene," Merit said.

They continued through the reception area and down the hall to Merit's office. Betty woke up the firm by flipping on light switches and turning on the copy machine as they passed each room.

"What happened?" Merit asked.

"Just said he was found tortured and dead in one of those old farm houses out by Bastrop. Seems he was hanging from a rafter and cut to bits," Betty said.

"His poor wife," Merit said.

"Shocking," Betty said.

Merit dropped her briefcase, picked up the remote, and turned on the flat screen TV on her credenza. Red, in a short purple dress with puffy sleeves stood before the crime scene with a microphone in her hand. The crawler along the bottom of the screen indicated that she was in Bastrop. Members of law enforcement were busy behind her on the other side of the yellow tape.

"It appears the killer called The Enforcer has once again tortured and killed a member of the Austin community," Red said, and she flipped her red hair over her shoulder. "Police are still unsure of the motive."

"How does something like this happen in Austin?" Merit asked.

"There's no place like Texas," Betty said.

"I better call Ag," Merit said.

At that moment, Merit's mobile rang, and Ag's face popped on the screen.

"Are you watching this?"

Chapter Twenty

Mark went to the pro shop and gave a full day's schedule of golf lessons. Bob Tom Jakes walked out as Mr. Shasta, a fat cat wearing a chunky gold Rolex and green plaid pants, handed Mark a wad of cash.

"Thanks, Mark." Mr. Shasta said.

"No problem, Mr. Shasta. Thank you for the generous tip. Keep that left arm straight."

"Right," grunted Mr. Shasta as he headed for the bar.

"Bob Tom, I'm rackin' it in today," Mark said.

Bob Tom looked at the wadded bills and said, "Johnson got twice that a few hours ago."

Joe, standing behind the counter, turned and straightened a rack of socks with orange longhorns, blue bears, and maroon ATM's embroidered on them.

No matter what Mark did, Bob Tom found a way to criticize or belittle him. He always fell just short of Bob Tom's expectations. Mark was starting to feel as if Check had moved to Austin and taken up camp in the pro shop.

Bob Tom even resembled Check with his slight paunch over his belt.

I just can't do this anymore. Mark thought as he cut through the pro shop and down the hall. He liked most of the people he worked with and heaven knows loved golf, but at the end of the day, he was still in the same place, doing the same thing and facing the next day of sameness. His morning self-pep talks were becoming less and less enthusiastic and all but ineffective.

Mark went into the men's room and sat on the toilet. He rested his head on the top of the chrome tissue holder and sighed with relief as the metal cooled his forehead.

He heard a couple of golfers come in and unzip at the urinal. They chatted over the sound of tinkling liquid.

"Did you hear the one about the lawyers playing golf? They had a fifty-dollar bet. After a few holes, the first lawyer is ahead by a few strokes, but hits his shot into the rough. He asks his buddy to help him find the ball, but neither can find it. So, the first lawyer pulls another ball out of his pocket, tosses it on the ground and says, 'I've found my ball.' The second lawyer says, 'After all these years, you'd cheat me for a lousy fifty bucks? And you're a liar, too. I've been standing on your ball for the last five minutes.'"

Mark rolled his eyes at the ceiling as he heard them laugh and zip up.

As they washed their hands, one asked, "Did you see the Colonial in San Antonio on TV this weekend?"

"Yeah," replied the other, "and what a score by Spieth. Did you see that last shot when he knew he had a sixty-five? I'd give my left nut for a sixty-five on that course."

Mark quietly banged his head against the stall wall as the men left. Mark rested his forehead back on the chrome.

"I can shoot sixty-five on that course any day," Mark groaned to himself.

Chapter Twenty-One

Merit arrived home late and tired. She took care of the dog's needs and started a bath for herself. She turned the hot water on full blast and squirted grapefruit body wash under the stream. The citrus scent rose on the steam and revived her a bit.

Merit heard a noise from her bedroom. It was her son's ring tone on her mobile. Merit pulled on a robe as she answered.

"Hey, Ace. How are things in Houston?"

"Great, Mom. How are you?"

"I'm busy as always, but things are running smoothly," Merit said.

Don't think I'll replay my day.

"I wanted to let you know that the school is planning a ski trip to Colorado over Thanksgiving break. I'd like to go."

"Oh, Peaches. I was so looking forward to spending some time with you. I miss you."

"Me too, Mom, but I thought I might ask Rachel to go along."

Merit bit her lip. Ace had been moving further and further away the past year. It was inevitable, but it still grabbed her heart every time she realized it.

"That sounds like fun," she said. "Is Rachel the new girl?"

"Yeah. We've been out for burgers a couple of times. So far so good," Ace said.

"That's great, Ace," Merit said.

"Mom, do you think I could get a little extra money this month? Only if it's not a problem."

"I'll put some extra cash in your checking account."

"Women are expensive," Ace said.

"They are. Text me the trip info. I'll call the chaperone and make the arrangements."

"Thanks. Talk soon."

"Love you, bye."

Merit sat on the side of her bed and heard a resounding *SNIP! SNIP!* The sounds of the umbilical cord being severed once again. She knew it was healthy and normal, but the grief that welled up in her each time Ace took another step into manhood and away from her was bittersweet.

Pepper put her front legs on the bed and nestled her head between her paws. She looked for a long time into Merit's wet eyes.

Chapter Twenty-Two

Merit entered the club house for a lesson just in time to see Mark almost run into a burly man in bright plaid golf pants.

"Sorry, Mr. Zars. How are you?" Mark asked.

"*Oke'n*. Browno, please. How goes it with you? You ready to pay me?"

"Not yet. I'm working on it." Mark said.

"Juice it is running, eh? You remember?"

Mark knew that juice was interest. He'd seen enough mob movies to pick up the lingo.

"How much are we talking?" Mark asked.

"Fifteen thousand."

Mark blanched.

Mark seemed to force a smile on his face. "Of course, Browno. I'll have it soon."

Browno smiled again and slapped Mark on the shoulder.

"Time to pay the piper," Browno said.

Merit could only hear bits and pieces of their conversation.

Mark looked up, saw Merit, and turned to Browno.

"Could we talk later? I have a lesson," Mark said.

"You bet. Pretty lady," Browno said. "Just don't forget."

"How could I?" Mark said and walked over to Merit.

"Who's that?" Merit asked.

"One of my clients," Mark said avoiding her eyes. "Ready for your lesson?"

Merit let it slide and walked out to the practice area.

"I saw you had a few problems on Saturday when you were playing with Natalie," Mark said. "When you got stuck in the thick rough a couple of times, you couldn't get out."

"I felt like I was hitting the tar baby. The more I whacked at it, the worse it got," Merit said.

"Okay, let's move over to the short game area and I'll show you a few tricks," Mark said.

They took a few balls over to two grassy mounds, which had been flattened at the top. Mark threw the balls into the ruff at the edge of the chipping area.

"See that first ball?"

"Yes."

"Your goal is to get it out of the rough in one shot. So, the first thing you want to do is assess the line. Is the grass around it growing toward or away from the hole you're aiming for?" Mark asked.

"The grass is growing toward the hole, but mostly straight up," Merit said.

"I agree. So, come over here." He pointed to a spot on the ground near the ball. "See how this looks like a similar situation?"

"Yes." Merit said.

"Wait," Mark said as he took the club from Merit's hand. "Use your sand wedge, it's heavier."

Mark switched the club out of his bag and handed it to her. She stepped over to the spot he'd indicated.

"When would I use my regular wedge if I'm using my sand wedge and I'm not in the sand?"

"As a general rule, use the sand wedge when you've got more drag on the club like this heavy grass or sand. Use the regular wedge when you're in short rough or close to the pin. Just keep working with both in different topography and you'll start to develop a sense of which one will work in each situation," Mark said.

"Got it," Merit said.

"Now, take a few practice swings in this similar spot to see how much resistance there is. Feel the grass and the amount of loft you'll need," Mark said. "And, remember, grass changes directions as the sun moves, so where it might have been facing east in the morning, it may be facing west in the evening."

Merit took a few swings in the grass.

"Now, address the ball, but don't hit it yet," Mark instructed.

Merit stood over the ball with her sand wedge and got into striking position.

"Take a small step closer to the ball, and grip down an inch or two on the club."

Merit followed instructions.

"Get ready to swing, and when you do, go as deep as you can without tearing a big divot in the ground. At the same time, keep your weight forward. Really hit it," Mark said.

Merit tossed up a chunk of grassy ground that flew out with the ball. The ball rolled up on the mound and stopped next to the hole.

"A little deep, but good job," Mark complimented. "The more timid players are afraid to tear a hole in the ground, but this grass grows upward, and the only way to get to the bottom of the ball is to dig deep. If you make a divot, you can always repair it afterward with this."

Mark pulled a plastic gadget with two prongs on one end out of his pocket and handed it to her. It had the ACCC logo on the round end.

Mark squatted down and repaired the divot.

"Thanks," Merit said.

If only everything could be fixed so easily, Mark thought.

Chapter Twenty-Three

Merit met Ag for dinner at Jack Allen's Kitchen in Oak Hill. While they waited in line, they found a spot at the bar. Merit ordered a dark red wine and Ag had a local IPA. The beautiful people mixed with the retirees and families all around them.

"I've checked out Terrence Long's background, and I can't find a single thing that would lead to his murder," Ag said. "His family isn't wealthy. He married a name, but no money, and he was respected by other developers around town."

"What about his wife?" Merit asked.

"She entertains at home, does charity work, takes care of the kids. Nothing I can find there," Ag said.

"Is The Enforcer striking these people at random or is there some commonality to all of them?" Merit asked.

"I haven't looked at the other victims, but Chaplain has and he is stumped," Ag said.

"Well, someone wanted him dead and they wanted him to suffer first," Merit said.

Chapter Twenty-Four

Merit met Mark for another golf lesson at the driving range. It was a lovely November day. Cool. Crisp. One of the reasons people relocated to Texas. The beautiful weather seemed lost on Mark.

Merit had on a red polo shirt and black golf shorts. Her legs were tanned from the hours outdoors. Mark greeted her without comment on her outfit, or even a once over.

"What's up?" Merit asked.

"Oh, nothing," Mark replied, and smiled. But Merit could tell that something was wrong; normally Mark was so personable, so fun to be around.

"Did you see the new bumper sticker on Joe's car in the lot?" Merit asked.

"No, does he have a new one?"

"It says IT TAKES A LOT OF BALLS TO GOLF LIKE I DO!" Merit laughed.

Mark laughed a little.

"Are you sure nothing's wrong?" she asked.

"I'm sure," Mark responded.

"Okay." Merit grabbed a bucket of balls from Dave at the range stand while Mark set out her clubs. When she returned Mark looked absent.

"Ace's not going to make it home for Thanksgiving," Merit said.

"That's nice," Mark said.

"Okay. I give up," Merit said.

No quickies today, I guess.

"What? Let's work with your driver again today. Your putting is looking pretty good, but your driving is weak. You're not getting enough distance off the tee," Mark said.

"Good idea," Merit said. "I notice on a par four it takes me three shots to make four hundred yards instead of two, like the guys. I'm already one over par before I even chip or putt."

"Exactly, but your accuracy is pretty good, so I'm betting the people you're playing with are hitting wide or in the rough and having to take another shot anyway."

"Right, it's the only way I can compete."

Mark perched a ball on the tee for her.

"Okay, let it rip."

Merit set up and swung, knocking the ball just short of the one-hundred-yard marker.

"Okay, that's good, but you're not fully winding up for the swing. Here, set up and I'll show you."

Mark put a fresh ball on the tee. Merit addressed the ball with her driver.

"Now, wind up but don't swing."

Merit pulled the club over her right shoulder and held the position. Mark faced her and pulled her body around further to the right, giving her a much larger circle to swing through.

"Okay, hold that." Mark stepped back. "Now, let it go, and be sure to follow through at the end."

Merit swung the club and smacked the ball. It sailed well past the one-hundred-yard marker, taking a right along the way due to a gust of wind.

"That's great. You got a lot more distance. Did you feel it?"

"Yes, I got it."

"Try another," Mark set a ball on the tee and pointed to the flag blowing north. "See that flag? Since it's not flapping too much, the wind must not be blowing very hard, so just move your stance a tad before you hit."

Merit looked at the flags, adjusted her stance to the right and wound up fully. She struck the ball perfectly. It sailed out to the left, caught the wind, curved to the right, and landed close to the one-hundred-and-fifty-yard marker.

"Like that?" Merit asked.

"Exactly. Now do it until it's in your muscle memory," Mark said.

Merit hit most of the balls in the bucket, checking the flags and placing the shots around the range with increasing accuracy.

"You'll be beating Natalie before you know it," Mark said.

"Thanks," Merit winked at him.

Mark gave her a quick smile, then became serious again.

"Let's call it a day," Mark said.

"What about my etiquette tip? I don't want to get shortchanged on my lesson," Merit said.

"Oh, right. Let's see. Here's another one for putting. On most courses, when the player who's furthest out putts close to the hole, but doesn't make it in, the player can either clear their ball by putting in right away, or they can mark the ball and putt after those still further out."

"I see."

"Either way, they are clearing the area around the hole for the other players."

"Thanks, good one," she said. "Do you want some lunch?"

Mark didn't respond.

"Hey golfboy, where are you today?" Merit asked.

"Merit, I think I'm going to try to get on the tour again." Mark sounded as if he were spitting the words.

"Fantastic!"

"I don't want anyone to know yet, especially Bob Tom. He's already scheduled me for folding clothes in the pro shop two afternoons a week. If he thinks I might actually accomplish something, who knows what he'll have me doing. Maybe cleaning toilets."

"Okay, your secret's safe with me. Until a TV camera shows up, I guess," Merit laughed.

"Oh, God. TV." Mark shrunk back.

"Okay, wait a minute, I was kidding. That's a long way off, right? What's involved to play the tour? What do you have to do? The Tin Cup movie guy seemed to do it pretty quickly," Merit laughed.

"Kevin Costner? Yeah, he made it look easy. It's a long process.

"Nix that. What's your plan?"

"Well, there are several ways to go. I could start with the mini-tours," Mark said.

"Is that the Nike Tour and the Hooter's Tour I've heard about?" Merit asked.

"Yeah, but it's a rough life, a different town every week, and I already tried that before. It didn't work out."

"What are your other options?" Merit asked.

"I could go to Qualifying School, but I'd have to quit my job, and I don't have the bucks. Only about thirty-five of the players in Q school get their PGA cards. I figure I've only got one more shot at this, and I don't want time to slip away."

"Two off the list. What are your other options?" Merit asked.

"Being a member of the PGA of America, I can play in the PGA Championship in August if I jump through a few hoops first."

"Such as?"

"I am already a PGA professional. I took all the classes and tests over the last year. Maybe one or two small things left. I played the locals for fun in July and survived that fine. Right before we met, I played the Regional Club Pro Championship. I finished one hundred and five and that qualifies me to go onto the PGA Pro Championship," Mark summarized.

"When is that?"

"It's in June in Frisco near Dallas. That would give me several months to train, get in shape, and see how I progress."

"Aren't you in shape now?"

"Yes, but I'd really have to train, lift weights, eat differently, find a pro to work with. Step up everything. I need your help."

"Yes. What can I do?" Merit asked.

"Just hear me out first."

"Okay."

"No one has ever won the PGA Championship who wasn't already on the tour and pretty high on the money list. And, I'd be putting all my eggs in one basket. I don't know if I have more than one shot left in me."

"Remember our first date when we went to eat pizza?"

"Yeah?"

"We didn't eat the whole thing in one mouthful. Let's eat one bite at a time, then one slice at a time. Pretty soon done - the whole pie."

"Good point. I guess if I decide I've had enough, I can always stop along the way. I don't know if this is what I should be doing. Maybe I'd be better off just to enjoy my pro work and play golf for fun. I could lose my job," Mark said. He didn't mention that if he lost his job he'd never pay Browno back.

"That's not a very positive attitude. What's really bothering you?"

"I don't want to bomb in front of everyone again like I did in Wisconsin." Mark said. "That's another reason to choose the PGA Pro Championship. I can just appear to play for fun. If I can't do it, nobody will be the wiser."

"Not going for it doesn't make you safe, Mark. It only holds you captive," Merit said.

Chapter Twenty-Five

M erit knocked on the door of deceased Terrence Long's large beautiful home in Westlake Hills. His widow, Jessica Hogg Long answered the door wearing a flowing black caftan. Her long platinum hair hug over one shoulder and chandelier earrings dangled from her earlobes and danced around her neck.

Merit knew that although Jessica was a descendent of Jim Hogg, the Texas governor of around 1890, there was no money following that legacy, only history and bad j"Thank you for coming," Jessica said.

"I'm sorry about Terrence. It must have been a terrible shock to you," Merit said as she entered the foyer.

"He was just starting to perk up after all the stress surrounding Hill Country Homestead," Jessica said.

Merit accompanied her into the living room where they sat before a huge marble fireplace on Design Within Reach type furniture.

"I checked with the bank, and Terrence made a payment of two-hundred-thousand dollars just before his death," Merit said. "Do you know where he got the money?"

"No. Chaplain from APD asked the same thing. I told Chaplain to ask you. We didn't sell anything. Not that we had much left to sell. The house is mortgaged, the cars are rentals. Just between us, it's all smoke and mirrors at this point," Jessica said. "Maybe he got it from a friend."

"Terrence probably didn't want me to know where the money came from. I've ordered title work to see if he took a second lien," Merit said.

"It's the only collateral he could have used," Jessica said.

"Has APD determined who might have caused his death or why?" Merit asked.

"No, and when I identified the body at the morgue, they wouldn't let me see his torso. His face was sliced in several places, so if the torso was worse, I can only imagine what he went through," Jessica said.

"I'm sorry you had to go through that," Merit said.

"The children are being teased at school, and my friends are whispering," Jessica said.

"Hang onto your dignity, Jessica," Merit said. "We'll find a way out of this."

"That's why I wanted to see you. I need to preserve my home for the children and keep as much of the life insurance as I can. I haven't had a job since just after college. I'll need some time to establish an income."

Or get married again. Merit thought.

"I've spoken with the bank and they are willing to give us a little time to re-arrange the mortgage on the property," Merit said. "It's really not a nice gesture on their part. They know the probate will tie them up anyway, so they might as well appear gracious."

"I'll take it any way we can get it, but how can we do anything without some cash?" Jessica asked. "I'm worried about foreclosure."

"I think I can find another developer to complete the project. If I can get the bank to sign off on the change-over, we might be able to get you a percentage as well as relief from the loan," Merit said.

"So, the children and I can live off of the life insurance until the development is sold out?" Jessica asked.

"That's the goal," Merit said.

"Who would you approach?" Jessica asked.

"There are two large developers in Austin who already have relationships with the bank. I'll go to them first since they are credit worthy. It will speed things along if we don't have to qualify a new corporation for a line of credit to take over the loan," Merit said. "The bank will be more comfortable working with someone they already have a relationship with. The probate court, too."

"That sounds like an excellent plan," Jessica said. "I'm so glad I called you."

"Let's not get too far ahead of ourselves. I'll have to negotiate your retention percentage and I'll need you to be flexible on that," Merit said.

"Terrence trusted you, so I do, too," Jessica said. "Do the best you can."

Fingers crossed, they both thought.

Chapter Twenty-Six

Merit sat back in her chair at the ACCC's award winning restaurant. Across from her was new friend and golf buddy, Natalie. They had both just finished a long day at work and were enjoying a glass of wine while they studied the menu. The chef had been nominated for a James Beard Award and was known for his sauces.

"Penny for your thoughts," Natalie said. "You look like you're thinking about something important."

"A client of mine passed away recently and there's a lot on my plate at work right now. You must have crunch times too."

"Absolutely. Here's to strong women," Natalie said.

Merit raised her glass to tap against Natalie's.

"So, you had a long day, too. What is it that you do for work?" Merit asked.

"I'm in public relations," Natalie said.

"That covers a lot of territory." Merit smiled. The wine was a nice Pinot Noir, full of flavor. She hadn't blinked when Natalie ordered one of the best wines on the list. Good wine was at the top of Merit's favorite things.

"I saw you at the driving range with that handsome young pro. Is he any good? What was his name again?"

Merit tipped her head and swirled the wine in her glass. "Mark Green. He's an excellent instructor," Merit said.

The waiter came and stood unobtrusively over Natalie's shoulder, waiting for her order. Other than his oversized ears, he almost blended into the background.

"Salmon special," Natalie said.

"And for you, Madam?" he said to Merit.

"I'll have the same."

As the waiter slid away gracefully, the young man in the Z-Ro cap that Merit had seen around the course emerged from the bar area and cut through the restaurant to the patio doors. She thought he was looking at her. Her armpits prickled, and she shivered.

"You know him?" Natalie asked.

Merit shook her head. She chided herself.

Danger is not around every corner. Especially in the middle of a fine-dining establishment like this.

Natalie asked a few more questions about Mark, and Merit parried expertly, even though she was on her second glass of wine. For the next hour or two, she focused on Natalie, and they shared their war stories about clients. No names, of course.

Desert was fresh fruit and crème fraiche, and they both enjoyed it with a pot of French press coffee.

"I'm normally a tea drinker, but there's nothing like a good cup of coffee after a nice meal," Merit said.

"Mm. I'd like to get you out on the course again this week," Natalie said. "I think we play very well together."

"Coolio," Merit said.

When the server deposited the bill on the table, strategically in the middle, both Natalie and Merit reached for it, but Natalie got it first. She signed the receipt with a set to her mouth that showed Merit that she liked to get her way. It irked Merit for a minute, and then not so much.

Natalie had gotten it first; she'd won fair and square. Merit respected that. She'd get it next time.

They walked out to the parking lot arm in arm like school girls who'd found a new secret pal.

Chapter Twenty-Seven

Mark went south to the Woodlands in Houston for a regional qualifier. Merit joined him the next day after she wrapped up some work projects. It was their first trip out of town together, and Merit was enjoying the escape from scrutinizing eyes. They knew virtually no one at the tournament, but Merit thought if Mark went on to achieve his goal of playing the PGA tour, people might remember seeing them together. She enjoyed herself but played it cool when with him in public.

Mark, on the other hand, acted as if Merit were his high school girlfriend and had been grabbing her hand all weekend. They stayed at a small hotel near the course, nothing fancy, but clean and accessible. Merit would have preferred something at the Galleria, or near Rice University, her old alma mater, but it was too far a drive to accommodate early tee times. Besides, she knew Mark didn't have the bucks. If he won, he could cover the expenses of the trip but not much beyond that. She didn't want him to feel like a kept man, and she didn't want to feel as though she were paying for sex.

The first day of the tournament had been great, putting Mark in a good position for the rest of the weekend. He played well on Saturday and started Sunday with seeming enthusiasm, which gradually waned until the end of the day, when he appeared to have nothing left. He barely made the qualifying score he needed, but there was not much other than that to be proud of.

Merit found an outdoor seat at the clubhouse to wait for Mark to sign his scorecard and wrap up paperwork. She ordered a glass of Malbec for herself and a margarita for Mark and stretched in the afternoon sun. George Strait sang over the outdoor speakers about his "Love Without End, Amen".

Typical Gulf Coast humidity was keeping the weather nice and warm. The course lay out before her, serene and wooded with beautiful water spots and stylized hedges. The white wooden tables and chairs made a sharp contrast to the aqua water and green grass.

Mark walked over and sat down at the table with Merit. He scooped the lime and umbrella decoration out of his margarita with two fingers and flung it on the table. He downed half the drink in one gulp.

"I showed my ass out there today," Mark said, his face as red as the flag on the last hole. "I couldn't feel any rhythm, and I never clicked into my pattern."

"You played fine overall." Merit smiled at Mark. "Remember what they say, there's no such thing as a bad day on the golf course."

"Some say that. Mark Twain said it was a good walk spoiled. I just didn't get it done," Mark said. He flexed his hands, massaging first one and then the other.

"Everyone has an off day. You'll make it up next time," Merit said.

More golfers walked off the course.

"Let's get out of here. I can't stand to face these people." Mark frowned at his drink.

"Let's have our drinks. Relax for a minute. They've all had bad days too," Merit said. She took a long sip.

"I can't relax," Mark said and scowled at the stragglers coming in from the eighteenth hole. The sounds of the course echoed around them as they sat in contemplative silence. Merit searched her mind for something wise to say.

Mark sulked on.

Mark broke his pouting silence and said, "I'll never play like Tiger or Phil. I can't make that clutch two-iron or spin the ball. I will never be able to do what they do. I'll never be like Jack Nicklaus."

Merit placed her hand over his scared fingers on the table. Her eyes wandered over to a blue pond dotted with white swans and green ducks. A peacock emerged from behind the trees and walked toward the clubhouse fanning its brilliant turquoise tail.

"Look!" she said, gesturing toward the magnificent bird.

Mark was not impressed and hung his head further.

"What if every peacock tried to be a duck or an elephant or a dog? Wouldn't that be ridiculous? It just wouldn't work," she said.

"Your point?" Mark said, downing the last of his drink.

"Well, a peacock can only be a peacock, and you can only be Mark."

"What are you talking about?"

"You have to be you, Mark, play the way you play, the way your body moves, the way your hands work, the way your swing flows. You can't be anyone else, and to imitate any one of them is being a poor second to what they are. You have to be the best you."

"I guess," Mark said.

"When we're in bed and you move your body just so, or put your hands on me just right, there's no one else who can do that in exactly that way. Play golf like you make love, Mark. All your own."

Mark caught her mood, "You mean like..." He leaned over and whispered in her ear then nipped at her earlobe.

"Exactly." Merit smiled at him. "Now, I'm ready to go."

They laughed.

Mark gestured toward the waitress. "Check please!"

Chapter Twenty-Eight

M ark drove back to Austin and Merit stayed an extra day in Houston to visit Ace. She moved into Joy and Tucker's house and got two for one with friends and family during the time in H Town.

Merit picked up Ace at school and they drove downtown to the Market area to the second oldest building in Houston for Cajun food at Treebeards. Ace was bubbly, and it did Merit's heart good to see him happy. The waiter seated them by the window and they watched the parade of commerce go by while alternating looks at the menu.

"Betty sent you her world-famous lemon squares. They're in the car. I ate one on the drive down. Couldn't resist," Merit said.

"I was hoping for some Betty snacks," Ace said, grinning.

After they ordered, Merit said, "Tell me about Rachel. Is she nice?"

"Yeah, and sweet. I have a picture on my phone. Wanna' see it?" Ace asked.

"Sure," Merit said.

Ace scrolled his finger over his iPhone and selected a snap. He handed the phone to Merit.

"Oh. Cute!" Merit said looking at a petite girl with pixie blonde hair and a sweet smile.

"She is, isn't she," Ace grinned.

"Is this getting serious?" Merit asked.

Merit tilted her head and gave him her best I-am-your-mother look.

"Maybe, I like her a lot. We haven't gone all the way if that's what you mean." Ace said.

"No, I…"

Nothing had prepared her for these moments. Sometimes you couldn't learn something unless you lived it.

"Let's order," Merit said, snapping her menu open.

The server deposited drinks for them and they ordered. Jambalaya for Ace and seafood gumbo for Merit.

Ace kept checking his phone and texting while they waited for the food.

"I'd appreciate it if we could spend this time alone," Merit said.

"It's Rachel. She wants to know if we're having a good time," Ace said.

"You can tell her later," Merit said.

Ace's smile faded. The food arrived, and the discussion ended as Ace dug in and they both sopped up the sauce with crunchy French bread.

Merit wasn't sure if it was the fact that Ace hadn't asked for her opinion about Rachel, or that he seemed out of balance with his priorities. Ace was a good kid, and they never argued, except that now they were.

Merit drove Ace to his dorm and hugged him. He held her for a minute and then slipped out of her embrace.

Chapter Twenty-Nine

The next day, Mark entered the pro shop at ACCC on time, but before he could punch in, Joe sidetracked him.

"Mark, could you help Mr. Jameson here with a question about the course?" Joe asked.

Joe proceeded to administer WD-40 to his elbows while Mark answered the player's questions.

"Hello, Mark. Did they fix that soggy spot on the back nine?" asked Mr. Jameson.

"Yes, sir, they did," Mark said. "There was a low spot where the holding pond was spilling over. The groundskeepers shored up the mound on the left side and it holds the water now."

"Great, that was an eyesore, "Mr. Jameson said as he headed toward the door.

"Not to mention the fact that every ball he hit on that hole went right to that spot," Mark commented to Joe. They both chuckled.

"How are things going with that pretty lady lawyer?" Joe asked.

"She's a great student," Mark said.

"Does she know about your agreement with Browno Zars?" Joe asked.

Mark made a non-commital face. "How did you know that? Excuse me. I need to do my time card." Mark pushed his thoughts of Browno away. He didn't want to think about how he was going to come up with his upcoming payment. He especially didn't want to think about how he was going to raise the funds for his PGA attempt. Why wasn't Browno getting him paying gigs? Maybe he should ask him.

Bob Tom came out of the office just in time to see Mark punch in, now about five minutes late.

"Eight o'clock means eight o'clock," Bob Tom scolded.

"I got waylaid on my way through the pro shop," Mark said.

"That's no excuse. Dawdling. You always have a reason," Bob Tom said.

Joe heard the commotion and piped up.

"Bob Tom, it was my fault. I asked Mark to field a question for a new member on his way in."

Mark proceeded to the back as Bob Tom walked up to Joe.

"Don't make excuses for him. You'll make him soft," Bob Tom said.

"The only reason you don't like Mark is because he looks like Bobby used to," Joe said.

"Mind your own business," Bob Tom said.

"Well, you can punish Mark all you want, but he's not Bobby, and it won't bring your son back."

"You have no idea what it's like not to know whether your son is gone for good, shooting up somewhere, or even dead," Bob Tom said.

"No, I don't. But, Mark is not Bobby. Mark comes to work every day, he tries hard, he doesn't lie or steal from you, and he truly wants to please you. Why do you want to hurt him?" Joe said.

Bob Tom's angry face changed to sadness. "Maybe it makes me feel better."

Mark listened in at the office door. He didn't know that Bob Tom had a son. That explained a lot. Fathers and sons, always a tricky area to navigate.

Chapter Thirty

Mark went to Florida for a qualifier a few weeks later. Merit stayed in Austin as she was working on the Long re-finance, and had a big deal coming together for Fiesta Tamales, one of her largest clients. Fiesta was working with two Texas based grocers, Whole Foods and HEB, to put their tamales in the stores and Merit was negotiating the contracts.

On Sunday, Merit met Mark at the airport. He was tan and handsome. Merit felt a tingle of longing when she first saw him. They caught up in the car on the way.

"Did you get your client's tamale deal done?" Mark asked.

"Most of it. Betty is working on the last paperwork now."

"That's great, Merit."

"How did the game go?" she asked.

"Much better than Houston. I saw some improvement. I really missed you, though," Mark said. He tugged on her ponytail.

"Good work," Merit said.

"You, too. I scored a sixty-seven," Mark said.

"Now, that's more like it," Merit said.

"Thanks. I'm going to need a coach to work with pretty soon. I wish I had the bucks for someone like Butch Harmon. He was Tiger Woods' swing guru in Tiger's heyday. I did talk with a guy named David Yee that I like, but he's tied up right now, and expensive, too."

"I saw you on television," Merit said.

"I avoided the cameras as much as I could. I didn't realize I was on."

"It was from a distance, but you looked great. You even got some nice comments from the announcer. I taped it for you," Merit said.

Merit didn't mention that they cameras had zoomed in on Mark's hands several times.

"What's next?" Merit asked as she took the back way to avoid the ever-increasing Austin traffic.

"I've got to work at ACCC most weekends until Christmas, so I'll need to play locally during the week most of the time. I need to sit down with a calendar and map out a plan."

"That sounds like a good idea. I'll try to be as involved as I can," Merit said.

"That's great. I need to find a caddie, and I've got to find a way to get off a week each for Frisco and then Wisconsin if I qualify. I'll only accrue part of the vacation days I need by summer. If I get that far I may have to quit or take a leave of absence. I can't really do without the paycheck."

"That's a lot of juggling," Merit said.

"Bob Tom will be a bear about it," Mark said. He was glad that Merit didn't ask how he was going to finance all of his big plans.

"What about the holidays?"

"Since I'm the new kid, I have to work Christmas, but I'm off the day after Christmas through New Year's," Mark said.

"Are you going home?" Merit asked.

"No. Mom is coming here for a few days before Christmas. I'll be working, but we'll have time at night, and she can go sightseeing during the day. Of course, I'll want to sneak over and see you."

Mark massaged her neck with his scarred fingers.

"And your Dad?" Merit asked.

"Check won't come to Texas. He thinks all Texans are like J.R. Ewing," Mark said.

Merit laughed. "Larry Hagman was a Texan. J.R. Ewing was a character."

"Try telling Check that," Mark said.

She pulled the car into his apartment complex driveway and pressed a code into the gate box.

"Do you have your plans set yet?" Mark asked.

"Ace will be home for Christmas or we'll meet at Joy and Tucker's in Houston. I also have some business for a client in L.A.," Merit said.

"I didn't know you had L.A. clients," Mark said.

"I handle the estate of a singer songwriter named Liam Nolan. The client takes me out to California now and then," Merit said.

"How long will you be gone?" He asked.

"A few days. Betty is working on my itinerary."

"I have to do a clinic for work and to wrap up the PGA school in Santa Fe. I thought we might meet there for New Year's," Mark said.

"Is it warm enough to play golf in January in Santa Fe?" she asked.

"Most of the clinic is indoors and meets only in the morning. There are some parts of the Club Pro program that aren't learned on the golf course. I have to do a clinic on club repair, and another on the basics of course management."

"What's the one in Santa Fe about?" Merit asked.

"It's on running a tournamen"There's more to it than I thought," Merit said.

"I really want you to come. You could sleep in. We could ski after," Mark said.

"Sounds fun. I could fly back from California through New Mexico. If you'll e-mail me your schedule, I'll see if I can match it," Merit said.

"It will be perfect," Mark said.

"How about a sex lesson?" Merit said.

"Don't tease me. Can you stay?" Mark asked.

"Tee it up," Merit said.

Chapter Thirty-One

Merit and Ag sat in her office after hours with a beer, a glass of wine, and three files on the desk before them. The TV was on KNEW 9 on low volume. The lead was about the torture killings around town, including Terrence Long. Red Thallon, decked out in a skimpy black and white blocked mini-dress stood outside of an old house with crime scene tape stretched around it.

"It appears that The Enforcer has struck again," Red said.

Mayor Burke Lee walked nearby, and Red scooted over to him.

"Mayor Lee. Are there any new developments in the attempt to catch this monster?" Red asked.

"Police are having a hard time determining the link between these murders, but they all have the same M.O. All the victims bear ligature marks from being tied up and hung from their arms. Various sharp objects have been used to torture and kill them," Mayor Lee said into the hand-held mic.

"We'll have more on the five o'clock news. This is Red Thallon for KNEW 9."

Merit muted the sound.

"What happened to sleepy little Austin?" Merit asked.

"It grew up and out. Chaplin and the boys at APD are going mental over this Enforcer guy. Someone else has gone missing, and they think it's related. His family says they don't know anything, so Chaplin has nothing to go on." He rubbed his hand over his eyes. "Whoever this guy is, he's good. He doesn't leave witnesses, he plans in advance, and he likes his work."

"Speaking of work. Let's go over these files," Merit said as she took a long sip of her wine.

"Right," Ag said.

Merit knew all about the climbing crime rates and victim stats. She knew that Austin was a safe place, but she knew that there was evil out there and what it looked like. Merit's armpits prickled ever so slightly.

Chapter Thirty-Two

Mark entered the parking lot at Austin Creek Country Club on a beautiful sunny day. The course maintenance crew was wrapping the trees with tiny white Christmas lights. He zipped up his light jacket and wondered how deep the snow was back in Wisconsin.

He looked out over the first nine and thanked his lucky stars for being a golfer, for meeting Merit, and for finding the courage to try again.

Mark asked for anything the god of golf could do to help him get to Frisco in June. He wasn't relying entirely on the golf god today. He needed the blessing, but Mark also had a plan.

He walked into the pro shop, said hi to Joe and punched in. Bob Tom came out of the back just in time to scowl at him. Mark gave him a smile.

"Do you have a minute?" Mark asked.

"Just a second," Bob Tom went over to Joe who was straightening a stack of shoeboxes. "If we don't get those inventory reports in by Friday, we'll be screwed and tattooed by the home office," Bob Tom said.

"Got it," Joe said.

Bob Tom nodded toward the office. Bob Tom sat behind his desk piled high with charts and order forms. Mark took the guest chair in front and looked out the window at the second hole, which wrapped around that side of the clubhouse. He fidgeted with his scarred hands on the arm of the chair.

"I've been thinking," Mark said.

"Yeah?" Bob Tom asked.

"It seems to me that we should make a three-part form for the stock room. When the inventory comes in, we'll only have to document it once. Then, we'd tear off one sheet send the other two out to the floor with the merchandise. When the item is stocked, we'll tear off another copy." He rushed on. "When the third part comes back after inventory or sale, Joanne could do a simple spreadsheet for you and corporate. That should save you about five or six hours a week." Mark finished and took a breath.

"Did you think of this on your own?" Bob Tom growled.

"Yes, sir, I did," Mark kept a smile on his face.

He'll either love it or attack me again, Mark thought.

"It's hotter than the dickens in here," Bob Tom said as he got out of his chair and crossed to the thermostat on the wall behind Mark's chair.

Mark looked straight ahead and waited.

"Well, it's a good idea," Bob Tom said.

"Bob Tom, sir, I know we haven't always seen eye to eye, but I'd really like to change that. I respect you and have learned a lot from you here."

"You don't say."

The tension seemed to break. Bob Tom returned to his seat.

"Anything I can do to prove that to you, just say the word," Mark said.

"Maybe I've been a little hard on you," Bob Tom said.

"I really care about this place and my job here," Mark said.

"I didn't realize that," Bob Tom said.

"Well, it's true, and if you'll give me a chance, I'll prove it to you," Mark said.

"All right," Bob Tom said. "Let's start fresh. We'll see if you follow through. Why don't you do a mockup of that form you described, and I'll see if I can get it printed up."

"I'm on it," Mark grinned.

Chapter Thirty-Three

M erit and Ace made up for their missed Thanksgiving during Christmas break. They enjoyed the Nutcracker Ballet, shopping at the Armadillo Bazaar, and parties in Austin. They avoided the topic of Rachel who had also gone home to her family for the holiday. Ace texted all day long but put the phone away during meals which was a good enough compromise for Merit.

While Ace spent some free time with his childhood Austin friends, Merit was able to slip over to Mark's a couple of times.

Christmas day was spent with Betty. She had insisted that they holiday at her home since it was bustling with people and they wouldn't have time to think too much about Ace's dad and his absence.

Betty needn't have worried. Merit made an effort to remind Ace of the good times they'd all had with Tony around the holidays and had intentionally made light and smiled as if it was the best way to remember the lost one.

After Christmas, Merit and Ace ran down to Port Aransas for a couple of days and enjoyed the sun, walked Pepper on the beach, and ate a lot of seafood. Merit made her famous soft-shell crab and deep-fried shrimp for Ace, his favorite.

Merit aired out the beach house as they'd not used it in a while and she hadn't required her cleaning lady to do it since it was the holidays. After a nice visit, Merit drove back to Austin via Houston and dropped Ace at school.

Time to get back to work for both of them.

Chapter Thirty-Four

M ark was supposed to join Browno on the course for a lesson, but he was late and unhappy to be seeing him. Mark finally made his feet move.

Browno was waiting, leaning on a club, and Mark wondered where he'd managed to get golf gloves big enough to cover his ham-sized hands. He decided not to ask Browno this particular question.

Browno was ending a call and Mark heard him say, "Just take care of it, Petrov."

Mark stood patiently at a polite distance.

"Mark, you late. You doing good?" Browno asked.

"I am. How are you?"

Browno guffawed, a low, Slavic sound.

"Let's roll. Mark did not want to give Browno time to bring up the issue of the money. Mark had never owed anyone anything before except a car payment. His parents, Check especially, didn't believe in debt. It was wearing on him like a constant pressure that he couldn't escape.

They started their lesson, Mark giving pointers to Browno, and Browno ignoring all of them and continuing to slug his way through. Mark had always loved golf, partly because it was something that everybody could enjoy. He was starting to think that Browno might be the exception to that rule. Since Mark didn't want to share that particular tidbit, he kept a smile on his face and murmured encouragement to the hefty Russian.

The hour-long lesson felt like it took three weeks, but when it was finally over, Mark took his hat off and wiped the sweat off his brow with his forearm.

"Good work, Browno."

"*Der'mo*," Browno said.

Mark's forehead wrinkled. "What?"

"Bullshit."

There was a beat while Mark tried to figure out the expression on Browno's face. He had never seen anything quite like it before. It wasn't a look that people from Wisconsin used.

"No tip for you today. I apply it to your juice," Browno said.

After a long moment, Browno smiled his crooked smile. Then he reached over, and clasped Mark's arm, pulling him towards him.

"Why I have to keep reminding you of my money?"

"I just don't have it. If I did, I'd give it to you. I thought you were going to set up some ways for me to make money so I could pay you back. Wasn't that the deal?" Mark asked.

"The deal is you have my money," Browno said.

Mark shrunk. "I know. I just don't have any place to get it. There are a lot of travel expenses right now and with the holidays."

"You spend less attention on your little lawyer girlfriend and more on paying me back. We be friends again," Browno said.

"I'll work on it," Mark said.

"Maybe I take care of that distraction," Browno said.

Chapter Thirty-Five

Mark wrapped up the day's lessons and went to the driving range to hit a bucket of balls before he called it a night at Austin Creek. He was secretly preparing for the PGA Professional in Frisco, just north of Dallas.

His long game was important due to the quartet of par fours he'd been studying, using drawings and paintings of the course. Artwork conveyed more details of topography than photos, so Mark used them instead of pictures when he could find them.

Frisco was a monster course and he'd never played there. He was further stressed because he was currently ranked below the top one hundred golfers. That meant his game had to shift significantly before he got to Frisco, or he was just playing for fun, and right now, that wasn't his goal.

He got a bucket of balls from Dave and set up for practice at the driving range while he thought of Merit. She was so beautiful. He couldn't wait to see her later that night. He forced himself to focus on the task at hand and began hitting with his driver.

Bob Tom delivered some paper work to Dave and stopped to watch Mark for a while.

"That boy can play some golf," Bob Tom said.

"He sure can. Look at that swing," Dave said.

"He needs to bend his right knee a little more at the end there," Bob Tom observed.

"Go tell him."

"Nah, I don't think so," Bob Tom said.

"Go ahead," Dave encouraged.

Bob Tom walked over to Mark. "What's up?"

"Just hitting a few before it gets dark," Mark said.

"If you don't mind a tip?" Bob Tom said.

"No, I mean yeah, great," Mark said.

"When you come to the end of the swing, push your hip out just a bit more."

Bob Tom put his hand on Mark's hip and pushed as Mark mimicked a swing.

"Like that?" Mark asked.

"Right."

"Thanks."

"Don't mention it. Now, let the big dog hunt," Bob Tom said.

Mark scalded his driver as Bob Tom watched.

"Better."

Mark grinned like a kid with a jawbreaker in each cheek.

"Bob Tom, I've decided to play in Frisco. I'd like to take some time off to go up there, but I'm on a tight budget, and I don't want to jeopardize my job. Do you think we could work something out for me to get off?" Mark finished quickly and took a breath.

"Ambitious plan," Bob Tom said.

"I guess."

"How much time would you need?"

"About a week. The junior class I'm teaching ends the day before I'd leave." Mark sounded hopeful. "Plus, I'll have to cover two days I volunteer with The First Tee charity, but I'm sure I can find a replacement."

"I think we can work something out." Bob Tom arched an eyebrow. "Do you think you're ready?"

"I've got a few more months to work on it. I'm doing the clinic in Santa Fe during my post-Christmas break, and if you have any more tips, I'd be grateful to have them."

"Why don't we meet out here tomorrow night. Same time? I'll give you what I've got."

"Really?"

"Yeah."

"Woo hoo!" Mark shouted, scaring up a few birds from the nearby bushes.

"You know, I played the PGA back in nineteen seventy-two. It was one of the highlights of my life. Of course, I didn't finish in the top twenty, but I played it, by golly, and the memory is mine forever," Bob Tom said.

"I didn't know that," Mark said.

"Those were the glory days. Jack Nicklaus and Arnold Palmer were in their prime."

∞

Mark and Bob Tom met every possible moment and worked on the game. Mark had followed through with the inventory form and had been coming in on time and limiting his dawdling. Bob Tom took note, and it had increased their mutual respect. Bob Tom's old bear persona slowly disappeared as Mark marched toward his PGA goal.

Mark finally found the courage to ask about Bobby.

"I understand you have a son. Did he ever play golf?" Mark asked.

"No, I'd always hoped that Bobby would try to go beyond my game, but no matter how often I took him out, he never grew to love golf. He liked it okay, but he didn't crave it like I did. It just never got in his blood."

"Too bad," Mark said.

"Yeah, he got in some trouble later on with drugs and such. I haven't seen him in a while. I don't know if he's dead or alive. I don't even know if I'd recognize him between the age and drugs.

I've read it can take the vitality right out of one's face."

"I'm sorry to hear that. You know, that's one of the main goals of The First Tee charity. It gets kids involved in golf so that they have something to hold their attention instead of drugs and gangs."

"I wish it had been around back then," Bob Tom said.

At the end of the week, Bob Tom said, "I've been doing some checking on Frisco. I know a little about the course designer."

"Anything you can tell me would be great."

"Well, I thought I might go along. Maybe carry your bag. Unless you already have someone, that is. You can decide when you get back from the New Year's break if you like."

"Really? No. I mean, yes. I don't have anyone. I can decide now. That would be great. You've helped me so much, Bob Tom. I really appreciate it, but I can't pay you."

"Like I didn't already know that, bonehead."

Mark laughed. "Then you're hired."

Chapter Thirty-Six

Mark met Merit on her return trip from California at the Santa Fe Airport with a basket of mangos sporting a big plaid Christmas bow. She exited the departure ramp from the terminal wearing a red Bogner ski jacket over her jeans and white turtleneck.

Mark grabbed her up and swung her around and around, hugging so hard she couldn't breathe. At last, he put her down and looked into her eyes.

"You're finally here," Mark said.

"Hello golfboy, those for me?" Merit asked.

"Of course. How was your flight?" Mark asked, smiling his disarming smile down at her. Mark had on jeans that fit just right on his cute behind, and a chocolate brown sweater that deepened his eyes. He handed Merit the basket of fruit and she sniffed the skins and smiled at him.

"Thank you. The trip was pretty normal," Merit said. "Pretty standard except for the lady breast feeding her baby in the seat next to me. The kid ate for the whole two-hour flight. At least he wasn't crying."

"Mm. Breakfast of champions," Mark said.

They laughed as they got her luggage in baggage claim. Merit retrieved a long tube and pointed to a black Tumi bag with wheels. Marked grabbed the bag as it came by on the turnstile, and they walked toward the exit door.

"What's in the tube?" Mark asked.

"Can't tell you," Merit said as she handed her claim checks to the attendant who compared the numbers and motioned them through.

"Why not?" Mark grinned.

"Then it wouldn't be a surprise."

"I love surprises. How about a hint?"

"No," Merit said. "How was your Christmas? How are your Mother and Check?"

"Great, Mom cooked and fussed the whole time she was in Austin. We called Check on the phone. He was grouchy as usual with Mom gone."

"I bet she enjoyed seeing you," Merit said.

"Yeah, it was nice. After she left, we all had Christmas day at the club. Mr. Shasta brought by a big ham and Joe cooked up some cornbread dressing. Mom left a couple of pecan pies and I took those."

"Sounds yummy."

"We had a lot of golfers, mostly early. After the football games started, the crowd thinned out. How about you?" Mark asked.

"Wonderful. It was so good to see Ace and catch up on all of his news. California was profitable." Merit said.

"Sounds great," Mark said.

"I got in a few days at the gym too, so don't plan on beating me down the mountain. I'm one step ahead of you," Merit said.

"We'll see about that," Mark said.

They exited the airport terminal into the crisp air and bright sunshine. The mountains rose up to the north, climaxing in breath taking snow-capped peaks.

"Beautiful," Merit said.

∞

Merit and Mark checked into La Fonda on the Plaza. They had the Rio Grande room, which was cozy with a huge Mexican fireplace built into one corner of the adobe walls. Rough-hewn logs supported the ceiling, and a log ladder was displayed in the corner. The bed sported down pillows and two thousand thread count cotton sheets.

"Let's try this out," Merit said as she tested the mattress.

Mark pushed her down and they did their version of the New Mexico Salsa.

After napping and getting cleaned up they walked down Don Gaspar Avenue under chili pepper Christmas lights and over to the Loretto Chapel. The entry sign said *The Chapel of Our Lady of Light*. There was a golden statue of Mary above the ornate alter.

"The Golden Virgin," Mark read on a plaque.

Merit wandered over to a circular staircase that wound up to the choir loft, which housed a huge pipe organ. A velvet rope barred her entry onto the steps. The stairs were made of wood, with intricately carved spindles, and had no apparent means of support. A nun in a black and white habit walked over to answer questions.

"How does this stand up?" Merit asked.

"It is the miraculous staircase built in 1878," said the nun. "There's no center pole, yet it doesn't fall."

"That doesn't seem possible," Mark commented.

The nun continued, "The story goes that the nuns back then needed a new stairway to the choir loft. A lanky carpenter with long hair came out of the desert looking for work. He built the staircase and left mysteriously without receiving his payment."

"Fascinating," Merit said.

They lit a candle, deciding that world peace was the worthy prayer, dropped a donation in the box by the door, and made their way toward the town square past shops and shoppers bundled in their winter coats. The store windows displayed turquoise jewelry, handmade Indian artifacts, leather goods, and artwork.

"I'm hungry, let's eat." Mark said.

They made their way over a few streets to the Coyote Café where they sat under a heater on the outdoor deck overlooking the busy street below. They ordered margaritas and blue corn enchiladas with rice and beans.

"So much for fine dining," Merit laughed as Mark wolfed down his food.

"The mountain air and great sex," he smiled.

She laughed, and they ordered two more margaritas.

After dinner they strolled back by the Hotel St. Frances and observed through the window a cozy bar with a good crowd.

"I could use a nightcap," Merit said.

"Looks like the place to be," Mark responded.

They sat by the window, watching the tourists stroll by and sipped smoked sage margaritas.

"Heavenly," Merit said.

"It can be like this all the time," Mark said. "I love you, Merit."

Uh oh. I meant the drink, Merit thought.

"Cheers," she said.

Chapter Thirty-Seven

The next morning, Mark wrapped up the golf clinic and brought breakfast tacos from Pasqual's to Merit, who was still in bed at eleven.

"Wake up sleepy head, time to hit the streets," Mark rubbed her thigh as he sat on the side of the bed. He opened the bag and fanned the aroma over to her nose.

"Mm, that smells good," Merit mumbled, but didn't open her eyes. "Come back to bed."

"Yes, ma'am," Mark replied and pulled his shirt over his head. He climbed in beside her warm body.

"Do anything you want. I'm not waking up." Merit said. She kept her eyes closed and stayed relaxed.

Mark gently ran his hands over her warm skin as he spooned in behind her. As his erection intensified, he slipped into her, repeating a position she'd taught him in Austin. Afterwards, she relaxed against him and he dozedMerit gently moved away and lay awake thinking.

This is not play, this is relationship stuff.

Merit thought about the future for a while, what might happen next. She wondered how much Mark was going to be gone while he made his PGA attempt. It seemed like a lot of planning and organization.

She shifted her leg under the covers. With such a big operation, how was Mark going to pay for all of this? She smiled inwardly. She couldn't help it, she was a born problem-solver.

"Penny for your thoughts," Mark said as he opened his eyes.

"I was just thinking about the tour, how it would all work, how you would finance such a big endeavor."

"I have some help," he said, and then moved closer to her. "Want to try again?"

Merit smiled and shook her head. She was perfectly happy as she was.

He shifted his weight and came closer.

"You trying to change the subject?" Merit asked.

She couldn't quite place the look on his face, why he was so reticent.

"No, yeah. I had a plan. There's a guy who's promised to help me, but he's not doing it."

"What guy?" Merit sat up to face him and hugged a pillow across her chest. She was fully awake now.

"A guy in Austin. He plays golf at the club. The big guy you saw me talking to." Mark propped up on one elbow and looked at her.

"Go on."

"Well, I sort of signed a contract with him," Mark said.

"Mark, this is like pulling teeth, just tell me what's up," Merit said.

"Okay, this guy, Browno Zars, lent me some money when I first got to Austin. I wouldn't ask Check to help me, assuming he even would. I was just starting the job, and Browno offered to lend me some money and do some promotion. So, I signed up with him."

"What does that mean? Did you sign a contract? Did you have an attorney look at it?" Merit couldn't help herself, her lawyer brain went on high alert.

"Check never had a lot of time for lawyers when I was growing up," Mark said.

He ran his hand down her leg.

She put her hand over his, feeling the roughness of the scars.

"Do you have the document with you?"

Mark got up and went to his bag. He took out a folded eight and a half by eleven document, several pages long. It had coffee stains on the back and was crumpled around the edges.

She took the document and checked his face.

"Okay, okay, let's take a look," she said.

Merit read the document once quickly through, then a second time word for word. Mark watched her reading, then paced, then went into the bathroom.

After Merit finished reading, she said, "Did you read this all the way through?"

He nodded. He didn't want to admit that he hadn't understood all of the paragraphs in the entire document. But the look on Merit's face was starting to worry him.

"This was obviously drafted by a lawyer." Merit said.

"Is something wrong?"

"I have to process this for a bit," Merit said, in a voice that did nothing to reassure Mark, who was starting to feel like a teenager who'd just wrecked his first car.

∞

The next night they ordered room service and dined by the flickering firelight. After dinner, Merit brought out the tube she'd brought on the plane and handed it to Mark.

"Sorry it's not wrapped, but I wanted to keep it protected," Merit said.

"What could this be?" Mark said as he used a car key to slice through the tape at the end. He pulled off the plastic cap and slid a long velvet bag out the end of the tube. He opened the bag and pulled out a vintage Arnold Palmer putter.

"Merit, it's fantastic."

"You like it?"

"Love it. Love you." He leaned over and kissed her.

He ran his hands over the shiny metal and stood up to take a few practice swings on the tile.

"Thank you so much." He returned to his seat beside Merit and picked up his champagne glass.

"Happy new year, Merit," Mark said as they clinked champagne glasses and gazed into each other's eyes.

"Happy new year to you, golfboy." Merit whispered. "This has been special, Mark."

"I'm glad you liked your Christmas trip." Mark smiled.

"Listen, I've been thinking about that. I'll let you pay for skiing, but I'm picking up the tab here. I can't let you spend this money when you've got a lot to pay for this year."

"If you pay here, then it's a trade, and I didn't really give you a gift." Mark looked wounded but had to admit he was not in great shape to argue.

∞

The next day they were up and out of the hotel early and headed for the Santa Fe Ski Basin.

Merit and Mark stopped at Tia Sophia's for breakfast of seasoned omelets heaped with green chile. They continued coffee in the car as they headed up Hyde Park Road, Mark behind the steering wheel as Merit juggled the hot drinks. After they were rolling, Merit got out the contract. As Mark wound the SUV through the mountains, Merit studied the document further.

"Tell me about this Browno Zars guy." Merit said.

"He's just a Russian guy I teach at the club."

"Go on," Merit said.

"To take the job, I had to move. I ran up a lot of debt and I didn't want to ask Check for money. I kept falling further behind and Browno offered me this deal. It seemed like a good idea at the time." Mark said.

"Is he associated with Austin Creek in any way?"

"No, he just plays there and drinks in the bar, when he's in town," Mark said.

"Where is he when he's not in town?"

"I don't know. New York? Brighton beach I think it's called," Mark said.

Merit was familiar with the area. "Mark," she said gently. "Did you read the section where you have to give Browno fifty percent of all of your purses?"

Mark looked at the road in front of him, his gaze steady. "Just the ones where he promotes me."

"Why do you think that?"

"He said he can get me exhibitions and exposure. He has connections."

"Okay. Here's my take on it," Merit began. "It appears to be a binding contract, and that you owe him fifty percent of all your purses. Period."

"But he hasn't done anything. He's not put me into one game. I've made no money from him at all," Mark said.

"Then it lacks partial consideration. He did pay you some money, but he hasn't provided you with any service, not yet. Also, there may be a case for fraudulent inducement here. He lied to you to get you to sign the agreement. I took a look at him online this morning. He's promoted some boxers in the past, but never any golfers. Promoting a boxer and a golfer are two different things. And a standard commission for this type of work would be fifteen percent, not fifty."

"Can I get out of it?" Mark asked. A muscle jumped in his jaw as he spoke.

"Maybe, but that's not your biggest problem."

"It's not?" Mark frowned.

"No, the biggest problem is that you've got tournaments coming up with money purses if you win or finish well. Under this agreement, if you don't pay him, he can stop you from playing until you do. So, your main issue is timing. Even if you can get out of it, he can string you along in court until the season ends. Your chances to qualify this year, so you can play the tour next year, would be gone."

"Can he do that?" Mark asked. He looked ashen and his hands were squeezing the wheel.

"Yes and no. The law frowns on anything that prevents a person from making a living at their chosen profession. But he did give you money and can expect some type of return," Merit said. "All that said, he can still file an injunction, drag you into court, and let the judge decide whether you get to play."

"I don't want to steal from him. I planned to pay him back, but I never got a chance to win any money at the games he promised to set up. What can I do?" Mark pleaded.

"First of all, you have a dollar on you?" Merit asked.

"Yeah."

"Get it out." She held out her hand.

Mark shifted his seat belt and pulled a smashed dollar bill out of his blue jeans pocket while watching the yellow stripe on the road.

"Do you trust me?" she asked.

"Yes," he answered.

"Okay, then if you want to hire me, give me the dollar," she said.

Mark handed it over.

"Now, I'm your lawyer, and can act on your behalf. I'll call this sleaze bag Zars when we get back to Austin and see what I can do. Until then, just keep working on your game and try not to worry."

"Okay," Mark said, as he took a sharp curve and looked more worried than ever.

Chapter Thirty-Eight

Merit and Mark hit the ski lift and plowed down the mountain in the fresh white powder among a sprinkling of early skiers in rainbow colored jackets. Merit stayed on the blues and an occasional black trail, but diligently avoided the moguls. Mark was a good skier and they occasionally passed each other playing leapfrog down the slopes.

Late in the afternoon Merit rounded a curve between a stand of trees and a severe drop off and cut down Upper Broadway to the Tesuque Peak triple chair lift. Mark lost sight of her on the curve and took a trail over the drop off and hit a patch of moguls that turned his legs to rubber bands.

Merit looked back, but Mark wasn't visible. She slowed down, but he still didn't catch up, so she snow plowed along and finally stopped. She waited for a few minutes, and when he didn't show, she continued down the mountain.

Merit sat at the bottom waiting for him to make his way down, and finally decided he must have beat her down and gone back up to the top. She double checked her cell phone, but still had no bars. She clicked her boots back into her skis and got in the lift line, cursing under her breath for not renting walkie-talkies like she and Ace had done on their last ski trip.

Merit waited in the single skier's line until the attendant signaled her over and found herself riding with a cute male college student from California. He looked more like a surfer than a skier with his tan face and bleached out hair.

"I just came in from California, too." Merit made chit chat.

"I'm on winter break," he said. "Berkeley."

As they occupied the ride up the mountain, Merit kept her eye peeled for Mark. She spotted his yellow ski jacket and striped hat below them and called down. Mark looked up and Merit pointed to the mountain top. He gave her the circled okay sign with his gloved forefinger and thumb.

Merit got off up top and snow plowed over to the side to wait for Mark. He soon arrived and skied off the lift. Instead of snow plowing to keep his speed under control, he did a swish around her and sprayed a rooster tail of snow onto her boots and pant legs, winding up on her other side.

She laughed. "Where have you been, Hot Shot?"

"Looking for you. Where have you been?" he said with a scowl.

"I waited and waited. Hey, what's this aggressive look? I didn't lose you on purpose," Merit stiffened.

"I saw you with that guy."

"What guy?"

"On the lift."

"So."

"You were flirting with him."

"And you know that because you could read my lips from the ground when I was twenty feet above you? Besides, what if I did?"

Mark's face contorted in anger.

"Wait, I didn't mean that last part," Merit apologized. "I rode with him, that's all. Why am I explaining myself to you? This is silly." Merit skied off and down the mountain.

Mark followed, calling after her, "Merit, Merit, wait."

She pulled over to the side as a stream of skiers coming off the lift whizzed by.

"I'm sorry," he said as he skied up beside her.

"Mark, we just got separated. It happens to skiers all the time."

"I know. I just couldn't find you, and then I saw you with that guy, and I've been worrying about things, and I just didn't like any of it." Mark said.

"Let's just forget about it and enjoy the rest of the day." Merit said.

"Okay."

They skied down again, working out their frustrations on the slope. They wrapped up the day without further incident, but Merit couldn't get it out of her mind. She shouldn't have been so mean to Mark, but there was no promise between them that warranted his comments, and even if there were, she hadn't done anything wrong. What was Mark thinking that he felt he could claim ownership to her?

And, he'd said the L word more and more lately. This was supposed to be light and fun, not serious and committed.

That night at The Shed, they had red and green chile enchiladas called Christmas when the two chiles are mixed. After a short stroll around the plaza, they returned to the hotel where they fell asleep early without making love for the first time in their relationship.

They drove to the airport the next morning to catch their return flight without saying much.

Chapter Thirty-Nine

Merit opened the glass doors to her office and saw Val, her law clerk, leaving the break room with a tray of coffee cups and a pot of coffee. Valentine Louis was petit and buff, with streaked blond hair and wearing natural colored lip gloss. Maybe a little mascara. Merit was never quite sure. He wore a classic single button, single vent navy suit and yellow bowtie.

"Good morning Val. You look snazzy, as usual."

"Thanks," Val said as he headed toward the conference room.

"Do I have a meeting? What's going on?" she asked and followed him into the room.

Ag sat at the head of the conference table before a half-dozen clowns all in full costume.

"Hi," Ag said.

"Betty signed you up to do pro-bono for the Austin Lawyers for the Arts," Val said.

"Did they send all the clients at once?" Merit asked.

"No," a blue-faced clown with a turned down mouth volunteered. "I have an appointment. I brought my buddies along. People are stealing our faces."

"Yeah," a white-faced smiley clown said.

"They're taking our livelihood," another clown with purple cheeks said.

"See, our faces are all different. It's our brand," a blue-faced clown said.

"I'll do what I can. I, uh," Merit said. Betty came into the area from her office.

Val and Ag looked at each other, then at Merit.

Val giggled until the whole room, clowns, lawyers, staff, and Merit joined in. All of them rolled with laughter.

"Good lord," Betty said.

Merit said to the clowns, "I'll be right with you." Then to Ag, "I'll meet you in my office."

Merit followed Ag to her office and Betty appeared with two big-ass glasses of iced tea, which she placed before them.

"Thanks, darlin'," Ag said with a smile. Betty gave him a grin in return and then left, closing the door behind her.

"You rang?" Ag asked.

"Yes. I have a client named Mark Green. He's also my golf pro. He's gotten himself tangled up with a shady Russian character named Browno Zars. Supposed to be from Brighton Beach, New York."

"New York - get a rope!" Ag said.

Merit laughed.

"I'd like for you to check him out and see if he's dangerous or just greedy," Merit said. "Please talk to Betty on your way out and get the background info, but don't go around the clubhouse. You might be recognized," Merit said.

"Can do. Report?" Ag asked.

"Nothing written yet, just get your head around it," Merit said.

Merit passed a picture of Mark to Ag along with his contact information on a post-it note in Betty's handwriting.

"He's a kid. How did you meet this guy Mark Green?" Ag asked.

"He's my golf instructor. It's a long story," Merit said.

Ag tilted his head. "I bet."

Eager to change the subject, Merit said, "How's Chaplain?"

Ag's smile faded. "He's putting in twelve-hour shifts, trying to get a grip on this Enforcer situation. I've never seen Chaplain like this; whoever it is must be well funded and 'enthusiastic' is the word he used."

It was Merit's turn to raise her eyebrows. "Why does he say that?"

"This Enforcer seems to enjoy hurting people. The families of the victims are really suffering, too," Ag said.

After Ag was gone Merit sighed and turned back to her computer. She was putting the finishing touches on her letter to Browno.

She hit the intercom on her desk and called in Val. He perched on the edge of a chair before her desk with a pen and tablet in hand.

"I've read over your memo on failure of consideration and it's good. One question," Merit said.

"Shoot," Val said.

"It's this part about whether the contract is treated as if it never was or if it's voided after the fact."

"From what I researched, if there is fraudulent inducement, the contract is treated as if it never happened. The law doesn't recognize it as a contract from inception," Val said.

"I vaguely remember that from law school. What I don't recall is if the entire contract is null and void or whether only parts of it are," Merit said.

"It would appear that the parts where the contractor relied on the fraudulent mis-representations are null and the other parts are valid," Val said. "I printed out the case law. It's in the file."

"I looks like we don't have any other parts in this contract," Merit said.

"I agree," Val said.

After Val left, she did some research of her own online.

She typed in failure of consideration and found too many cases to count. In the event she couldn't sell the fraudulent inducement argument, she was going to rely on the fact that the contract failed because there wasn't enough money or services paid to secure it.

She quit the search program and began to type general legal phrases into the Browno letter. If it went any further, she planned to consult with her mentor, Woody Woodard.

She'd told Mark on the trip back that she would be sending the letter out today. Embedded in the legalese was a simple request: release Mark from his contract.

She had no idea who she was dealing with.

Chapter Forty

Merit called Mark at the pro shop and asked him to stop by her office when he got off work that day. When Mark arrived, Val steered him to the client chairs before Merit's desk.

"Thanks, Val," Merit said to his back as he left the office.

Val turned at the door, gave her a mischievous look, shook his hand at the wrist and mouthed *Hubba Hubba*.

Merit gave him a dismissive look. She walked around her desk and sat beside Mark. She gave him a few minutes to settle in before she broke the news.

"I wrote the letter we discussed to Browno Zars letting him know you had hired me and demanding that you be released from your contract. Today I was served with this." She held up a legal looking document with a blue cover and seals stamped on it.

"What is it?" Mark asked.

"It's notice of a hearing for a temporary injunction to keep you from playing golf until you pay Browno half the money you've won since you started playing competitively again," Merit said.

Mark sat quietly for a moment, stewing.

"How could I have been so stupid to get mixed up with that gangster? Damn. Damn."

"It's not a lot of money, but we don't want to establish the contract again by paying him anything. Of course, the court may see it his way," Merit said.

"Can he do that? Establish the contract again? How did it get unestablished?"

"At this point, we can assert that there is no contract because of his failure to perform and his lies about being a promoter. If you pay him something, that defense is waived, because you've re-affirmed the contract with the payment."

"It's complicated, the law," Mark mused.

"It's not really a surprise that he would try this. He can file anything in court, but whether he can win or not is a different story. If we can hold him off on this injunction, the only thing left for him to do is settle with you or file a full lawsuit to enforce the contract. I think he's trying to avoid that."

"I don't have the money to settle with him. I can probably get part of it, but how much are we talking about?" Mark asked. "There are few places I can beg, borrow, or steal thousands of dollars."

"I don't know how much, or if he will settle at all. This is one of those legal situations where we have to play it through and strategize each step as we get information from the other side," Merit said.

"I understand," Mark said. "I understand that I was a big jerk and need my head examined."

"Mark, I don't normally do extensive trial work, but since this is just a hearing on the temporary injunction, I'll handle it. If we go to trial later, I'll have to bring in a litigator. My friend Kim Wan Thibodeaux is really top notch."

"Litigator? How did I get myself into this mess?" Mark said.

"Don't let the legal jargon scare you. This is like a chess game. You have to think two or three steps ahead. Just trust me," Merit said.

"I do, but I can't pay your bill, and I don't like taking your time," Mark said"I'll keep a tab running. When you win the championship, you can pay me," Merit said. "For now, keep your eye on the ball."

"Yeah, right."

Chapter Forty-One

Merit took a quick drive to Houston to see Ace and meet with her mentor, Woody Woodward. She stayed with Joy and Tucker in their spare bedroom she called the "Out of Africa" room because it reminded her of the scenes in the book by Karen Blixen.

Woody had agreed to come by on his way home from the office and Merit greeted him warmly at the door.

"It's been so long, dear," Woody said.

"Too long. Let's sit," Merit said. "Joy and Tucker will be back in time for dinner. They're looking forward to seeing you, too."

"And Ace?" Woody asked.

"He's coming along as well," Merit said.

They went into the beautifully appointed living room and Woody found a big cushy leather chair while Merit went to the corner bar and fixed him his favorite scotch with one big round ice cube. She joined him, sipped a glass of Malbec, and smiled at the only positive father figure she'd ever known.

"What are you working on?" Woody said. "You didn't say much on the phone."

"I need to get my client, Mark Green, out of a contract. A Brighton Beach Russian lent him some money and now he wants not only skin, but blood, too."

"All the basics of a contract met? Offer, acceptance, consideration?" Woody asked.

"To a point. The loan shark offered money, Mark accepted, the money was given," Merit said.

"Sounds binding. Where's the rub?" Woody asked.

"The payback is hell. Fifty percent of all the earnings," Merit said.

"It's usury if it's interest, but not since it's a sort of gamble on the golfer's career," Woody said. "Smart way to get around the usury laws."

"Yes, this guy is very smart. He may have one weak spot, however," Merit said.

"What's that?"

"He held himself out as a golf promoter and promised to get Mark exhibition games and charity appearances, so Mark could earn the money to pay him back. He didn't do any of those things," Merit said.

"You actually have two weak spots there," Woody said. "The first is fraudulent inducement if he led Mark to believe he had a higher skill level than he had as a promoter. The second is partial failure of consideration since he didn't provide the services. The two together give you a pretty strong case. It will all depend on who the judge believes."

"It's a hearing for injunctive relief. The Russian wants to prevent Mark from playing until he pays the money he's already earned and agrees to start paying if he wins anything. So far, all he's won is enough to cover the expenses of a few small tournaments. No real profit," Merit said.

"Since it's only an injunction, I don't know if you'll even get to the he said, he said. Most judges don't want to hear a lot of testimony at a hearing," Woody said. "Maybe you can use that to your advantage and force him to either settle or go to trial."

"Bingo," Merit said. "That's just the strategy I need."

The door opened and in walked Joy, Tucker and Ace.

"Welcome home," Merit said.

Hugs and greetings went around the group. Joy went to the bar to pour cocktails and Ace checked his phone for a place nearby to eat.

"Call me if you need me," Woody said.

"I think you've given me a good start," Merit said.

"Don't count your bingo card yet," Woody said. "It all depends on the judge."

Then, Woody turned to Ace and Tucker, "What's for dinner?"

Chapter Forty-Two

Back in Austin, Ag met with Merit after hours in her office. Betty served up a beer for Ag and wine for Merit.

"I'm going home," Betty said. "You two don't work too late."

Betty gave Merit a knowing look and departed.

"What did you find out about Browno Zars?" Merit asked.

"His reputation is that he makes his money off of usurious loans in the black market to desperate businesses. Publicly, he preys on the labors of others by tricking them into service contracts, first boxers, and now golfers and tennis players. Seems he can sniff out a young sucker in need of money from a mile away."

"If he's anonymous, only lending to these business men and women, why does he mess with the public figures?" Merit asked.

"He likes to be the big shot at the events where the athletes perform." Ag said.

"I've seen him throw his weight around. It's not attractive. What a bully," Merit said.

Ag took a sip of his beer.

"Keep everything in the public eye and you should be okay," Ag said.

"Don't worry," Merit said.

Chapter Forty-Three

Merit and Mark sat in the viewing area of Courtroom Number Three of the Travis County Courthouse. Merit wore a navy-blue blazer with a cream colored pencil skirt that made her look very businesslike, and Mark had on a gray suit and tie for the first time in Austin.

"You look nice," Merit said.

"You're a knockout in that blue. Makes me want to forget this whole mess and take you to bed," Mark whispered.

"You want to forget this whole mess with or without bedding me," Merit laughed.

"You got that right."

Across the aisle they saw Browno and his attorney Steven Boor take a seat. Boor was a dark, wiry little man with a pencil thin moustache and accountant-looking thick lensed black glasses. Browno looked like his usual slovenly unmade bed.

Boor acknowledged Merit with a nod. She nodded in return.

The court clerk, sitting beside the empty judge's bench, called the docket and then signaled to the security guard that they were ready to get started.

"Settle down," the guard called out.

The gallery stopped buzzing and all eyes turned to the clerk.

"All rise."

Everyone stood as the judge entered the court in black robes and took his seat on the bench.

Mark sucked in a gulp of air.

"Oyez, Oyez, this court is now in session. The Honorable Judge Harold Jameson presiding."

"You may be seated," Judge Jameson said.

As they took their seats, Mark whispered to Merit, "That's Mr. Jameson. I didn't know he was a judge. He's a new club member. I've given him lessons." Jameson was the golfer who'd asked about the sitting water on the course. The one he'd been hitting balls into.

"Is that good or bad?" Merit asked.

"He likes me, if that's what you mean, but he's played golf with Browno before."

"Oh, shit," Merit swore under her breath.

The docket was called. Judge Jameson disposed of all the short items first - requests for continuance, written pleadings and motions. Attorneys came and went through the swinging doors as each was called in turn. Finally, the judge got to the part of the morning where he had to hear oral argument.

The clerk called the case, "Browno Zars vs. Mark Green, request for temporary injunction."

Merit and Mark moved through the swinging gate to the defendant's table, and Browno and Boor took their places on the plaintiff's side.

The judge started, "Mr. Boor…"

Merit jumped up from her chair, "Your honor, before we begin, may I have a sidebar?"

The judge looked annoyed, but agreed, "Yes, Ms. Bridges. What is it?"

Merit and Boor approached the judge's stand. "Your Honor, my client tells me that you've played golf with Mr. Zars, as well as taken lessons from Mr. Green at Austin Creek Country Club. While I trust your honor's ability to remain impartial, I feel it my duty to my client to get it on the record that the issue of recusal was raised."

Boor chimed in, "Your Honor, we have no objection to your impartiality."

"Very diplomatic, Ms. Bridges, Mr. Boor. Step back." The attorneys returned to their respective positions.

The judge spoke toward the court reporter. "For the record, Ms. Bridges has pointed out that I've played golf with Mr. Zars and I've taken golf lessons from Mr. Green. That makes me equally acquainted with both parties, and I choose not to recuse myself from this hearing. The court docket is crowded enough in Travis County without wasting time re-setting this with another judge. I have no doubt I can decide this matter impartially, however, it is now on the record in the event that someone wishes to take it up on appeal. Everyone okay with that?"

All four nodded in unison without speaking.

"Out loud for the record, please," the judge said.

"Yes, your honor," Merit and Boor said in unison.

The judge looked at the file. "Mr. Boor, would you like to begin?"

Boor stood up and walked toward the Judge, "Yes, Your Honor."

"That's far enough," the judge said, holding up his palm. "And keep it short. I've read the file and know what this is about."

"Yes, sir. If it please the court, my client, Browno Zars has a contract with Mark Green for fifty percent of his professional player earnings. We have evidence that Mr. Green has been playing golf and earning small purses. Even though it's not a lot of money at this point, Mr. Zars did advance quite a bit of money to Mr. Green and is entitled to his cut under the contract." Boor took a breath.

"Stop right there. Ms. Bridges, what is your response?" the judge asked.

Merit rose and circled the table but stayed a good distance from the judge. "Your Honor, my client, Mark Green was fraudulently induced into signing the contract at hand. In addition, he should not be enjoined from earning his living while we sort this out through other means. At this time, he's spending more on going to the tournaments than he's earning. There's been nothing to share because there's been virtually no profit. The contract, if it were enforceable, specifically defines earnings as after expenses."

The judge directed his question at Browno and Boor. "Do you intend to file a lawsuit to recover half of what he's earned, which doesn't look like much so far?"

"No sir, we don't intend to file suit until he earns some substantial winnings, unless we have to."

Merit addressed the court. "Your Honor, this is just a cheap way for them to avoid a lawsuit. They're hoping you'll enforce the injunction and ignore the other elements of the case so that they can hold my client hostage and judicially reinforce a fraudulent contract."

"I'm beginning to see that, Ms. Bridges," the judge said.

"Your honor," Boor said, "the purpose of an injunction is to enforce contractual provisions without having to go to court for a full lawsuit."

Merit looked at him and smiled, "No, your honor, the purpose of an injunction is to prevent someone from doing irreparable harm. That's something that can't be undone, such as chopping down a tree, or selling a piece of property. Mr. Zars has the remedy of going to court at any time to enforce his contract and collect his money against Mr. Green if we lose."

"She's right," said the judge.

"Your Honor…" Boor began.

"Finding for the defendant. Next case." The judge rapped his gavel and reached for the next file.

"But, Your Honor," began Boor.

"I've made my ruling, Mr. Boor."

"Thank you, Your Honor," said Merit. She gathered her files and briefcase.

"Thank you, Your Honor," Boor said and returned to his table.

"You ass, you walked right into that one." Browno said to Boor as they exited the courtroom.

"Let's talk outside," Boor replied.

Browno and Boor went into the hall, followed by Merit and Mark. Browno and Boor entered the elevator, talking rapidly in hushed tones. Merit took Mark's arm and steered him toward the stairs.

"We won," Mark said.

"For now," Merit said. "He still has the contract and arguably, some rights to enforce it. You did take his money. He's entitled to some remedy, we just have to establish what that is."

They went down the stairs, exited onto the main floor, and proceeded through the double doors outside. Browno and Boor were standing on the courthouse steps as Merit and Mark exited into the bright sunshine.

"Hey, Mr. Zars," Merit said. "When you're finished being mad, why don't you come over to the office and let's get this settled. You don't have time to deal with a lawsuit, do you?"

"Don't bet on it," Boor responded.

"Shut up," Browno said to Boor.

"No one's going to play golf with you at the club until you let Mark off the hook," Merit said.

"We'll see about that," Browno shot back.

Chapter Forty-Four

Later that week, Merit met Natalie for dinner at The Grove on East Sixth. Merit chose it because it was locally owned and famous for their wine offerings. Natalie was sitting with her back to the wall at a corner table. Merit admired her designer outfit as she crossed the floor. It had been a long day and she was tired, but she'd decided not to cancel dinner, so she could have some girl time.

Natalie's angular hairstyle picked up light from all the candles in the room.

Merit returned her smile and situated herself in her chair. It was incredibly comfortable; perfect after a long day.

"Hello there. How goes the battle?" Natalie asked.

"Some days better than others. I've asked my friend, Red Thallon, to join us. She's a journalist. She's a lot of fun."

Natalie stiffened and looked down at her leather-bound menu, her eyes running over the options. Merit sensed her displeasure.

"I would have let you know in advance, but it just happened as I was walking out the door," Merit said.

"No worries. Anything we should talk about before she arrives?"

"Wine first," Merit said, and they both laughed. Natalie's laugh may have been less genuine than Merit's.

Red arrived in her usual very sparse outfit with stacked wedge heels. Natalie seemed to go out of her way to be nice to Merit's friend.

"Any chance you're free for a golf game this weekend?" Natalie asked as they finished their entrees. "Or is your schedule too tight? Red, do you play?"

"No, I'm not a golfer. I work too many odd hours to keep a tee time," Red said. "In fact, I may have to leave earlier than I'd planned today." Sure enough, a couple of minutes later Red made apologies, traded air kisses on each cheek with Merit, shook hands with Natalie, and left the same way she'd arrived.

"She's a doll," Natalie said.

"A good friend. She's bailed me out of trouble more than once," Merit said.

"Well, invite her any time. A friend of yours is a friend of mine," Natalie said.

What a relief to have such a nice new addition to my life, Merit thought.

"Good, now we can chat," Natalie said. "What are you working on these days, anyway? I find the law so fascinating. I even read an article about how you're one of the best lawyers in the city."

Merit thought about the lineup she had at the moment: her clown faces copyright case made her giggle a little, so she told the story.

Natalie laughed.

"I always have real estate and oil and gas clients. I have a fraudulent inducement case I'm working on, some management work. It's been a crazy week."

"Sounds interesting," Natalie said. "How is your, what did you call it?"

"Fraudulent inducement." Merit took a sip of her wine. "I have a Russian gangster who hoodwinked a small-town boy into signing his life away, basically."

Natalie moved her dessert around her plate. "Shouldn't the small-town boy have gotten a lawyer? Did the Russian force him to do anything?"

Merit smiled. "It's a little more complicated than that, unfortunately."

"Unfortunately," Natalie echoed. "I don't believe I understand the law well enough to know, of course. But I did Google you this week. Interesting history you have."

"Yes, life is a highway," Merit said. "I checked you out as well, Natalie. Nice website. Impressive client list. Do you go to New York often?"

"I do. It's where the big deals are made," Natalie said.

"I tend to go more in the other direction to L.A.," Merit said.

"So, what about that golf game?" Natalie asked.

"I'm in," Merit said.

Chapter Forty-Five

Merit and Mark sat in Merit's office preparing for their settlement meeting with Browno Zars. Merit had called Boor after the courthouse coup and later she'd sent an email and requested to see him and his client. Might as well go for it while she had them on the run.

The meeting was scheduled in Merit's conference room. Betty would let them know when the parties arrived.

"I had my investigator, Ag Malone, do some research. It seems Browno was run out of Brighton Beach on a rail. When he goes back to visit, he sees his family, but no one else has much to do with him," Merit said.

"Really," Mark said.

"My investigator reported that Browno makes his money off of usurious loans to desperate companies. He also tricks boxers, and now golfers and tennis players. Seems he can spot a target from a mile away."

"Gee, thanks." Mark frowned.

"Sorry. You deserved a little punch in the ribs. Let's not worry about what was and put our energy on Zars from now on," Merit said.

"Good," Mark said.

"Browno Zars isn't his real name. Browno was a nickname from Brighton. He got it for brown nosing mob guys. The gangsters started calling him 'Brown Nose'. Zars is short for Zarov. His full name is Bronislav Zarov."

"Sounds like an alien," Mark said.

"He also has a record. He extorted some money from several boxers in Miami. One was gay and Browno punched him, then had him stripped and humiliated in a gay bar. Told the police the kid propositioned him. Later the boxer disappeared, but the police never found who did it."

"I had no idea he was dangerous," Mark said.

"If he's a homophobe, you're safe," Merit said.

Mark laughed nervously.

"Still, I'm going to use it to throw him off guard."

"How?"

Merit's phone rang, and she answered it.

"Thanks. Please ask Val to show him to the conference room."

Merit hung up and turned to Mark.

"Speak of the devil. Mark, whatever I say, I want you to go along with it until we're alone again. Trust me. Okay?"

"Okay." Mark looked as if he were going to his own funeral.

Merit and Mark walked down the hall and into the conference room. It had two glass outer walls, one facing the reception area, and one with a magnificent view of downtown Austin. It was late in the day, and tourists were already gathering on the Congress Avenue Bridge, waiting for the bats to fly out.

Val placed a tray with water and glasses on the table with a flourish. He was not wearing his usual haute couture. He wore jeans with rips in them, letting his pink boxers peak through. His shredded t-shirt was held together with safety pins, and he had a gold hoop earring in his right ear. His makeup was perfect, hot pink lips.

Merit said, "Thank you, Val."

Val stopped in Browno's eye line, patted Mark's arm and winked at Browno on the way out. Browno recoiled.

Mark blushed and turned toward Merit with a question mark on his face.

She gave him a look that said, "Later."

Browno sat at the head of the table with his back to the wall. Merit walked over and extended her hand.

"Hello Mr. Zars. How are you?"

"Ms. Bridges, Mark." Zars shook hands with Merit without standing up. He avoided eye contact with Mark.

"Brown Nose." Mark nodded back but couldn't resist the slur. Merit gave Mark a warning look.

Browno didn't seem to catch it.

"Is Mr. Boor coming?" Merit asked. "I can't speak with you if you are still retaining legal counsel."

"No more Boor," Browno said. "I fire him."

"Okay, Mr. Zars." Merit said.

"Call me Browno." Zars said.

"Okay, Browno, call me Merit then."

"Right. That makes us pals," Browno said.

"Like hell it does," Mark said.

Merit gave him a look meaning settle down, bit her tongue, and smiled at Browno.

"That's right, pals, so there's no reason we shouldn't be able to work something out here," Merit said.

"Listening," Browno said.

"We would like to return your money and end this contract. You haven't done any promoting for Mr. Green, Mark, and he hasn't even seen you except at the country club since the contract was signed," Merit said.

"I invested in him and he owes me more than the initial ten thousand," Browno said.

"You'll be hard pressed to prove that in court, and your attorney must have told you that," Merit said.

"I'm representing myself now, and when I go to court, I won't be using that idiot Boor," Browno said.

"How much will it take for you not to go to court?" Merit asked.

"I want a hundred thousand dollars, and I'll cut the kid loose," Browno said.

"A hundred thousand dollars!" Mark choked.

"If you win the PGA spot and play the tour next year, you'll win well over that, and I'm giving up the chance to collect on even more," Browno said.

"I don't..." Mark beMerit put her hand on Mark's arm.

"Mr. Zars, Browno, let's be reasonable. You know Mark doesn't make that kind of money, and besides, Mark has not declared for the tour."

"Nu'," Browno grunted.

"One-hundred thousand is a steep return on ten-thousand-dollar investment, don't you think? How about ten thousand and ten percent interest."

Browno stared at Merit.

"What about all the money he been making? I come down to eighty thousand, but that's it."

"He's not making much money and what he makes pays for hotel, travel, entry fees. How about ten thousand and twenty percent interest," Merit offered.

"No, seventy-five thousand or court, and that is final offer," Browno snarled.

Merit considered for a moment. She didn't think he'd go any further without a threat, but she knew it had to be well played.

"No. There's a third option here. The contract says you get half of what Mark makes if he plays. You can't make him play. He won't play."

Mark swallowed several times, causing his Adam's apple to bob up and down in his throat.

"Mark won't do that. I know how much he love the golf," Browno said.

"He can wait a year. We'll take you to court and sue you for failure of consideration in promoting him or setting up any exhibition games. We'll terminate the contract, you'll get nothing, and he'll play next year." Merit stared back.

"You can't," Browno said.

"Hell, we might even get damages from you," Merit said.

Mark squirmed in his big leather seat like a little boy in church.

"You not do that." Browno said.

"He won't play," Merit said.

Browno looked at Mark.

"I won't play," Mark stated less firmly.

Browno poured a glass of water from the crystal pitcher in a tray on the table. He sized them up.

"Okay, I'll take fifty-thousand. It will cost you more than that to go to court."

"No, it won't cost more than that. I'll do it for free, and you'll be paying your lawyer for every deposition, discovery motion, and court date we put you through. You'll pay through the nose," Merit said.

"You work for your boyfriend for free?" Browno said.

Merit didn't flinch.

"We haven't even gotten into fraudulent inducement. You have no experience with golf promotion, and you can't prove in court that you do. Thirty thousand. Final offer," Merit said.

"Okay, thirty-five thousand, and that is last offer. I got bigger fish to fry," Browno said.

Mark started to interject, but Merit cut him off, happy to have gotten to a number she could work with. She didn't want to push Browno to the point of leaving. Besides, she had a good idea that was close to his magic number as well. He was cagey.

"If we can find the money, you have a deal. I'll send over a draft of a release late next week. I have to go to Los Angeles on Friday and won't get to it before I leave."

"Fine. I give you until Friday of next week," Browno said. His face was suddenly affable, his voice friendly. "I know when I've been beat."

"No hard feelings, Browno," Mark said.

"Sounds good," Browno said, clapping Mark on the back.

Browno left the conference room, and Mark turned to Merit. "That was a good bluff about not playing, but thirty-five thousand dollars?"

"It would cost you more than that to take him to court, and you do want to play this year, don't you?"

Mark did the mental math.

"Yes, but what if I don't win enough to cover it? We've spent this for nothing, if I can even find the thirty-five thousand. I'd be better off to split with him in case I don't win. Giving him half of nothing is nothing," Mark said.

"Yes, but I have faith in you. You're going to win, and you don't need this Brownnose Marzipan tainting your reputation with his bad business," Merit said.

"But I don't have that kind of money," Mark said.

"Give me a few days to work on the money, and you think, too," Merit said.

"I guess I better up my two-dollar Nassau," Mark said.

"We'll talk about it when I get back," Merit said.

"I didn't know you were going to L.A."

"I am now," Merit said.

Chapter Forty-Six

M erit marched into the offices of Fairway Shoes in Los Angeles and dropped her business card on the receptionist's desk.

"May I help you?"

"I'm here to see Mr. Baker. He's expecting me." Merit pointed more to "Attorney at Law" than her name on the card.

"Please have a seat." The receptionist indicated the Eames black and chrome chair and ottoman - one of Merit's favorite designs - so clean and symmetrical.

Merit sat down and picked up a copy of *Sports Illustrated* with Lindy Duncan on the cover and flipped to the article. Seems Duncan had won the Dell Women's Championship and had pocketed over half a million last year.

Mark can do that, she thought, and the men make more than the women. He just needs a little more confidence. A woman opened the door at the end of the room and interrupted her fantasy.

Mr. Baker's assistant invited Merit in with a wave of her hand.

"Mr. Baker will see you now."

"Thanks. "Merit gathered her belongings and got into her battle mode.

Baker's office was clean and contemporary, dotted with bits of nostalgia honoring the greats of golf. There was a photo of Jack Nicklaus at Augusta, and another of Tom Kite with Arnold Palmer at Pebble Beach.

As Fairway's head of advertising, Baker had his work cut out for him. Fairway had been trying to catch Footjoy, Ecco, and Nike in the golf shoe market for about five years with little headway.

"Hello, Merit, long time." Baker indicated a chair before his desk.

"Hello. It's good to see you." Merit smiled as she shook his hand in both of hers.

"It's good to see you, Merit. Are you here about this Green kid?" Baker said.

"Good guess. Mr. Baker, Mark Green is the next big star in golf. He's smart and savvy, and golf is in his blood."

"He's just a pup," responded Mr. Baker.

"I know he's young, but he's been playing since he was five. Remember Ben Curtis. He wasn't on anyone's radar either until he won the one hundred and thirty-second British Open. His name went on the Claret Jug along with Jack Nicklaus, Arnold Palmer, Ben Hogan. Everyone has to start somewhere."

"You have no way of knowing that Green will go that far. From what I've heard, he sounds like an Iowa Polack fresh off the corn field."

"Wisconsin Polack - cheese." Merit laughed.

"Cheese?"

"I know you've seen him on television. Did you ever see a swing that fluid, or that kind of power behind his driver? You were impressed, admit it," Merit said.

"Yeah, I saw, but what if he's just a flash in the pan?" Baker asked.

"I know he's only had a bit of success so far but let me tell you —Nike and Footjoy are going to come knocking once he proves himself, and then it will be too late for Fairway. Get in now and follow him to the top. Think Lance Armstrong and the United States Postal Service."

"Look how that turned out. What's your interest in this guy? You his lawyer?"

"Yes, and his student, and friend," Merit said.

"Hmm," Baker said.

"I've been following his games. I know he can do it," Merit said.

She laid several eight-by-tens of Mark across his desk.

"Just look at this kid. He looks like a young Leonardo Di-Caprio on a Wheaties box."

Baker caught her enthusiasm and stared off into space for a moment. Merit wondered what visions he was conjuring in his mind. She waited, knowing there was a time for selling, and a time for letting things sink in.

"Okay, we'll do a small budget to try six months with him. If he moves up, we'll take him on for a year. If not, we won't take any more exposure from a loser. Understand?"

"Thank you, Mr. Baker. I understand. When can I have that in writing?"

"Anxious, aren't we?" Mr. Baker laughed.

"He plays Frisco, Texas soon, and if he does well, you'll want to have your logo on his shirt and your shoes on his feet, won't you?"

"Right. So, he needs money?"

"Well, that too," Merit said.

Knowing he had already jumped to that conclusion, Merit went for the gold. They talked price for a while. Merit knew she had to get at least fifty-thousand to make her plan work.

"If it's okay with you, I'd like to keep this under wraps until we actually sign the contract. I have a few things to clean up for Mark," Merit said.

"Anything I should know about?" Baker asked.

"Not at this time. If I can't work it out, I'll let you know before we execute the agreement," Merit assured him.

"Okay," Baker said.

"One more thing. I think he should work with David Yee, don't you?"

Baker looked pensive.

"Well, first of all, Yee is expensive, and secondly, he's working with Jon Handom. I doubt he has time to take on another student."

"Handom's out. Back injury. He hasn't announced yet, but he will. That's why I selected Yee. He's suddenly available, and he met Mark recently. Yee said he saw promise in his game. I think he might take him on for a trial run."

Baker smiled and appeared to give up.

"Right, I suppose you want us to pay for that as well."

Merit nodded and smiled.

"Okay. But the first time he shoots a snowman, he's history with me."

"Yes, Sir," Merit saluted.

No snowmen, got it.

∞

Merit returned to Austin the next day and Mark met her at the airport. They held their affection at bay through the baggage claim process and had a big hug and kiss when they reached the parking garage.

"I'm glad to pick you up either way. But it sounds like you have something to tell me," Mark said.

Merit could hardly contain her excitement.

"I do. I do. Let's sit in the car for a minute. When you hear this, you're not going to want to be driving."

"Good or bad?" Mark asked.

"Good, good, it's all good," Merit said.

They got in the Jeep and she pulled the notes from the meeting with Baker up on her iPad.

"If you agree to the terms, I've gotten you a deal with Fairway Shoes," Merit said.

"You're kidding!"

"No, I'm not. I met with an old business associate while I was in L.A. He's in charge of their promotions, and he likes the looks of you and your game."

"How did you do this?"

Mark looked incredulous.

"It's what agents and lawyers do. Just because Browno was a jerk doesn't mean everyone else is going to let you down," Merit said.

Merit ran over the basic terms of the agreement.

"There's only two things left that I haven't told you. One is good news, one is bad news. Which one do you want first?"

"I thought it was all good. Okay, I'll take the good news first, although I can't imagine what could be bad. If the bubble's going to burst, let me enjoy this a little longer," Mark said.

"Okay, the good news is that Fairway is going to pay David Yee to work with you before you go to Frisco. He'll continue to work with you afterward to get ready for the PGA Championship in Wisconsin if you make the cut. All on Fairway's dime."

"Be still my heart. David Yee, that's fantastic! Here in Austin? When can we start?"

"I spoke with Yee, and he's ready at any time since he's lost his gig with Handom. Only thing is, he's on hold until we sign the contract with Fairway, which brings me to the bad news."

Mark held his breath.

"Problem is Browno Zars. The Fairway contract has a provision that requires you to have good moral character, blah, blah, and no undisclosed encumbrances against your playing," Merit said.

"Okay, what do we do?"

"With part of the money you'll get from Fairway, we can pay off the thirty-five thousand to Browno, but we'll have to get him to sign an agreement in advance of getting the money, and not let him find out about Fairway in the process. It will be tricky."

"I see." Mark frowned.

"Both have to go at once to avoid triggering the contract clauses, and if Browno hears of the deal with Fairway and backs out, it's off."

Mark pondered the catch twenty-two. "If he hears about Fairway, he'll want more money."

"You got it," Merit said.

"How could he hear?" Mark asked.

"We hope he won't, especially if we move fast. Baker has promised to keep it under his hat, but you know how small the golf community is. When it gets around that you're working with Yee, it will be big news."

"Yeeeeeeee!" Mark said.

∞

It was Monday, Valentine's Day, and a dozen red Intuition Roses sat on Merit's credenza. The enhanced variety was one of her favorites. She didn't remember telling Mark that. Perhaps he guessed because she often had them at home. A sweet note from him was tucked inside her desk drawer, hidden from prying eyes.

There was also a box of Tiff's Treats brownies from Ag. Just a reminder that he was around. More like a disguised client gift, which was a relief to Merit.

Merit and Betty were geared up for the Browno Zars settlement payoff. Merit had Federal Expressed the executed contract to Fairway Shoes in L.A. the day before. The contract contained a clause that required Fairway to wire the funds to Merit's escrow account by ten o'clock that morning in order for the contract to be valid and binding.

Merit had also sent a different contract to Browno Zars a few days earlier. They had been going back and forth on terms and conditions until the day before, when he'd signed it. Now, it was Mark's turn to sign and pay the thirty-five thousand.

Betty was standing downstairs at the bank at nine-thirty a.m., waiting for the wire from Fairway, and Val was waiting in the reception area of Merit's office.

Merit paced in her office and looked at the phone, willing it to ring.

"Betty on line two," Val told Merit over the intercom.

Merit punched line two, "Tell me we have good funds?"

"Just came in. Good to go," Betty said.

"Thanks, come back up. I'm sending Val out now." Merit hung up, signed the check, and handed the package to Val.

"Take this over to Browno, and make sure nothing happens with the delivery. Timing is everything on this one," Merit said.

Val had on his duster overcoat, doing his usual Young Guns imitation when clandestine matters were at hand.

"On it," Val said.

"Wait for him to sign it, and then bring it back," Merit said.

"I know," Val said.

"If he gives you any trouble, don't argue with him. Just call me from there and I'll see what I can do. Don't faux flirt with him either. We need him calm and happy today."

"Okay, boss." Val said.

Merit watched his perfectly groomed body disappear into the elevator and crossed her fingers for good timing.

Betty got off the second elevator.

"In motion?" Betty asked.

"If Browno just follows through, we'll have this all put to bed in time for lunch," Merit said. "If he doesn't, my name is mud with Baker and Fairway, and Mark is out of luck."

"Surely, Browno knows better than to back out now," Betty said.

"He's not stupid. Greedy, but not stupid," Merit said.

"Let's see if smarts or greed wins out," Betty said.

Merit and Betty returned to Merit's office, and they sat on pins and needles, unable to turn their attention to anything else.

"This is what my mother would call begging from Peter to pay Paul," Betty said.

"I call it creative lawyering. Big difference," Merit said.

"You're a genius to orchestrate this whole thing," Betty said.

"Let's just hope it pans out," Merit said.

They chatted until Val returned about an hour later. Val handed the package to Betty who opened the clasp. She pulled out the documents and handed them to Merit.

Merit flipped through to the release and read the signature 'Browno Zars'. She let go of a held breath and smiled.

"Thank goodness. Signed, sealed, and delivered," Merit said.

"Happier than a tornado in a trailer park! I think this calls for lunch out," Betty said.

"I agree, and maybe a glass of wine to boot," Merit said patting the page against her chest.

"Am I invited?" said Val.

∞

That night, Merit met Mark for dinner at Weird Pizza on South Congress for Valentine's Day. They'd decided to go back to the place they had met.

Since it was February, they sat inside in a green vinyl booth, foregoing their former spot on the deck. The table was covered in a red-checkered tablecloth, and candles flickered around the room. Lyle Lovett sang on the jukebox. They ordered salads and pizza just as they had that first night, with wine for Merit and a beer for Mark.

Merit hummed along with the music to, "Ain't it Somethin'".

"Don't give up your day job," Mark said.

Merit play punched him on the arm.

"Did I ever tell you that *Mrs. Robinson* by Simon and Garfunkel played on the radio when I was driving over to meet you that first night?" Merit laughed.

"You're kidding," Mark said, sipping his suds.

"No, I'm not. I was so nervous I thought I was going to have a wreck," Merit said.

"You were nervous! I changed my clothes ten times that night," Mark laughed.

"That was exciting," Merit said.

"Still is," Mark said.

Merit smiled at him and reflected back on the past months. So much had happened - fast. A fire burning too hot? She put those thoughts aside and enjoyed the evening and her surprise for him.

"After dinner, I have a gift for you," Merit said.

"You've done so much for me already. The flowers I sent weren't nearly enough," Mark said.

"Yes, they were. They are, and you are. You're enough, just being who you are."

She put her hands on his scarred fingers.

"Okay, give me my present," Mark laughed.

"After dinner."

"Now."

"Okay." Merit took a large manila envelope out of her tote and handed it to Mark. She'd drawn a big red bow on the front with a felt tipped marker.

"Is this what I think it is?" Mark asked.

"It is," Merit said.

"All done?" Mark asked.

"Executed and notarized. The check cleared. Browno is probably spending his money right now."

Mark moved around to her side of the booth and sat next to her. She looked around the room uncomfortably. He kissed her right on the mouth.

"Thank you."

"You're welcome."

"Don't look so nervous, it's dark, nobody's watching, and besides, it's Valentine's Day. They don't exactly think we're having a business meeting here." Mark laughed.

Merit laughed too, a little from nerves, but more with glee at their accomplishment.

Mark moved back to his side of the table and took her hand.

"Thank you so much. I feel like a hundred pounds has been lifted off my shoulders," Mark said.

"Just play. Play your best, that's all the thanks I want."

Chapter Forty-Seven

David Yee met Mark and Bob Tom at the driving range. Dave, Joe, and about half a dozen players who'd heard through the grapevine that he was coming milled around the ball stand acting as if they'd casually dropped by.

It was a beautiful spring morning, clear, sunny, cool, and filled with the sounds of baby birds chirping in the trees. Yee walked toward Mark carrying a bag of oddly matched clubs over his right shoulder and a Starbucks cup in his left hand with a tea bag tag hanging on a string from under the lid. He was slim, had traditional Asian features, and creamy skin.

Yee smiled at Mark and inspected the new blue shirt with the Fairway Shoes logo on the sleeve. They shook hands.

"David, this is Bob Tom - my boss, coach, caddie, and friend. Bob Tom, this is David Yee. You know who he is," Mark said.

Yee shook hands with Bob Tom. "You've done a good job with him," Yee said.

"Thanks, but the credit is his. We've only been working together for a few months," Bob Tom said. "Basically, he's a natural. Lots of raw talent."

"Let's see if we can harness some of that talent and win a few," Yee said.

"Great," Mark said. "What is your method or philosophy for doing that?"

"First, I do all my teaching in accordance with the laws of nature, Buddhist concepts, and traditional Chinese energy paths," Yee said seriously.

"What?" Mark asked, his eyes crossed.

"Gotcha'," Yee laughed. "I'm more of the grip it and rip it school with a little I Ching thrown in for good measure."

"Whew," Mark laughed. "That's a relief. I was worried I might have to chant before each tee shot."

"Horse feathers," Bob Tom said. "You had me going there for a minute."

"Seriously," Yee said, "we'll take a look at your swing and get you started on whatever techniques are needed to improve it. Then, we'll look at your overall game and try to increase your stamina and distance. Mostly, we'll just try to fine tune everything and increase your control. I already studied some tape from Houston."

"Houston? That was the worst game I've played all year," Mark moaned"I know, that's why I chose it," Yee said.

"Let's win a few and make sure Fairway Shoes continues to foot the bill. Pun intended," Mark said.

"My thoughts, exactly. Are you ready to get to work?"

Chapter Forty-Eight

Across the range, in the shade of the tree line, Browno and the young man wearing the Z-Ro cap watched the men fawning over Yee and Mark. It made Browno furious to hear all the club members talking about Yee.

It had been going on all Spring and he was getting sick of it. The passing of time didn't make things better, it festered and stewed in Browno until he felt like a fool who'd been taken advantage of by a Texas lady lawyer and a Wisconsin cheese farmer.

Browno could feel his blood pressure skyrocketing, although that might be related to the Cubano that he was smoking and the vodka he was sipping from his flask. He offered the drink to his companion who refused.

Browno was angry at everybody, including himself. He hadn't believed that the lady lawyer would be able to get the money together so quickly. The Fairway shoes money came in fast. This meant that she had a plan in place before they had met, before she had tied things down with Browno. This made him especially angry.

He took a drag on the Cubano and watched the trio on the golf course. Mark's strokes were powerful and accurate. He looked like a champion. Legally, Browno no longer had any hold over Mark. But he was going to fix that.

Browno's companion in the cap stared at him. Browno pointed toward the parking lot and the young man moved away down the tree line.

Browno cursed and ground the Cubano out in the grass with his foot.

Chapter Forty-Nine

Mark worked hard all Spring to get ready for his big move toward the PGA tour. He walked into the pro shop for his last day of work before going to Frisco. In the morning he was scheduled to give a few lessons. In the afternoon, he was running the last day of the summer clinic for juniors. He loved working with the young golfers. He might even have a few young golfers of his own someday. He wondered if Merit wanted more children. She had one child already. Did she want any more?

Mark walked up the sidewalk to the club house, and into the pro shop, still distracted.

"Surprise!" a chorus of voices yelled out. A banner over the counter read: *GOOD LUCK MARK!*

"Oh!"

Mark looked around the room. Standing before him were Joe, Bob Tom, Dave, about a dozen of his adult students, the junior clinic members, The First Tee students, and Merit with the big-haired older woman from her office. All were smiling like jackasses.

"Wow!"

Joe came forward, shook Mark's hand, clapped him on the back, and signaled the group for attention.

"Mark, as you know, The PGA Championship is the working man's tourney. It's the only place where the golf pros get to rub elbows with the big boys. We decided to take up a collection for some mad money for your trip. We want you to qualify. We want you to play for all of us."

Joe handed Mark an envelope. "Don't spend it all in one place."

Everyone applauded, as Mark's look changed from shock to gratitude.

"We're behind you all the way."

"Don't take any wooden nickels."

"Take care of him, Bob Tom."

"Good luck up there. Give 'em hell."

"Thanks," Mark said.

"Make us proud, Mark," Dave said. "We're with you."

Cans of soft drinks and plates of brownies were passed around. Everyone munched and celebrated. As the crowd began to thin, each person passed by to shake Mark's hand on the way out.

When it was Merit's turn to congratulate Mark she said, "Joe called me."

Joe came up behind her. "Well, she is your lawyer, isn't she?" Joe winked.

"Yeah, I needed advice," Mark responded awkwardly.

Merit kept quiet. She wasn't quite sure how comfortable she was with someone else knowing about them – even good-hearted Joe.

Adding to her discomfort, Bob Tom walked over and said to Mark, "Who's this tall cool drink of water?"

"Bob Tom, this is my friend and attorney Merit Bridges. Merit, this is Bob Tom." Mark said.

Merit and Bob Tom shook hands.

"I've heard what you did with Browno. Good job." Bob Tom said.

"Thanks," Merit said.

"But, I meant this pretty little filly," Bob Tom indicated toward Betty.

"This is my office manager and right hand, Betty." Merit said.

Betty shook hands and smiled all around.

"Nice weather we're having," Bob Tom said to Betty.

"Yeah, but that rainstorm last night was a real turd floater," Betty said.

Bob Tom focused on Betty and turned on the charm, "Are you a golfer?"

"No, my late husband was a golfer," Betty said. "There's almost nothing he'd rather do than play golf."

"Almost?" Bob Tom grinned. "What would he rather do?"

"Here comes trouble, Darlin'," Betty said to Merit.

"You betcha'," Bob Tom said.

"Lord have mercy," Betty said.

"I tell you what, you're as fresh as a spring breeze," Bob Tom said.

"Well, don't let this baby face fool you, Darlin'. This ain't my first rodeo." Betty smiled through crinkly eyes.

"Shew wee," Bob Tom said. "I was fixin' to get myself a co-cola. You want one?" He offered his arm.

"I need one Darlin', I think I'm havin' a hot flash," Betty said as she hooked her wrist through his elbow.

Merit grinned at them and then slipped away to get some fresh air and check her messages. At the edge of the parking lot, she could see two figures talking, their voices raised. One was pointing at her.

She nonchalantly held her phone to her ear and pretended to be checking her voicemail. The two men were walking now, but it was hard to make them out because they were so far away. She put on the zoom on her phone camera and turned to the side as if she were listening while she snapped a couple of pics.

She checked her texts next: one from Ace saying he'd call her tonight, a few from Val.

She was about to go back in when she got a better look at the two men; one was Browno, who was now heading to the main clubhouse. The other was the young man wearing Z-Ro ball cap she'd seen hanging around lately.

Betty appeared at her elbow. "Who's that?"

"I'm beginning to wonder myself," Merit said.

Chapter Fifty

Browno was sitting in the dark in his black SUV across town near the warehouses he used from time to time. His wife had made borscht for dinner, but even his favorite dish wouldn't fix his mood today. He was waiting for The Enforcer to meet him, and The Enforcer was late.

He gritted his teeth, adjusted his bulk, and waited.

Seventeen minutes later, The Enforcer drove up, parked beside him and rolled down the window. "*Prosti*, Browno. I was caught in traffic."

"*Prosti*, eh? You're sorry? You waste my time and all you have to say is sorry?" Browno said across the vehicles.

Browno brought his fist down on the steering wheel. "Sorry? This woman has messed with my business. We are going to mess with her. And after that, I am getting this fish, this Mark, back on my payroll. I want him working for me," Browno took a hefty swig from his flask. "Pronto. And you are going to make it happen. No more late, no more excuses."

"Of course," The Enforcer said smoothly.

"What do you have on this woman?"

"Photos, inside information, a complete workup," The Enforcer said.

"And her schedule, you have this?"

The Enforcer's eyes narrowed. Then, a nod.

"I want her stopped, *nu*? I want her business to stop, and I want her away from my fish."

"Browno, with respect, what is the focus on this man? We have three more fish that need to be reeled in."

"She think she tricked me. She think she smarty pants."

The Enforcer's head bent forward in acknowledgment and to hide a smile.

"Don't you question me, *nu?*"

The Enforcer nodded. "I'll make sure she's taken care of, boss."

"If you don't." Browno raised his shoulders in a shrug. "I don't need to remind you what happens when people think you are weak."

Browno slid an envelope across the two car windows. The Enforcer took it and dropped it on the passenger seat.

"Nu?" Browno asked.

"No problem. I appreciate the dough-re-mi, but I'd do this one for free. I plan to enjoy it."

Chapter Fifty-One

Mark and Bob Tom drove north through Dallas in Bob Tom's SUV that held all the clubs, baggage, and equipment. They travelled onto Frisco to possibly the most important tournament Mark would ever play. Yes, Wisconsin was looming large, but first, he had a job to do here in the Lone Star State.

They arrived on Tuesday as did most players. Coming in early gave Bob Tom time to survey the course and compare it to yardage books by Gorjus George, the unofficial surveyor of tour courses.

After driving about an hour, they turned into the gates and drove down the long entrance under a banner that said *WELCOME TO THE PGA PRO CHAMPIONSHIP.*

They pulled up to the unloading zone and saw an announcer talking into a microphone with The Golf Network logo. A cameraman made hand motions as the announcer spoke. The cameras zoomed in for a close up on the mustached face of the announcer.

"Hundreds of PGA Professionals qualify for the Club Pro Championship each year. To get to the tourney, the club pros have survived several qualifying steps making them the best of the pros," Mustache said.

Mark was thrilled to be one of those players. Bob Tom smiled at him and held up his thumb.

"The rough here is fierce, and the greens are hard, thin and slick," Mustache said. "The Stimpmeter shows the average at Frisco at nine point five. Fast. Very fast. The twenty low scores of this weekend will go to Wisconsin."

"You just need your ticket to get on the bus," Bob Tom said.

The sun sparkled in the leaves as a soft wind moved the tree-tops. Mark looked up at the huge clubhouse that seemed more like a resort or fancy hotel.

"I don't know what I was expecting, but it wasn't this big," Mark said.

"Yeah, and you get a free towel in the locker room," Bob Tom teased.

Mark smiled.

The bag handlers unloaded the clubs and equipment and put them on a cart under Bob Tom's supervision.

"Nice touch," Mark said.

Other players pulled up and followed the same procedure.

They've all got the dream, Mark thought.

Mark felt the history of the event down to his bones. He'd been watching the PGA tournaments with Check since he was a boy, and the full impact of the week unnerved him.

As he walked, he began to settle down and self-talk under his breath about the week.

Just play my game. No muss, no fuss.

Mark knew making the top group at the end of this tournament would be a small miracle, but he felt it was his time. If he didn't do the job here, there was no going to Wisconsin. He would not be invited.

Near the pro shop, The Golf Network was advertising later coverage on a large television that was placed in front of four big comfy chairs imitating someone's fancy living room. The dark wood reminded him of an English library. Mark sat down and rubbed his hands on the arms of the chair, then jumped up and looked around.

Do I belong here? Is this wishful thinking? Just play my game. Go low, go deep – low score.

Mark turned to the television set on the wall above him.

"Frisco Golf Club," the TV announcer promoted, "is said to define how much you really love golf."

The announcer continued, "Frisco is eighteen holes and nineteen acres of bent grass. Golf & Travel Magazine ranked it twenty-third in its list of the top forty daily fee courses in the country. All twenty-one-thousand of the season's tee-times are usually filled by May."

Mark and Bob Tom spent most of Tuesday getting organized and taking care of paperwork. Wednesday morning Mark got in a practice round and by Wednesday afternoon, the driving range was packed solid. Bob Tom found a spot for Mark between a pair of familiar faces from the regionals. Mark felt a spark of nerves, but he tried to look, if not be, cool and collected.

The player hitting balls on his right was Brian Fierce of Tampa, Florida. On his left was Paul Swallow of Phoenix, Arizona. Bob Tom chatted with Fierce's and Swallow's caddies. He got the scoop on their golf histories and filled them in on Mark's four-one-one.

Mark fell into rhythm with the group and got in a good hour of practice before he had to relinquish his spot to another PGA wannabe.

∞

The tournament was set up with practice rounds on Monday through Wednesday, and elimination play on Thursday and Friday. Those who made the cut on Friday, top ninety and ties, were going into play on Saturday. Top seventy and ties would play on Sunday.

"You'll have no trouble making the cut on Friday." Bob Tom said as they walked across the course to the starting area.

"The first two days aren't what I'm worried about." Mark responded. "It's being in the low scores on Sunday that I want."

"Exactly."

"Let's take it one day at a time."

"Right."

The TV announcer Mark had watched in the pro shop was running commentary at the first hole.

"Playing Frisco can be a humbling experience, but it is also a thrilling playground. The PGA of America selected the course with challenge and excitement in mind."

Mark was paired with veteran Paul Swallow and followed a couple of young players. As all four players walked on, delight showed on their faces.

Mark had concentrated on his long game in preparation. In addition, he'd modified his diet, by adding more high-water content food to help deal with dehydration. Mark and Bob Tom further monitored water consumption beginning in the locker room and through the day's play.

At the end of day one, he and Bob Tom assessed.

"You played well all day," Bob Tom said.

"Yeah, but is it enough?" Mark asked.

∞

Mark played well on Friday and smiled as he got up early on Saturday for the third day of play at Frisco. He'd played respectably so far and had kept his nerves under control. Mark didn't start until later in the day. Players, camera crews, the increasing crowds, and any unexpected mishaps slowed players drawing later slots, but that's the way it was done.

Most uncomfortable for Mark was that the cameras followed the afternoon players the most, and he wanted to avoid being on television as much as possible. He got the shakes when a camera showed up. It reminded him of Whistling, Check, and bad times. Mark wondered if Check was aware that he was playing. Maybe Check would be proud that he'd tried again.

From his practice play and the first two days of the championship, Mark knew that the fourth hole was his biggest challenge. He'd handled it well on Thursday and Friday, but he knew not to take that for granted. The hole played five hundred and sixty-three yards from the blacks. The tee shot was downhill to the fairway, but if he missed the short grass, there were perils on both sides.

Bob Tom had informed him earlier in the week that the hole was so difficult, a course marshal was posted on the tee for regular players to show them where to hit their tee shot. The green looked inviting.

"Don't be seduced," Bob Tom said.

"I know. The trick is not to go for it," Mark said.

Mark's strategy was to lay up short of the water, then take it to the green with a short iron.

"Exactly," Bob Tom said.

The player ahead of him hit the water, and Mark got nervous.

"Just do it the same way you did yesterday." Bob Tom stated calmly.

"Just give me a second." Mark responded. He did some serious self-talk, took a deep breath, and reached for his driver. His first shot took him to the middle of the fairway, and he exhaled with relief.

Mark prepared for the second shot, set up, and hit.

Whack! The ball soared out straight toward the water. Mark held his breath and Bob Tom clutched the bag as the ball struck the ground, then began rolling backwards. It rolled just inches short of the blue pond and stopped. They both let out air at once.

Mark took another shot to put the ball on the green, and handled the putt without issue for one under par.

"One shot less than we expected," Mark said.

"A blessing," Bob Tom said.

Mark played through to the twelfth hole with competence, missing a couple of putts he should have made, but overall handling each hole in turn. Mark made up for missed putts with his long game, but with a course rating of seventy-five point two, it was a challenge.

Mark approached the thirteenth hole with trepidation. The hole was four hundred and eighty yards long, with a dogleg to the right around a huge bunker. If he sliced the ball and came up short, he'd be in thick rough with an uphill lie, and unable to see the green. Even if he got to the fairway, it would still be a difficult second shot.

Bob Tom and Mark had a pow-wow.

"I could play the hole as a par five, lay up on the second shot, then use a wedge to the green," Mark strategized.

"Yeah, but that would cost you a stroke, and your long game is better than your short," Bob Tom filled in the other side of the equation, even though Mark was well aware of it.

"I won't rely on my putt. I'll take the chance of getting to the green in two," Mark said.

His drive sailed out about halfway to the green and rolled a few feet. Perfect set up for the second shot. He took his two-iron from Bob Tom, and set his sights on the green, about two hundred and thirty-five yards away at a diagonal across the fairway.

"I'll have to stick it," Mark said.

He put a hard launch on the ball and shaded his eyes to watch it land. Halfway through, he knew he'd blown it. The ball landed on the green about two feet from the hole, then rolled to the right and would not stop.

"I was thinking of exactly what I was afraid of, instead of what I wanted." Mark grumbled.

"You can make it up at the putt," Bob Tom said. "If you'd laid up, you would have come out with par anyway. No problem."

When they got to the hole, Mark squatted in the rough to eyeball the line to the flag. To make it in one, he'd have to curve to the right for about half the distance, then back to the left and in. He lined up, stood up, took a short swing, and held his breath. The ball curved to the right as planned, but didn't swing far enough back, and he was left with a two-footer to the hole.

"Darn," Mark said.

"Damn," Bob Tom echoed under his breath.

He sunk the two-foot putt without issue but was still grumbling when he reached the next tee.

"Shake it off," Bob Tom said.

Mark recovered well on the fourteenth hole, and his confidence was somewhat restored. He finished with a seventy, and most importantly, he'd avoided the television cameras except for a couple of distant shots late in the day.

"I have no advice to give. Good job," Bob Tom said.

"I'll have to kick up my game tomorrow if I'm going to finish in the top twenty."

"Yes, you'll have to take a few more chances, but one thing you have in your favor, the more you play a course, the better you get at it," Bob Tom said.

I still have a shot at the brass ring.

Chapter Fifty-Two

B ack in Austin, The Enforcer surveyed the lair, trying to ignore the smell of rotted wood that was always so bothersome. It was a good place, a favorite place. The building looked as if it should be condemned. It was a property owned by Browno that was sheltered by a zigzag of numbered companies, and that worked perfectly for its intended purpose. There was nothing worse than getting interrupted if you were in The Enforcer's line of work.

The Enforcer was still thinking of yesterday's conversation with Browno. Then there was a smile. It was really too bad the blond had to die.

The Enforcer's heavy footsteps thudded as the first door was checked, and then the lock. It would imprison the lawyer perfectly. The second door was checked too; solid metal and sturdy. As Browno would say: This was good. The outside door was left as it was; almost falling apart. It would not do to fix up the door so that it looked shiny and new. Besides, who would ever dare enter this building?

The Enforcer thought about toying with Merit for a while first. Merit had a son, a teenager. Maybe that would be a good soft spot to aim for. Playing with Merit would be fun but torturing someone Merit loved in front of her would be even more pleasant.

The room had no windows, and the only piece of good furniture was a table that held a few tools of The Enforcer's trade. The Enforcer turned back to the table. It really was too bad they couldn't snatch Mark and show him who he was really dealing with. Then The Enforcer shrugged. The woman would be just as good, with her fancy shoes and her fancy life. They'd take her down a few pegs.

A surgical scalpel called to The Enforcer from the table: shiny, oiled, and ready. Not too long now.

Chapter Fifty-Three

Mark, Bob Tom, and Yee sat in the clubhouse cafe in Frisco on Saturday night. Mark looked at his score card. He had shaved off a point that day, easily placing him in the top seventy to go into Sunday's play.

Unfortunately, several of his new friends got hung up at various holes and never recovered. He wished them a fond farewell and they each caught a flight home that night.

"Can you handle a one beer and a burger to celebrate?" Bob Tom asked.

Yee look disapproving, but no need. Mark was in training mode.

"I'll have it tomorrow night after I've secured my place in Wisconsin," Mark said.

Bob Tom nodded.

"I'll have the broiled fish, whole grain pasta, and loads of vegetables," Mark said.

Yee smiled. "I'll have the same."

They didn't invite anyone along to dinner, as Bob Tom's philosophy was to isolate Mark from the other players who might have the jitters and give them to Mark like the measles. After dinner, they retired early.

Mark called Merit from his room before he went to sleep to let her know he'd made the first cut, and to see how she was doing. During their chat, she diplomatically skirted the topic of television, although she intended to watch The Golf Network the next day to try for a glimpse of him. She knew Mark would be avoiding the cameras, and she also knew Mr. Baker wouldn't be happy unless Mark showed his face and the Fairway Shoes logo around.

"Are you getting tired of traveling yet?" Merit asked.

"It's okay. If I make the tour, it will be worse than this. I'll be traveling all the time."

"Not if, when. When you make the tour," Merit said.

"I just wish you were here," Mark said.

"Me too, but we agreed it was best if you stay focused, and I'd be a distraction."

"Yes, you would," Mark laughed. "A welcome one for sure. I could use a little stress relief right now."

"You say that when I'm a thousand miles away," Merit laughed. "Good luck tomorrow."

I'll need it.

Chapter Fifty-Four

Merit and Ag met for lunch at Hyde Park Bar and Grill in South Austin. She had subconsciously worn his favorite color, dark blue. Ag had on his traditional Aggie maroon shirt and jeans.

They smiled at each other and shared an order of the house famous battered French fries while they waited on fish tacos for Merit and the choice burger for Ag.

"I got the reports from New York I'd sent for on Browno and his gang," Ag said.

"Let's tidy up the file with the reports, but I think that's handled," Merit said. "We settled and paid Browno a nice sum. He should be happy."

"Browno has muscle, a guy named Petrov. He has quite a rap sheet. Most crimes were committed in the Brighton Beach area," Ag said. "I'd like to give this information to Chaplain if it's okay with you.

"Browno's out of the picture, so the client confidentiality is covered. If you think it's wise, go ahead, then you can wrap up that file and send your final bill," Merit said.

"Just watch out. It's never good to get on the bad side of a crew like Browno's," Ag said.

Chapter Fifty-Five

Sunday at Frisco should have been a fun day for Mark. It was the last day of the PGA Pro. He'd played well the first three days, he knew the course, he was making few errors, and he still had a shot at a slot in the top twenty. *BUT.* The "but" today was The Golf Network.

"I can't play well and escape the cameras today," Mark said.

The Golf Network producers were searching out the players they thought would finish in the top twenty and highlighting their play-by-play throughout the day.

Bob Tom looked at an information sheet.

"Prepare yourself. You're behind Brian Fierce who is a shoo-in for a top spot. The producers will be following Fierce, and that means they'll be near you, too," Bob Tom said.

Mark cringed. He wished he could wear two gloves instead of one. He wished he could putt with his gloves on, too. That would be too obvious, and not very professional.

"We're here for the last day at Frisco, a humbling and exciting course. It's said that you can play badly and enjoy Frisco only if you don't care about your score," Mustache said.

Bob Tom wiggled his nose at Mark like Charlie Chaplin, imitating the announcer's moustache. Mark cracked a smile, and it broke the tension for the moment.

Mark played through the first hole without issue and approached the second.

Moustache on the TV camera piped up, "The par-four second hole here plays four hundred and seventy-four yards."

Mark made it to the landing area, then looked out over the two hundred remaining yards to a small green. The fairway was pencil-thin to the green, so no room for error.

Fierce, ahead of Mark, placed his second shot less than a foot from the hole. Moustache went bananas on camera.

Mark placed his second shot about three feet out and breathed a sigh of relief that this hole was handled with a short putt remaining.

"Good job." Bob Tom patted him on the back after the easy putt. As they passed the camera crew on the way to the next hole, Bob Tom intentionally steered him away and kept him walking and talking.

Play progressed to the infamous fourth hole for the last time during the Championship. Mark and Fierce navigated around the water avoiding the rough along the way.

Then Moustache announced in a hushed voice, "This is purported to be the toughest hole of the day."

Mark found himself having trouble on the green, as he almost rolled the ball down the drop-off on the backside to the rough, but the ball held. Mark had to take two putts to put the ball in the cup. He made par, and he'd been counting on one under. He'd have to make that up somewhere along the way.

Moustache announced their approach to the eighth hole. "This par-four eighth hole received an honorable mention from Golf Digest as one of America's best." Moustache pointed downhill and added, "See the green in the distance that looks like another state over there."

Mark could see the green surrounded by water, but he knew it was an illusion and that there was fairway short of the water. He had to hit over about two hundred yards of deep grasses to get there. He set up and aimed his ball to the left of a big tree on the hillside of the fairway. His ball didn't stick. It rolled, and rolled and rolled, out of sight into the rough.

Mark made his way down the slope, and with the help of Bob Tom discovered his ball. He knocked it out of the rough, taking a big chunk of ground with the ball.

Mark finally got it up on the green and putted in one. This put him at par for the hole.

He'd have to make that up too, and soon. He was able to do just that on the ninth and tenth with two consecutive birdies. Bob Tom let out a huge sigh and patted Mark on the back as they walked to the thirteenth.

Bob Tom and Mark consulted.

"You can play it safe as a par five and lay up on the second shot or try again to get to the green in two," Bob Tom said.

"That hasn't worked before, but I have to chance it or kiss a spot in the top twenty goodbye," Mark said.

His drive sailed out about halfway down the fairway and rolled a few feet. He took his mind off the earlier slice and focused on hitting the flag.

He sailed the ball out over the fairway. It landed on the green about three feet from the hole, and stuck. "Yes!"

Bob Tom smiled. "One hole to go."

The crowd moved with the players down the course. Picnic baskets came out and children used large cardboard boxes as make-shift sleds to slide down the hillsides. A party atmosphere took over.

But, Mark wasn't taking part in the fun. Mark knew that on the next hole, there was a long carry to reach the fairway, which curved like a boomerang around a large tree in the left rough. At this point Mark's score was good. He wasn't sure where he ranked among the other players, but Bob Tom got some intel from the cameraman. Using Fierce as his high guide, and another player, Toad, as the low, Bob Tom thought Mark was somewhere between them.

Mark needed to make this hole in three, and it was a tough par four.

Fierce hit his tee shot into the fairway and was left with a three-wood to the green. A tough shot, but he grabbed a piece of the green at the edge and moved up to putt in two. He had par on the hole.

Mark could have tried the same, but he wanted birdie, not par. He needed to be sure he had the score to make the cut. He hit his tee shot onto the fairway, and mimicked Fierce's use of a three-wood to the green. Mark landed squarely on the green, putted in one, and made birdie.

Moustache announced, "Nice. Mark Green just showed some real talent there. He's in!"

The crowd cheered and Mark got the ball from the last cup and held it up in triumph.

After confirming that Mark had indeed finished in the bottom twenty scores, Mark and Bob Tom celebrated with the much-anticipated beer and burger.

Mark had achieved his goal and, more importantly, he'd not been questioned about his hands. Bob Tom raised his glass, "Top twenty! You kept your cool and played your game. I couldn't be prouder."

"Thanks, it feels great," Mark drank a long cold draw on his beer and looked up with foam on his face, grinning from ear to ear.

"On to Wisconsin."

Chapter Fifty-Six

M ark slipped into Bob Tom's empty office to make a private call. The young man with the Z-Ro cap started into the office. Mark looked up and smiled, but the young man backed out and passed on by.

"Hi, Mom. How are things?" Mark asked.

"Great, Sweetie. I saw you on TV. Good job," she said.

"Thanks, Mom. Did Dad watch? Could I speak to him?" Mark said.

"He's outside right now." Mark heard the screen door slam through the phone.

"Don't lie for him, Mom. I can take it if he still doesn't want to talk to me."

"He's really proud of you. He's just stubborn. You know how he is," she said. "What are you up to?"

"I'm working today. Thankfully, Bob Tom is letting me work enough hours to keep me on the payroll and my health insurance coverage going. The rest of the week I'll be working with Bob Tom on the course layout."

"That's wonderful, dear."

"Thanks for the try, Mom. I'll call you later in the week."

"Okay. Take care of yourself."

Mark hit the end button on his phone and sat quietly for a moment. He left the office and slammed the door behind him.

He returned to the reception desk and checked the book for his next lesson. The clients were starting to blur into one big mixed personality.

Same song second verse.

Mark grabbed the keys to a cart and headed over to the driving range to bang some balls as hard as he could.

∞

Yee found Mark at the driving range knocking the balls wildly and using very little form.

"If you're in that frame of mind, come with me," Yee said.

They loaded a set of clubs into Mark's Jeep and drove out to Windy Point on Lake Travis. It was a weekday and not very busy. Yee took Mark to an area behind a closed restaurant.

"What's up?" Mark asked.

"You know how the weather was second nature to you on the farm?" Yee asked.

"Yes, how did you know that?" Mark asked.

"I grew up on a farm too. Soybeans," Yee said.

"I want you to remember how that felt and apply it to golf. We'll practice here, out of view," Yee said.

"Why?" Mark asked.

"I haven't done this before," Yee said. "If it works, I don't want anyone else to know about it before we go to Wisconsin. If it doesn't work, we'll forget about it."

"What is it?"

"I want you to hit this bucket of balls into the wind. The wind whips up here every afternoon around this time," Yee said, pointing toward the ripples on the water.

"I don't get it," Mark said.

"You'll see," Yee said.

Mark hit the balls one by one until the bucket was empty.

"This is exhausting. I don't have much control."

Yee gave him another bucket of balls. "Try again."

"Okay." Mark hit the balls into the wind again.

"That's better," Yee said. "How do you feel?"

"Like I've been lifting weights," Mark said.

"Now, turn around and hit this bucket with the wind at your back," Yee said. Mark hit the next bucket, then another to the right side, and another to the left. By the time he had finished, he'd begun to place his shots.

"Now, how do you feel," Yee asked.

"Like a wind expert," Mark said. "Exhausted."

"Good work. We need to go. The restaurant is opening for dinner soon," Yee said.

They walked toward the Jeep, stopping by the restaurant. Yee gave the manager a check and thanked him for the use of his property.

"I put a little extra in there for someone to pick up the balls on land. The ones in the water will dissolve," Yee said.

They drove back to Austin in silence. Both had a lot invested in the next stage of Mark's journey.

Chapter Fifty-Seven

Merit met Mark for lunch at Hula Hut on Lake Austin. She had been doing a good job of avoiding him at night without invoking a discussion of their non-sex life. They sat on the deck over the water near a bar surrounded by thatched palapas. A big art deco fish was poised as if jumping from the lake below.

"It's good to see you," Merit said as Mark pulled her chair out for her.

"You too. I feel like it's been an age since we've been together," Mark responded. "How long since we've made love?"

"I know. How's it going with Yee?" Merit asked.

"Great. He's got me doing visualization exercises, and he's fine tuning a few details on my swing, but we're pretty much ready to go."

"Fantastic," Merit said.

"You're coming up to Wisconsin for the last few days of the tournament, right?"

"Yes, I can't wait to see you play. I'll also meet with Fairway Shoes and the Nano people, but I won't bother you with that. I know you'll be busy and focused. Just leave all the sponsorship work to me."

"I don't know what I'd do without you," Mark said and touched her hand.

Merit pulled the latest copy of Golf Pro Magazine out of her bag. "Have you seen this?" She opened it to a page with a yellow post-it hanging off the edge and handed it to Mark. "It's a story on Frisco. Says you are the up and coming to watch."

"They were talking about this at work today, but I hadn't seen it. Hope I can live up to it," Mark didn't smile. "Joe told me I was mentioned on golfplay.com too."

"I'll get Betty to pull the article off the net. Pretty heady stuff," Merit said. "Isn't this what you wanted? You don't look happy."

"I am, I mean… I'm just a little nervous. So much is at stake."

"I have faith in you," Merit touched his hand.

"Not having to work a full schedule at the club has given me so much freedom to practice and having Fairway has given me relief from money worries, not to mention your getting Browno off my back."

"Speaking of, I had lunch with my investigator Ag and he told me that Browno has a right-hand man, Petrov. Ever seen him?" Merit asked.

"No, should I be worried?" Mark said.

"I don't think so. Browno's in the past. Good riddance."

"Do you see Ag a lot out of the office?" Mark asked. "Seems like you like him a lot."

"Sometimes, and I do like him and respect him. Regardless, that should not be a problem. Remember, we are supposed to be casual. And, now you're a client." Merit said.

"I don't feel like a client, but I do thank you for all the work you've been doing lately," Mark said.

And thank you, too," she said.

"For?"

"For being my first full-fledged sports law client. I've taken on several others, an Austin Ice Bat hockey player and a minor league baseball player. My entertainment client list has expanded beyond Liam Nolan's estate as well. I had a gaggle of clowns in my office looking for help. Pro bono, of course."

"Clowns?" Mark asked.

"Yes. Did you know that clowns register their faces just like a copyright? Fascinating area of the law."

"That's great, Merit. Isn't it funny how things work out?"

They ordered tubular tacos and big sweating glasses of iced tea. They ate quickly while Merit ran through a few minor details.

"I've coordinated Yee's payment with Fairway Shoes, and all the expenses for the hotels and meals in Wisconsin are being handled by Betty. We're splitting the costs between the three sponsors," Merit said. "I'm looking for an accountant for you to keep your taxes and records straight. It's starting to get a little complicated."

"Great, but if I don't win, it won't be complicated at all, will it?"

"No chance of that," Merit said, and motioned for the check.

"That's right, positive attitude, no room for doubt," Mark said.

"Sorry this is such a rush," Merit said as she paid the bill. "I have a new client at one- thirty, and I can't be late."

"No problem," Mark said. "I've got a lot on my list to get ready to go. We'll find some time when we get back from Wisconsin."

Merit avoided his eyes, stood, and picked up her purse. "Let's go.

Chapter Fifty-Eight

Merit finished another long day at the office and left for home. She hummed "The Bluest Eyes in Texas" by Restless Heart as she entered the garage. Someone had thrown down a bag of fast food leftovers and the smell caused her to cover her mouth and skirt the walkway.

Merit didn't notice Petrov watching her as she walked to her parking space. Merit had no idea the security cameras had been shifted just a tad with gloved hands to leave a blind spot. She didn't know she was in danger at all.

Merit had her keys to her SUV in her hand with her briefcase and her purse on her shoulder. Her ponytail swung in rhythm with her walk and her heels clicked on the pavement. She opened her SUV and placed her briefcase on the back seat then walked around the car to the driver's side.

A figure moved around the edge of the garage in the shadows and advanced toward her. Her armpits prickled. She suddenly stopped and looked down the ramp. A truck was coming up to her parking level. She stepped back, then recognized it as Ag's truck and waited for him to pull up beside her.

"Hello there," Merit said.

"Just the woman I wanted to see," Ag said.

"Close call. You almost missed me," Merit said.

"Glad I didn't. I thought I'd catch you working late and grab a drink," Ag said.

"Sounds great," Merit said.

"Hop in," Ag said and reached across the seat to open her door.

Ag drove off as Petrov watched his chance disappear.

Chapter Fifty-Nine

Mark met Merit and a photographer at her office to do some new headshots for the sponsors and press. He arrived with a garment bag full of the changes of clothes Merit had requested he bring.

The photographer was set up in the conference room with a thirty-five millimeter, a digital camera, and a video camera.

"What's the video for?" Mark asked.

"I think it's time we faced the demons. Maybe with a little practice, we can get you used to being interviewed."

"Oh, no."

"Sponsors expect exposure, and exposure means television. Just give it a try, no one will see it but us," Merit coaxed.

The photographer shot the still of Mark in various golf outfits and hats with each of the sponsor's logos featured in various pictures. Next, he set up the video camera on a tripod at the end of the conference table and hooked a cable into the television set.

"This is how you turn it on, and this is for playback," the photographer said. "I'll have these stills for you in a couple of days."

Merit turned on the video camera, took a pen in hand and stood in front of the tripod.

"Stand right here beside me and pretend I'm an announcer. This pen is my microphone."

"This is dumb," Mark said.

"Don't be a baby. Give it a try."

Merit held the pen to her mouth. "Mr. Green, may I have a moment?"

She put the pen to Mark's mouth, but he said nothing.

"Okay, Mark. Let's practice some standard answers, and even if the announcers don't ask you a question that matches, just use one of those. That way, you won't freeze up trying to think of appropriate responses. Okay?"

"Okay."

"And, don't forget to tip your hat or turn the shoulder with the logo to the camera. You get paid a bonus for each exposure. Got it?"

"Okay." Mark warmed up a little and put his arm around her waist.

"I wouldn't do that to the golf announcers," Merit laughed.

"Just tightening up the shot," Mark teased.

"Mr. Green, may I have a moment?" Merit began again.

"Yes, Ms. Brid"How do you feel about your game, Mr. Green? Now, no matter what they ask, just say something like 'It felt great out there today.' Or, for the future, 'I just plan to play the best golf I can.' Or, if it's about another player, 'He's the best, isn't he.' See?"

"How did you feel about your game, Mr. Green?"

"It felt great out there today." Mark said.

"The drive on blah blah hole was the best. What made you decide to hit the blah blah club?"

Mark fumbled for a moment and said, "I just want to play the best golf I can." He stopped. "That doesn't make sense."

"I know, it's a little off, but at least you'll have something to say at first, then you'll think of your own things after you get more comfortable."

"Can you hold onto your lead?"

Mark said, "I just plan to play the best golf I can."

"Good. When you've had enough and want to get away, just start walking and saying, 'thank you' until you're out of earshot."

"What are your plans for the coming year?"

"I just plan to play the best golf I can," Mark said and walked out of the conference room saying, "Thank you, thank you, thank you." He walked back in and kissed her on the cheek.

"Good job," Merit said.

"Until I do it for real."

Chapter Sixty

Mark and Merit went to the Café at Central Market North to have dinner, look over his play schedule, and have a little strategy meeting.

They placed their orders at the counter and found a clean table far enough from the band, so they could hear each other. Big House played Rhythm and Blues for the diners and kids jumped around the playscape outside. They noticed many colorful characters. Austin was never lacking in personalities.

"Keepin' Austin Weird," Merit said.

"Oh," Mark said and stared at a few interesting folks.

"How are things with Bob Tom?" Merit asked.

"Good. He's turned into my biggest supporter now that he sees I'm committed. Who knew the big old grouch was really a teddy bear?"

"Great to have the team come together," Merit said.

"Whistling Straits is the only thing left between me and next year's PGA Tour," Mark said.

"Don't let the big boys in Wisconsin freak you out," Merit said.

"That's a big enough problem, but being the old home state, I know what I'm up against. It's one thing to score bottom twenty-two against other club pros, but Whistling is a whole new level."

"I'll be in Wisconsin to cheer you on," Merit said.

After a quick lunch of eggplant and mozzarella on whole grain bread for Merit and a high protein stir fry for Mark, they left the café and walked toward the car. They let their arms and clothes occasionally brush.

Mark said, "I'm really looking forward to my next lesson with David Yee."

"You're about to get really busy again. I think I've got my end tied down. I'll try to keep the details at bay and let you keep your mind clear," Merit said. "If you wonder about anything, just bring up our online calendar and all your promo events will be there. Betty is keeping it up to date."

"Thanks for the support, Merit. What would I do without you?"

As they ventured further through the parking lot toward the car, a cute gray-haired couple split apart to let them walk through.

The little old man said, "Cut the butter," and smiled.

His wife of at least forty years, looked stressed. "We can't find our car."

Mark asked, "What are you driving?" Merit looked out over the parking lot.

"A blue Buick, license number W forty-two seven nine one," answered the husband. "Or is it seven nine two?"

"A blue Buick?" Mark searched for the color.

"There it is." The old man pointed to the next aisle over and joined hands with his wife. They walked away shouting "Good-bye, thanks."

Mark and Merit both chuckled and Mark took her hand. She did not withdraw it but was acutely aware that she was exposed. When they reached the Jeep, he opened her door and her armpits prickled slightly. As she slipped into the seat, she looked up fully into his face. It was the face of love.

In that moment, Merit realized that the relationship as they knew it was over.

She smiled at him and settled into the Jeep. As he went around the car to the driver's side, her stomach clutched. Why did he have to get so serious? They had been having so much fun, she hadn't taken time to evaluate her long-term goals with regard to the relationship. And, now he was a client.

Merit was forced to the sudden realization that this was not going to fill the longing of her heart on a long-term basis. Merit knew she would think it over, rationalize how wonderful he was, try to convince herself that time might change things. Under it all, she knew what she knew.

Damn.

Merit put on her sunglasses to hide pooling tears and swallowed the anguish in her throat. She just didn't love him like that, and she knew she never would.

217

Chapter Sixty-One

Merit spent the Fourth of July weekend relaxing and catching up with friends. Ace was in town and running around Austin having fun with his childhood buddies. Natalie was due back that night from New York. Merit had a golf date with her set for the next day.

Merit joined her dear friend and client Jean Springer and about a dozen other real estate and banker types to celebrate the holiday. It was hot. The Fourth in Texas can only be tolerated by submersion in water until the sun goes down, so the celebrants met at Lakeway Marina on Lake Travis. They hopped onto Jean's houseboat and set out past the buoyed boundaries of the marina into the open water.

The group consisted of the usual suspects, most of whom knew each other. There were a few newbies to the group, Dalton Broad being one of them. Jean, a beautiful woman in a bikini with perfect skin and teeth, introduced Merit, Dalton, and the other new members to the rest of the party. The boatload of guests settled into easy chitchat about lake levels, water temperature, and boat size.

Lake Travis was cool, pristine, and aglow with the sunlight reflecting on the water. The usual afternoon breeze picked up causing beautiful white sailboats to crisscross nearby with their sails puffed up like colorful robins' breasts.

Merit went to the upper deck to find a small group chatting about land prices, recent home sales, the economy and interest rates. A passing boat played Jimmy Buffet, "Changes in Latitude, Changes in Attitude."

After a polite interval, Merit took off her wrap revealing a baby blue maillot and soaked in the sun. She tuned out the conversation and relaxed in a solitary deck chair on the edge of the party. She noted the occasional drip of condensation on her arm from the cold white wine in the cup holder. Jimmy Buffet sang on.

The boat motored around the bend and dropped anchor at Marshall Ford within sight of a beautiful thirty-two-foot Columbian. The occupants of both boats waved, the usual boating etiquette. Merit and her new friends climbed in and out of the houseboat all day, bobbing in the lake on life preservers. Merit socialized for a while then returned to her lounge chair.

Merit's mind wandered to Mark. She gave a mental nod to the gods for luck for him at the tourney. Could she let him go? She had been feeling guilty for several days, until she'd realized that the truth was the truth, and facing it was the only way to handle it. She hated to end it.

It's inevitable isn't it?

And Mark was now a client. Timing, however, was another thing. He needed her support right now, and she wanted to help him. Events beyond both of their control had placed his golf career on the front burner, and she would focus there for now.

She gave herself a mental break from Mark, clients, parenting, everything. For the moment, she felt content, ageless, and at peace. All was well. The ridges of her mind were smooth for the first time in months. She nodded off.

Merit awoke before sunset to the sounds of the motor putting and opened one eye. They pulled up near the shoreline by a restaurant called Party on the Lake. The music from the outdoor dining place was easy to hear. Merit got up, tied on a colorful sarong, and found her hostess.

"Stealing music?" Merit asked Jean and laughed.

Jean laughed. "We give them plenty of business all year."

The captain anchored the boat and guests began to dance. Food appeared from below and blenders began whirring. Dalton Broad appeared beside her.

"Have a nice nap?" he asked and smiled orthodontically beautiful teeth out of his tan face. Teeth had always been one of Merit's weaknesses.

"I was hoping no one cared or noticed," she smiled back.

"Not notice you?" said. "No way." His eyes were twinkling with mischief.

Merit knew she was a captive audience for the night, so she decided to enjoy it, not a tough task to do looking at Dalton's handsome face.

He held up a beer from the ice chest. She pointed to a bottle of water. "Please".

Beneath her sunglasses, she checked him out – tall, lanky, around fifty. Dark hair with a bit of gray, and ceramic blue eyes. A little patch of chest hair peeked out of his open collar.

He smiled a brilliant smile and winked. A feeling of electricity caused her to suck in breath.

"What? Are you okay?" Dalton asked.

Fine, she coughed and gestured toward the water bottle. She composed herself.

"How do you know the group?" Merit asked.

"I develop property in Austin. I buy real estate occasionally through our hostess Jean," Dalton said.

"I've seen your name in the trades. Broad Development, right?" Merit asked. "Aren't you working on the renovation of the old Jones property down by Lake Austin?" Merit asked.

"That's right," Dalton said.

"I have you on my list of people to contact about a deal I'm trying to re-finance," Merit said.

"I'm always up for new business," Dalton said.

"Let's leave work for next week," Merit said. She had no desire to discuss Terrence Long's murder on her holiday weekend.

"Agreed," Dalton said.

"What else do you like to do?" Merit asked.

"I like to hike, travel, play golf, be outdoors," Dalton said.

Ouch! Merit thought. Golf. Mark. Mark? She had no commitment with Mark, and she knew they were heading for a change, but she wasn't prepared for the instant attraction to Dalton.

Merit thought about it. *I'll just go with it and have fun. Nothing is going to happen tonight, anyway. Why am I even thinking about him in that way? I've just met the guy. He could become part of a deal in her office.*

The tiny lights on the boat blinked to life and created a festive mood. The restaurant band Los Lobos' version of *La Bamba* and Dalton moved to the music. Merit caught the vibe and they danced, talked, and had a fine time.

The upper level filled in with expectant firework watchers. Dalton placed his arm in the middle of Merit's back and steered her toward an empty chair. "Marggy?"

"Absolutely."

He returned shortly with two frosty glasses. Limes hung on the edges and salt sparked like tiny jewel-stone chips in the Mexican lights. They chatted on and on about every ordinary thing.

Then the fireworks started.

Chapter Sixty-Two

Merit went into work the following Monday with a smile from the weekend.

Betty met her at the door with a stack of files and a puzzled look on her face. Merit passed the reception desk and went down the hall.

"Morning," she said to Betty and the receptionist at once.

"Did you get rest or sex this weekend, Darlin'?" Betty asked, following her back to Merit's office.

"Rest. I did go out with a new man, and I played a nice round of golf with Natalie."

"Honey, it don't get much better than that," Betty laughed and piled the files into the *IN* box. "Is this the guy you met on the boat?"

"Yep, Dalton," Merit sighed his name.

"Oh, dear. This is looking serious," Betty said.

"No, not serious, but I'd like to see where it goes. Whew, it's going to be hot again today." Merit took off her jacket.

"What about Mark?" Betty asked.

"What about him? He's a client now." Merit tried it out to see if it would fly.

"Right." Betty took Merit's jacket and hung it on a hook on the back of the door.

"What?" Merit asked.

"I'm just glad you're getting out again."

"If it's not Dalton, it will be someone else. I wish I didn't have to hurt Mark though," Merit said.

"If wishes were horses, then beggars would ride," Betty said.

"I know, I know."

"What did he expect? Didn't he realize it would end sometime?" Betty said.

"Yes, and we agreed to that in the beginning, but I think he's gone past that, and I don't want to talk to him right now with his big game coming up."

"There is that."

"Any advice?" Merit asked.

"What if you break it off with Mark and it doesn't work out with Dalton?" Betty asked.

"Either way, it's time to end it. Mark is in over his head with me. He needs to find someone his own age. Age isn't everything, but Dalton and I are the same life age, our homes, books, cooking, families, work."

"You're still going to Wisconsin, aren't you?" Betty asked.

"I wouldn't miss it, and I've got the Fairway, Nano Phone people, and several others meeting us there for the last few days of play," Merit said. She was happy that her career was going into this direction. It was exciting, the new opportunities in front of her.

"Mark's busy. Let it go until then. That's my two cents worth," Betty said.

"Thanks. Good advice. I better get to work. What is all this paper you've piled up here?" Merit pointed to the *IN* box.

"Grunt work if you ask me. Why don't you hire an associate to take some of the smaller things off your desk?"

"That's what I have you for," Merit smiled.

"Well, this is lawyer stuff, and besides, I don't have time for it all either with the office to run," Betty answered. "If you had someone else in here, you could develop more of the entertainment type clients you enjoy so much."

"I'll think about it. Maybe it's time." Merit said. "For now, could you print the new loan documents on the Long file for me?"

"Sure, darlin'. I'll handle it," Betty said. "You think about your end and handle that."

Chapter Sixty-Three

M erit was awakened around four a.m. by a distant ringing that became louder and louder. It was her mobile. She hit the speaker button.

"Hello," Merit said.

"Merit, it's Mark." He sounded frantic. She bolted awake, grabbed the phone off the nightstand, and switched off the speaker.

"Mark?"

"Merit, it's Check. He's dead."

"What?"

"Dad. He's gone."

"I'll be right there."

"No, I'm coming to you."

She got up and went to the toilet, she tried to wake up and make sense of the shock and the sweet lost sound of his voice. Tears misted her eyes for his pain.

She brushed her teeth and hair and put on a robe and some slippers. She made coffee and started to think. She wondered what flights were available to Wisconsin this early.

She put the coffee on a tray and took the tray, the phone, paper and pen, and her iPad to the dining room table. She searched Kayak and took notes on flight times until the desk called up to say Mark had arrived.

Merit opened the door and pulled him into her arms. She held him until his sobbing subsided and then led him to the dining room table. She placed a box of tissues on the table and poured him a cup of coffee, mixing in lots of sugar. Pepper sat quietly at Mark's feet and looked up at Merit.

Merit waited for Mark to speak.

He seemed dazed for a long time, blew his nose, then finally said, "I didn't think it would feel like this."

"I know."

"I've got to get to my mother."

"I know."

"I didn't really hate him."

"I know."

They sat in silence again and she gave him time to integrate his thoughts. Finally, when he looked more himself, she said, "There are two flights this morning that I think will work. One leaves at seven, the other at eight-thirty. It's four-thirty now."

"As soon as possible."

"Right, but if you leave at eight-thirty, we can get you packed and to the airport by seven and you can call the pro-shop and make some arrangements before you leave. And, it is a non-stop, so it gets in only about twenty minutes after the other flight."

Making plans seemed to help him. He clicked into action mode and said, "Yes, that's better."

"Drink your coffee while I get dressed, and I'll drive you to your place and then the airport. Okay?"

"The flight."

"I'll make your reservation while you pack. Okay?"

He picked up the coffee cup and said "Okay."

"Come with me, Merit?" Mark said.

"You know that's not a good idea," Merit said.

"I need you with me to face it."

"And, I'm here for you. If I go with you, your mother will have to deal with the loss of Check and this, too. It's not fair to her."

"Okay. You're right," Mark said.

They went through the motions of their plan and Mark took the flight to be with his mother. The next day he called Merit with information about funeral arrangements and the condition of his family. He seemed to swing between shock and getting things done.

Merit sent flowers, sent loving energy to Mark and his family, and kept her cell phone close by.

Chapter Sixty-Four

Mark stood over the grave of his father long after everyone else had gone. His mother had held up rather well. Mark had played the part of the supportive son for the past two days, and now his own feelings rolled over him like a bowling ball.

He cried, kicked at the dirt, and cursed the unfairness of it all. *How could you die without making things right with me? How could you leave and not say goodbye? How could God be so cruel to take Check away now just as I was about to show him I could be a winner?*

Mark cried until he was spent then returned to Mother's side at the farm in a state of confusion. He went through the motions of shaking hands and accepting condolences from family, friends, and neighbors.

After he had performed all of his duties, he brought his mother a cup of coffee. "Can you do without me for a few minutes? I need some air."

Margaret put her hand on his arm and said, "Sure honey. I'll be fine. I'm going to visit with your cousin Mac for a bit."

Mark squeezed her hand and went into the kitchen and took off his coat. He hung it on a hook by the cellar door and grabbed a beer from the refrigerator. Mark noticed a dozen store-bought eggs on the shelf beside various other super market purchases that had always been grown at home.

As Mark took off his tie and went out the back screen door, his cousin Mac yelled, "Want some company?"

Mark crossed the yard, turned back, and said, "Thanks Mac, but I need to walk on my own."

"I understand," Mac said. "Call if you need anything."

∞

Mark hooked his tie on the gatepost, unbuttoned his top button, and walked across the pasture adjoining the house. The grass was still green from the spring rains but crunched under his feet. It would soon turn brown and become feed for cattle.

Mark cut behind the house to the pasture where Check had taught him to play golf. He remembered how Check had cut off the old clubs and measured the shafts against Mark's height.

Mark passed the barn, rounded the old, uninhabited hen house, and found himself in the field where the fire had burned his hands so long ago. The area was still overgrown. Check had never mowed it in all these years. No signs of the fire remained.

As Mark looked at rusty chicken wire on the ground, he felt the wind blow his hair. His hands felt crampy.

The wind had been blowing that day long ago. Not at first, but that's what had made the fire flare up, wasn't it?

The wind took him back. Check was there, moving all the brush into the circle of wire. Little Mark found a puffball growing in the weeds and picked it. He blew the white fuzzy needles into the air and chased after them as they spewed around the pasture on light air. He picked up branches to help his father. Mark ran and jumped and helped and laughed. His vantage point was low to the ground. It looked like a wall of fire appeared before him. Where did that come from? It blurred and went black. Suddenly, Check was carrying him, and his mother was crying, and he didn't know why his hands hurt.

When Mark came into present time, his face was wet with tears. He was wringing his hands and stumbling. "Check. Dad. Daddy. I want my Dadd

Chapter Sixty-Five

Merit opened the e-file from the title company for the Hill Country Homestead closing for Jessica Hogg Long and the Estate of Terrence Long. She had worked hard to bring in Dalton and Broad Development to take over the floundering project and bring the bank on board to approve the sale to Broad and loan transfer.

She'd walked a fine line representing Jessica Long while making the deal work with Dalton Broad at the same time she was seeing him. But, if she hadn't met him, there would have been no deal, so everyone was winning. The bank's attorneys were watching the whole deal like hawks, so their scrutiny further validated her work on the deal.

Merit looked over the closing statement and did some quick math on her phone calculator to check the numbers. The bank was charging one percent to transfer the loan over and the title company was charging their usual junk fees: escrow, messenger, wire transfer, etc.

There was a second lien to Sem'ya Holdings for the money Terrence Long had borrowed and given to the bank. Merit had seen it in the preliminary title opinion, so she was not surprised to see it paid off now. She'd not heard of Sem'ya, but there were many lenders out there she hadn't heard of. Everything appeared to be in order.

The bridge loan was being converted to long term financing on the project with a mandatory take-down of five hundred thousand dollars per quarter for the next three years and a balloon note on the balance at the end of year three.

At the time of the last payment to the bank, the clock would start running on Jessica's portion of the deal. Broad would have one year from that date to pay her one million dollars.

"She'll just have to find a way to live on the million-dollar life insurance policy for the next four or five years or get a job," Merit said to the screen.

Don't think I'm cutting your bill because your husband died, Merit thought. *I earned every penny of my fee on this one.*

Chapter Sixty-Six

Ag checked his gun at APD and went into Chaplain's office. "Want a cup of joe?" Chaplain asked, stood up, and stretched his tall frame. His smile showed the crinkles around his eyes. Ag wasn't sure if they were from the Texas sun or worry over The Enforcer.

"Sure, thanks," Ag said, and they walked out to the coffee pot.

"What brings you in?" Chaplain asked.

"There's a guy who's popped up on my radar. I wonder if you're aware of him."

"What's his name?"

"Browno Zars. He's on the other side of a deal that Merit Bridges is handling. She's cleared me to tell you about him just in case he crosses your path," Ag said.

They took their coffee back to Chaplain's office and both stretched their long legs as they sat back in their chairs.

"Haven't run across him but email a few details and I'll put him in the computer data base if he's not already there," Chaplain said.

"Browno has a right-hand man named Petrov who goes back and forth from here to Brighton Beach as far as I can tell. Browno also has a daughter living in NYC. His wife moved here with him, but they travel back there a lot," Ag said.

"What should I be watching for?" Chaplain asked.

"He's skirting the law in this Bridges file. He's not crossed over into breaking it as far as I can tell, but something about him stinks a bit," Ag said.

"We've never had much of a Russian contingency here in Austin. They're just starting to get a foothold and it's hard to tell which ones to watch out for," Chaplain said.

"Just like all the others of us – good ones and bad ones," Ag said.

"Thanks for the heads up," Chaplain said.

Chapter Sixty-Seven

The next day, Merit sat in her office and looked out the window at a statue of a giant Mexican free-tailed bat by the South Congress Bridge. Beside it, rain was falling into the Colorado. The plunks were so heavy, they made a splash with each drop into the river.

With a sigh, she returned to the stack of files on her desk. She scribbled a note on one and put it in a box on the corner of her desk labeled "Betty." She turned back to the window, picked up the phone and called Mark at his Mother's home in Wisconsin.

"Hello," Mark's mother answered.

"Hello, Mrs. Green, this is Merit Bridges in Austin, Mark's friend? Is he there?"

"Hello, Merit, call me Margaret. I'll get him for you," she said.

"Mrs. Green, Margaret, before you do, I'd like to express my sympathies. I am truly sorry for your loss," Merit said.

"Thank you Merit and thank you for the flowers. I know Mark appreciated them too," she said. "I'll get him."

Merit stood up and pulled on the cord from the blinds as she moved back and forth in front of the window. She heard a screen door slam on the other end of the phone, and then Mark answered, "Hello."

"Hi, Mark, it's Merit. I'm just calling to check on you. I saw from the caller ID that you'd called last night. How are you?"

"Yeah, I was feeling low and thought I might catch you at home," he said.

Merit bit her lower lip and winced away a feeling of guilt. She had been with Dalton. "I'm sorry I wasn't there for you. I'm here now. Talk to me."

"Nothing in particular. I'm just thinking about Mom, and the farm and all that's left to do around here. She says she wants to sell it, but I don't know whether to believe her. I think she just doesn't want me to have to move home," Mark said.

"Move home? What about the tour? What about the PGA?"

"That may have to wait until another year," Mark said.

"Wait? What about all your hard work? You said yourself you may not get another shot at it."

"I don't know if I can play here in Wisconsin with Check gone. I thought he might come and watch since it's going to be close by. I thought he'd see how much I've changed," Mark said.

"Is that the real reason you went for the PGA Championship, because it's going to be near home and your Father?"

"It won't mean much with Check gone. I was doing it to prove to him that I could win," Mark said.

"I don't believe that. Golf is your life. The PGA tour is your dream. It may have started with Check, but it didn't die with him," Merit exclaimed.

"I don't know. I'm so confused. I can't think about it right now. I've got to go. I'll talk to you later." Mark rang off.

Merit sat for a long time looking at the rain.

∞

Mark sat in his mother's kitchen staring at the phone and thinking about what Merit had said. Why was he working toward the PGA? Was it about Check? Was it about pride? It just didn't seem to matter anymore. He felt numb.

Mark picked up the phone to call her back but stopped his hand in mid-air as his mother walked in the screen door.

"Do you need privacy?" Margaret asked.

"No, no. I'll call her later."

"Oh, then could I have a minute?" she asked.

"Sure."

Margaret poured two cups of coffee from the percolator on the old gas stove. She sat one cup in front of Mark at the kitchen table and pushed the sugar over in front of him. She untied her apron and wiped her hands on it. She folded it over the yellow vinyl chair back and sat down against it.

"I'd like to talk to you about the farm," she started.

"Okay."

"I know you think I love this old place, and I do. But this was Check's dream, not mine. I've thought for some years now if he went first, I'd like to move into town near my sister. I can't take care of this place alone, and I don't want you giving up your life to take care of it either. If you really loved the place, I'd give it to you, but in your heart, you know you don't want to live here." She gave him a minute to think.

"It's just so sudden," he said.

"If you really object, I won't sell it right away. I'll wait until you're ready. At some point though, I'll need the money. I've got some saved, and Check had the life insurance, but it won't last long without farming the land."

"I know. I just can't think about it anymore right now."

"I know, Son. Take some time, and we'll talk again. But, I know you need to get back to Austin to get ready for the PGA. I don't want you to miss this chance," she said. "Just think about it."

Mark's eyes blurred with tears. If his mother wanted to sell the farm, then there was no place for him here anymore. But did he belong on the PGA tour? And without that goal, did he really belong in his new life in Austin?

Mark got up and walked to the sink, then over to the table,

and tried to find his voice. Finally, he ran out the back door and got into Check's old red Chevy pickup. He ripped the gravel as he spun out and left dust swirling around the yard.

Mark drove into town and parked in front of Bomnskie's Tavern. He stood at the door for a moment, letting his eyes adjust to the dark and read the neon signs around the walls. Schlitz and Pearl Beer hadn't been served there in years, but the signs still recalled the days when they were.

Mark took a stool and motioned to Mo behind the bar, "Jack Daniel's, neat."

"Check's drink." Mo said as he poured. "I'm sorry about your dad, Mark."

"Thanks." Mark downed the whiskey in one gulp and pushed the glass forward. "Another."

"I can see where this is headed," Mo said as he poured the second drink and then a third.

Mark sat with the fourth drink before him and felt the booze numbing his brain, but not his heart. Mo moved away from the bar to the back room and made a phone call.

About ten minutes later, two of Check's poker buddies entered the bar and took the stools on each side of Mark. They ordered Jack Daniel's neat and clicked Mark's glass on the bar between them. Five minutes after that, Bud, the last poker player came in with Cousin Mac and joined them. They ordered the same, and Mo poured one for himself as well. The six of them clicked glasses again. "To Check," said Bud.

"To Check," they a
ll said in unison.

They drank for a while, listening to an old Johnny Mathis standard on the Juke Box, "In Wisconsin."

"You know, Mark," Bud began, "Check was really proud of you."

"Don't give me the old 'father was proud of you' speech," Mark slurred. "It just doesn't fit here."

"Fit or not," Mac said, "It's true."

"That's right," they all confirmed.

Bud put his hand on Mark's shoulder. "For the last three months, we've had to arrange poker time around The Golf Network. We all watched every televised game, and the ones that weren't televised, we watched the scoreboard report for the outcome."

"I didn't know he was keeping up with what I was doing," Mark looked surprised, and very drunk.

"He was a stubborn old coot, but he was your dad, and he couldn't wait for the PGA Championship. He never said, but I don't think he could have missed going to it, being right here in Wisconsin."

"Yeah?"

Too late now, Mark thought.

"Yeah."

The jukebox played on.

∞

Two days later, Bob Tom met Mark's plane at Bergstrom International Airport in Austin. Mark walked down the promenade under signs that said WELCOME TO AUSTIN, THE LIVE MUSIC CAPITAL OF THE WORLD. The public-address system played a grinding guitar instrumental by Stevie Ray Vaughn.

Bob Tom stood outside the security area and studied Mark's face as he approached. Mark broke from the exiting crowd and walked into Bob Tom's open arms. Mark shook as he sobbed, and Bob Tom pounded him on the back, as if sheer will would sooth him.

After a few moments, Mark became embarrassed that he was in a public place and swiped away tears. They moved toward the escalator going down to baggage claim. Bob Tom stayed beside him with his arm around Mark's shoulders.

"Merit called. She was worried about you. I asked her if I could meet your plane instead of her. She agreed, but wants to see you later," Bob Tom said.

"Thanks. I appreciate it. The flowers, too," Mark said.

"Well, we took up a collection, but Joe sent them."

They waited at the baggage turnstile for the luggage to come down the shoot. Mark watched the bags zip out of the chute and wondered where he really belonged now. He remembered how he felt driving into Austin, like anything was possible. He couldn't believe he'd ever been so young.

"How's your mother?" Bob Tom asked.

"She was better by the time I left."

"That's good."

Mark scooped his suitcase off the conveyer.

"You ready to get back to golf?" Bob Tom asked as they walked towards the exit.

There was an awkward silence. "I just can't anymore," Mark said finally.

∞

Later that night, Mark went to dinner at Merit's house. She was in the kitchen whipping dill into sour cream and mayonnaise when the doorman called. She turned the fire down under a sauté pan sizzling with red snapper. She wiped her hands on a towel, went to the foyer, and opened the door.

They grabbed each other and held on tight for a long time. She finally broke free and looked into his face. He smiled at her. She smiled at him and said, "Welcome back."

"It's good to be back. That smells good." Mark lifted the lid on a pot of steaming green beans with almond slivers sprinkled on top.

"Red snapper with dill sauce. Brown rice, and green beans almandine. Carrot cake for desert."

"Yum, carrot cake, my favorite."

"I know. Want to open the wine?" Merit winked at him. "There's a bottle of Conundrum in the fridge."

Mark opened the wine and pressed the bottle into an ice bucket set up on the dining table in the next room.

"Have a seat," Merit said. She brought two plates in from the kitchen and placed one before Mark and one on her placemat across from him, then took her seat.

Mark poured them each a glass of wine and looked at her as he raised his glass. "Thanks. For everything. For being there for me, and for all your support."

Merit smiled and clicked her glass to his. They ate in silence for a while and savored the food while it was hot.

"This is fantastic," Mark said. He was glad to get his mind off golf for a while.

"Thanks. I thought you could use a home cooked meal after traveling all day. Did Bob Tom explain why I didn't pick you up?"

"Yeah. It was good – the right call."

After dinner, they sat on the sofa and drank coffee with the sound muted on the television. A couple dropped into a lake from a helicopter after holding onto a bar for what seemed an excruciatingly long time. After a commercial for tampons and another for hemorrhoid crème, a different couple ate something that looked like worms in olive oil.

Mark stretched out on the sofa, put his head in her lap, and closed his eyes. Merit stroked his brow until he gave a deep sigh, then laid her hand on his chest. He turned over and scooted up, so their heads were even and kissed her softly. She kissed him back, then stood up and pulled him along with her. She led him to the bedroom where she slowly undressed him. She gave no lessons, just soothed and comforted him with her body and her soft cooing sounds. She knew, deep inside, that it was their last time.

Chapter Sixty-Eight

Merit pulled into the parking lot of the Lion's Municipal Golf Course on a beautiful Saturday morning. The eighteen holes were laid out in a tight footprint in central Austin. It had once been the site of the Austin Country Club, but now seemed small and pedestrian by comparison to the larger new clubs around town. Nevertheless, it was one of Merit's favorite courses because the fairways were short on most holes, and the matured trees and water features were beautiful.

Natalie parked an expensive convertible a few spots over. Merit waved when she exited the car.

"Have you ever played here before?" Merit asked.

"No, but I've wanted to," Natalie responded. "If I'm not at ACCC, I usually play at Star Ranch. The greens are really fast out there, and the facility is nice."

"I've only been there once. I've played mostly at ACCC." Merit said. "I usually come here when I'm short on time, or right after work to get in nine before the sun goes down."

"It's really pretty," Natalie said.

They each took their clubs out of their vehicles and propped them up on the pop-out stands. They rested their behinds against the rear bumper of Natalie's car to put on their socks and golf shoes.

Both threw their walking shoes into their back seats. They crossed the parking lot, with their clubs on their shoulders, toward the small unassuming clubhouse.

"No frills place," Natalie said.

"Pack your own gear," Merit said.

Natalie rested the golf bags in the metal holder provided for that purpose, and they went into the clubhouse.

"Tee time for Bridges at nine o'clock," Natalie told the man behind the counter.

The man looked at the appointment book, found the reservation, and made a check mark with his pencil.

Natalie turned to Merit, "Do you want to walk or ride?"

"Walk nine or ride eighteen, your choice," she said.

"Let's play the whole course. It's a beautiful day," Merit said.

"Good for me," Natalie said, then to the attendant, "We'll take a cart."

They went outside and loaded their clubs on the cart, each taking a putter, glove and balls from their respective bags. Merit walked over to the putting area and dropped three white Lady Precepts on the green. Natalie pulled on her glove and dropped two Titleist balls a few feet away.

They putted for a while, getting the speed of the greens, then chipped a few on the adjoining mound provided for that purpose.

"Do you want to hit a bucket on the driving range? We may have time." Merit asked as they walked back toward the cart.

"Let's just play," Natalie said.

"Sounds good," Merit said as she used her putter between two hands as a stretching tool. "I'll grab a couple of drinks. Tea okay, or do you want a beer?"

"No beer this early. I'll bring the cart forward. We should be up in less than ten," Natalie said.

The loudspeaker rang out, "Bridges party of two, Albertson party of two – ten minutes." They both laughed and went off to their respective chores.

Ten minutes later, they shook hands with a cute young couple who introduced themselves as Ralph and Clara Albertson. The foursome shared the Cliff Notes version of their life stories.

"Would you ladies like to go first?" Ralph asked. "I hit pretty long. I might bean one of those guys down there. Better give them some time to move on," he said, pointing to the four putting in on the first hole.

"I'll go," Merit said and drove a long white tee into the ground between the markers for the ladies tee box. She popped on a ball, set up with her Callaway driver, waggled, and whoosh! The ball sang out over the fairway and plunked down about two hundred yards out.

"Good one," Natalie said.

Clara hit next, then Natalie and Ralph. Natalie's ball went about two-fifty, and a little to the right of the fairway then just missed some tree roots. All jumped into the carts and took off to their respective balls lying in wait.

Natalie kept score with the stubby pencil and scorecard provided by the pro-shop which was clipped to the middle of the steering wheel. She and Merit alternated driving, depending on who was hitting next and where the balls lay.

They finished the first nine back at the clubhouse, switched to wine coolers, and waited at the tenth hole for the backlog to clear out and moved onto the course again.

"You're doing pretty well here," Natalie said and studied the scorecard. "If you keep this up, you'll break ninety."

"No way, I've never shot in the eighties. Ninety-four is the best score I've ever had on this course or any other," Merit said.

"Take a look," Natalie pointed.

"Well, not to worry, the water all over the back nine will eliminate any chance of that," Merit laughed.

Their turns came, and they teed off over a long sloping lawn trying to land the ball between two small lakes. Merit fell just short of the peninsula and Natalie hit perfectly between the water on the strip of land.

"Sweet," Merit complimented.

Merit and Natalie both hit fairly consistently until they got to the back-water holes.

Merit knew she didn't have the distance to clear the water, so she laid up by hitting a perfect shot to the right. Natalie's ball fell short, directly into the pond. Natalie decided to hit again rather than taking a drop, so Merit sipped wine and waited for her. With several shots, they both made it to the hole and putted in.

"Perfect play on that hole, Merit," Natalie admired"Thanks. Since I don't have the distance, I've been working on my accuracy with my golf pro."

"Mark Green?" Natalie laughed. "The work seems to be paying off."

They played through the last holes and headed toward the clubhouse to return the cart and get more wine. They entered the back double doors to the smell of greasy cheeseburgers and the sound of piped in music. Diana Krall sang a torch song that seemed more appropriate for a midnight rendezvous.

"What would you like?" Natalie asked.

"White, it's cooler," Merit said, shook out her glove and wiped her hands on a paper napkin. She found a table and sat down. Natalie brought the cold sweating glasses and began to tally the day's score.

"Let's see, I shot my usual low-eighties," Natalie said.

"Not bad for the first time on this course."

"Thanks. I'll do better next time, now that I've got the lay of the land." Natalie did some calculating in the margin of the card with the pencil. "Looks like you shot an eighty-nine."

"No. You must have added wrong. I've not broken ninety in my life," Merit said.

"Let me check. It's right. Eighty-nine."

"Are you sure you wrote down all the scores, right?"

"Yes, Merit, you shot an eighty-nine," Natalie laughed at her disbelief.

"Really? Wow!" She stood up and twirled around. "I broke ninety. I broke ninety," she said to the sales clerk, the other players, and the walls. Everyone smiled at her enthusiasm.

Merit and Natalie walked to the parking lot and made plans to meet up again to play the next week. It was great having a girlfriend to play and chat with. It was a bonus that Natalie loved wine as much as Merit did.

"See ya!" Natalie said as she hopped into her sports car and drove off.

Merit smiled and opened her door, thinking about a nice hot bath and something to eat. She was starving.

She retrieved her flip flops from the back then sat in the front seat bending over to untie her golf shoes.

Merit was still smiling when the club came down on her head and she fell from the car and crumpled on the concrete.

Chapter Sixty-Nine

Monday morning at the office, Betty checked the time again. It was nine seventeen, Merit wasn't there, and Betty made excuses to the client in the conference room.

"Something must have happened. She's rarely late and never a no-show. May I re-schedule? I'm so sorry," Betty said.

"No problem. Get this straightened out and call my office," the client said and left.

Betty went to her desk, picked up the phone and called Merit's cell again. When it clicked over to voice mail she hung up. She'd already called Merit at home and on her cell and left messages several times.

Val leaned up against the wall in front of her and raised his eyebrows. "Nothing?" He was caffeinating, a steaming mug in his hand.

Betty shook her head.

"Don't look so worried. Maybe she had a weekend with one of her boyfriends," Val said.

"No, something's wrong. I know it," Betty said.

"Go to your office and keep trying her mobile. I'll try a few of her other clients and friends," Betty said.

"Will do," Val said and scurried down the hall.

Betty shook her head. She felt helpless.

Betty flipped through a few client records and came up with Mark's number. She dialed it, getting Mark's voicemail. She left a message for him to call her asap.

She didn't have Dalton's number but knew he and Merit had been talking by phone. She logged into Merit's mobile account and searched the numbers for the last few days. One she didn't recognize looked promising and she dialed it.

"Dalton Broad," a deep voice said.

"I'm sorry to bother you," Betty said. "I'm Merit Bridges' office manager. She didn't show up for work today and I haven't been able to reach her. Not that you should know, but do you know where she is? I'm very worried or I wouldn't bother you."

"I've been trying to reach her since Saturday afternoon. We were supposed to get together on Sunday. I'm worried too. I'll be at your office in ten minutes."

Chapter Seventy

Merit's shoulders cried out in pain. She didn't know how long she had been hanging there, or where she was. It smelled damp and woody. Like decay.

A blindfold clamped down over her eyes. It had been tied so tightly that it was cutting into her skin. There was a dull throbbing in the back of her head.

She couldn't hear any of the noises of the city. No cars, no planes or people walking about.

She didn't cry out. She was afraid that someone she didn't want to know might be waiting for her to wake up.

What happened?

She searched through her memory, but nothing came to her. The last thing she remembered was leaving the golf course. Someone must have grabbed her in the parking lot.

But why?

She tried to ignore how thirsty she was.

What if they left her here?

Then Merit heard a skittering of claws against the floor.

Rats.

Merit shuddered as heard the little nails on their toes hitting the floor across the room.

She guessed that no one else was in the room with her. Rats would probably not come out if someone was there.

She decided to risk it and worked on getting free. She moved up and down on her toes to release the rope. She tried to rub off the blindfold by pushing her head against her shoulder. No luck.

She worked her toes on the floor until she turned herself all the way around. She could hear metal twisting above like a hook on a swivel. It didn't give any advantage.

Finally, she tried jumping up and down on her toes. She felt the bindings go slack and then grip when her weight came down. It didn't release her, but it gave her some relief on her arms for a few seconds. She jumped until she was exhausted and had to hang again and catch her breath.

She thought she heard a noise.

What was that?

Chapter Seventy-One

Mark was distracted as he drove into work. He hadn't slept the night before; he'd been tossing and turning and ended up watching TV as the sun came up and lit the room. He flipped through the stations and finally turned it off, disgusted. Bad news everywhere.

He forced his thoughts to turn to Merit and a softness fell over him. He was so lucky he'd met her. She'd done so much to help him, so much he could never repay. He felt bad that he was going to be letting her down after everything she'd done, but he just couldn't imagine going on with the tour now that Check was gone.

Before, there was always the chance that Check would tell Mark that he was proud of him. Check would never see Mark as a winner. Now that was all gone. And without it, Mark didn't have a definition of success anymore.

He drove to work, pulled into the parking lot too quickly, and startled a cluster of men who were heading to the clubhouse. Mark parked and sat, staring out at nothing.

"You goin' to stay in the car all day?"

The voice broke through Mark's thoughts and he flinched. When he looked up he took in Browno, all three hundred pounds of him, leaning against his Jeep. Before Mark could organize his thoughts, Browno opened the door. Mark was surprised how fast a man of that size could move.

"You and me? We gonna' have a talk," Browno said and jerked Mark from the seat.

Within seconds, Mark found himself pressed between Browno and another Russian. Browno sat in the passenger seat of the oversized SUV and the driver pushed against his thigh on the other side. The driver was large and muscular. He had two day's beard growth on his face and tattoos on his knuckles spelling out something in Cyrillic script.

"I…" Mark's voice broke as he tried to speak. "I'm going to be late to work."

"Is no problem," Browno said and nodded his head at the driver, who backed out slowly before heading away from the club. "Today, you call in sick. Is good plan, Petrov?"

Petrov grunted agreement.

Mark's belly hardened into a stone as they drove.

Petrov parked in the alley behind what looked like a restaurant or bar. Mark felt his arm squeezed as the driver pulled him out of the car.

∞

Mark was whisked inside and pushed into a booth in a shadowy corner. It smelled strange and foreign and that made Mark even more anxious. Petrov perched on the edge of the booth, blocked his exit, and lit a funky smelling cigarette. Browno filled up the booth across from them. After a rapid-fire exchange in Russian, Browno turned to Mark.

"We are buddies, *nu?*"

Mark didn't know what to say to that.

After a few more moments, Browno said, "So, this is what's gon' happen now. You sign a new contract for me. No lady friend, just we business."

The henchman deposited a one-page contract on the table in front of Mark.

Mark felt relief flood through him. They wanted his PGA money, not his blood. Well, there wasn't going to be any play money, not for him, not for anybody.

"I'm sorry, Mr. Zars. I dropped out of the tournament. And even if I wanted to, I can't sign this."

There was a shocked, tense silence while Browno took that in. "You drop out, when?"

"I…uh. Well, I haven't yet. But I'm going to."

Browno's smile covered his whole face. "I don't think so, Mark, I don't think so at all."

Petrov pushed the pen closer to Mark's hand.

Mark looked at the piece of paper. It was a single page that set out Browno as his sports agent, and that all purses would be paid directly to him to be disbursed and invested on Mark's behalf.

"I'm not signing this," Mark said. "And no one would believe it, anyway. We have a document ending our relationship on file with Merit Bridges."

"You say that you reconsidered," Browno smiled, satisfied with his word choice.

"No," Mark said, his tone defiant. "My dad just died. I'm not playing anymore." He pushed the paper back over the table to Browno and the henchman put his hand on Mark's arm. Just that small amount of pressure made a line of sweat run down the back of Mark's neck.

Browno smiled and then took out his phone and hit an icon with his sausage fingers.

"Come closer, Mark."

Mark narrowed his eyes but shifted in the booth as far as he could against the wall.

That's when he saw the picture of Merit. Blindfolded. Hanging like a piece of meat.

There was some more conversation and Browno talking about his big plans. Mark barely heard any of it.

"You tell anyone, I will know. You do anything you don't always do, I will know. You don't follow my orders, she's dead and you too," Browno said.

After Browno was finished, Mark signed.

∞

Browno and Petrov drove Mark back to ACCC and stopped at the street near the parking lot. Petrov got out of the driver's side and pulled Mark across the seat under the steering wheel and dropped him like a rag doll on the sidewalk.

Mark pulled himself up enough to sit on the curb. The concrete was hot from the summer sun. Sweat poured off of him.

"You be good boy, now," Browno said as Petrov got back behind the wheel.

As they drove away, Browno said to Petrov, "Take care of her."

"Nothing would give me greater pleasure," Petrov said.

∞

Mark sat at the curb for a long while as the adrenaline dissipated then composed himself and went inside.

I must act as if nothing has happened, for Merit's sake.

He went through his daily routine in a daze trying to figure out who he could call. What if Browno found out he'd asked for help and killed Merit?

What if Browno was watching? He became more paranoid with each person he encountered.

The guy with the Z-Ro ball cap moved around him and into the men's room.

Who is that guy?

Mark followed him, then stopped. He couldn't risk an

encounter. What if he wasn't the lookout and Browno's guys saw him. Even worse, what if he was.

He took his afternoon young adult class out for their weekly game still unwilling to risk alerting the police or Merit's office.

The kids played on and he half watched and worried the entire afternoon. Finally, he was spent and just put his head on the steering wheel of the golf cart.

No matter the pressure on him, he decided he would not let her down. He would focus. He would play until he could get someone to help him or find a way to get Browno to release her.

He would demand proof of life every day and keep her alive with each day that he played.

I must focus.

Mark picked up his iPhone and punched the speed dial for David Yee.

"I've got a problem," Mark said.

∞

Mark and Yee met on the course at ACCC.

"The mind game in golf is as important as any other aspect of the game. Can you get your mind on this?" Yee asked.

Mark was so scattered he could barely putt. He wanted to unburden to Yee and Bob Tom, but he dared not pull them into it. What if Browno sensed something or what if he tried to hurt one of them?

"I can. I will," Mark gritted his teeth.

"Today we'll work on that," Yee said. "You know life always throws problems our way, even before a tournament. Your concentration has to rise above the daily chatter in your mind. Golf is just like acting, writing, or snow skiing. Anything, really. If you want to do it well, you must be able to focus in the moment on what you're doing. Distractions can destroy your game."

"Right." Mark said.

Mark felt like a fish caught in a net. There was no one to turn to.

He forced himself to focus on Yee's voice. The only way to save Merit was to play. And he'd never do that unless he got his head in the game.

"Let's do an exercise to set it into your mind and muscles," Yee said as he dumped the bucket of balls on the grass.

"Okay."

"First, take your driver and look at that marker with the blue flag. See it? Okay, now do what Jack Nicklaus does. He calls it 'going to the movies'. See the blue flag where you want the ball to go. Now, see in your mind's eye the path the ball must take down to the flag. Visualize the way the ball moves to get there. Now, see your swing in your mind. What do your body and club need to do to get that exact shot? Feel it all the way through, then make the shot."

Mark lined up, did the visual imagery, and made the shot.

"Close. You've probably been doing some form of this all along or your game wouldn't be on the level it is but trust me for a minute to try it a little differently. Instead of using your will to make the shot, once you see it in your mind's eye, release to it. See it as already done, and then just let it flow into the pathway you made with your visualization."

Mark closed his eyes for a moment. "I think I get it." He looked up, spotted the flag again, swung the driver, and magic happened. It was effortless.

"That's it," Yee said. "Now, let's practice that until it's the only way you make a shot. Never again should you hit the ball unless you are in that space. That goes back to being able to focus under pressure and negate any distractions that might be hanging around in your monkey-mind."

"I understand. Let me try it again," Mark said as he selected a ball from the pile in front of him and set up. He hit the ball, then another, and another, until that bucket and several others were empty.

Yee was long gone. The day ended, light dimmed, and he was still visualizing and hitting the ball alone in the dark.

If he didn't, Merit was dead.

Chapter Seventy-Two

The next day, Mark went to the ACCC cafe looking for Browno. He sat in his regular booth acting as if he owned the world and no one could touch him.

Arrogant son of a bitch.

Browno looked up at Mark and smiled.

"What you want, boy?" Browno asked.

"I'm going to do what you say, but I want to know she's alive every day that I play. I want to know she isn't hurt any more than she already is," Mark said.

"You very strong now, defending your woman. Very demanding," Browno said.

"There's no incentive for me to play if she's dead, and I don't want to worry about her condition or I won't be able to focus," Mark said. "Golf is a mind game. You know that."

"Okay, I see point. I have a nice snapshot for you every day. It will remind you of our agreement and keep your mind on goal," Browno said.

Mark turned to leave.

"I give you pictures you never forget. Keep your phone handy," Browno said.

Chapter Seventy-Three

B etty was close to being frantic, although she was trying not to let on to Val, who was even more emotional than she was. Merit was officially missing.

Ag had a crew working out of the firm's conference room and was barking orders on the phone and to those who came and went with information. One man was dispatched to Houston to watch over Ace who had not been informed of Merit's absence yet. The school had been instructed by Betty not to let Ace out of their site until the guard arrived. Joy and Tucker were asked to be alert.

Betty finally reached Mark, who'd told her he hadn't seen Merit in days. Betty could hear the sadness in his tone. The poor kid, he was probably devastated by the loss of his father.

"I'll let you know if I see her or hear anything," Mark lied.

Dalton had come and gone several times trying to help, but not having known Merit for long, was not much help. There was a particularly awkward moment when Betty introduced him to Ag Malone.

That made two boyfriends that Merit was involved with. Ag didn't have time to dwell on it.

Betty and Val fed the troops and pleaded with Ag.

"Please find her. You have to find her," Betty said.

He had to find her.

∞

Betty puttered around Merit's desk off and on all day. It was clean as usual, but Betty tidied it anyway. She went back to her desk and worked up a spreadsheet.

"I made a list of her current clients." Betty handed the printout to Ag. "I sent it to you via email, too."

"This is great. Thanks. I'm going to get an update from Chaplain at APD. I'll be on my mobile," Ag said.

After Ag left, Betty and Val stared at the phone.

"You all right, Darlin'," Betty said softly to Val. He'd shed his blazer, his sleeves were pushed up, and his tie was askew.

He nodded. But the truth was, he looked as scared as a little kid.

Betty and Val sat in the disheveled conference room and prayed.

∞

Ag checked his gun and entered Chaplain's office at APD.

"Any news about Merit?" Chaplain asked.

"None. I was hoping your guys had found something," Ag said.

Chaplain looked exhausted.

"I've got as many men as I can spare looking for her. The serial killings around town have had us tied up for weeks."

"Did you get someone over to her SUV?" Betty had given the police the GPS coordinates when she'd filed the missing person's report.

"They're there now. The BMW is at Lion's Golf Course. Run by there before they leave. Maybe you'll see something they don't," Chaplain said.

"On it," Ag said.

"Any dangerous clients on her list?" Chaplain asked.

"They look like plain vanilla business people. A few celebrities, but no one looks dangerous," Ag said. "I just…" Ag put his head in his hands. "She would have told us if there was something going on."

"Use your men as much as you can. Coordinate with me and I'll keep my guys informed," Chaplain said.

Chaplain's phone rang, and he scooped it up. His face was stricken.

"Merit?" Ag asked.

Chaplin shook his head. "Looks like another body has turned up." He grimaced. "I've got to get over there."

"You don't think?" Ag asked.

"It's a man," Chaplain said. "It's not Merit."

Ag blew out the burst of air he'd been holding.

∞

Ag parked in the lot of the Lion's Municipal Golf Course. He raised the yellow crime scene tape and spoke with Chaplain's man, Rodriguez. Ag walked around Merit's BMW, looked underneath it, and then in the open door on the driver's side.

"Looks like she was hit here at the door. See the blood splatters on the concrete," the detective said.

"Some here on the seat back too," Ag said.

"Right. Here's one golf shoe by the door and a pair of flip flops by the accelerator. She must have bent over to change her shoes and taken the hit on the back of the head." Rodriguez pointed to each of the crime scene elements as he described them.

Ag's heart hurt at the thought of Merit's obviously painful encounter.

"Not a lot of blood," Ag said.

"Nope, she was intact at this point. Looks like a snatch job, not a murder," Rodriguez said.

Ag felt relieved

*Thank God. Now, talk to me Merit. Where are you?*Ag was up all night in the conference room at Merit's office going through all the reports and information of Merits last days before her disappearance.

Betty had refused to leave and was asleep on the sofa in the reception area. Dalton stopped by every evening to find out if they'd learned anything new, but didn't try to inject himself into the investigation. Val had gone home but was due back any time.

There was no evidence that Merit had been murdered, so he had to assume she was alive. The kidnappers could have killed her right in the parking lot in her SUV and didn't. They must need her for something. Betty or Val had been at the office every minute and no ransom calls or threats had come in.

What is this about?

Ag had investigated both Dalton and Mark, jealousy flapping around inside him as he went through his research. Dalton Broad was well known around Austin as a developer and a solid business man. Handsome and prosperous, Merit's type when she wasn't robbing the kindergarten class for lovers like Mark Green.

Ag had checked out as much as he could about Mark and he seemed clean as well. His mother had told Ag of his father's recent death. Could that have sent the kid off the deep end?

Mark. Ag looked at his picture again. How old is this kid, anyway? And how did Merit have enough time for two boyfriends?

Worry about that later, Ag told himself. *Find her, then yell at her.*

∞

Ag checked in with the doorman and took the elevator to Merit's condo. He used the key Betty had given him to unlock the door and was met with Pepper's sad face.

The doorman had already taken Pepper for a walk so Ag just topped off her water bowl and gave her a good rub. She drank some water then went to the door and stood staring at it while Ag went to work. He looked at the pics on the fridge but didn't recognize anyone there except Merit and Ace. There were a lot of golf photos with a group of women. She'd been playing more than he realized.

He looked around her home desk, and flipped through a stack of packages, magazines and mail on her dining table. He shook the packages. Probably books.

He went into her bedroom and could smell her scent. It hit him hard. He pulled himself together and looked around for anything out of the ordinary. He'd never been in the condo except for parties and social events so he wasn't quite sure what ordinary was. He hit a speed dial on his phone.

"Law Office of Merit Bridges," he heard Betty say.

"It's Ag. Can you meet me here at Merit's condo? I can't tell what's supposed to be here and what might be missing. Is Val still there to answer the phone?"

"Yes. I'll be right over," Betty said.

Ag went through Merit's closet and her dresser drawers until he heard Betty open the door.

"It's me," Betty said.

"Could you take a look around and see if everything looks normal and then open all that mail and see if anything stands out as odd or unusual?" Ag asked.

"Glad to be doing something to help," Betty said and began to move around the rooms and out onto the balcony. She totally ignored the downtown view.

"Her golf clubs are missing," Betty said.

"They weren't in her Bimmer," Ag said. "Her purse was missing but her Ruger was in the console."

"Not much use there," Betty said.

"I doubt she thought she'd need it at a golf course," Ag said as he opened a low credenza-looking piece of furniture that turned out to be china storage.

"Of course," Betty said as she ripped into the mail with a pair of kitchen shears.

Ag went through the trash cans in the kitchen, bath, and bedroom. He bagged it all up and tied the top but left it in the kitchen just in case. He checked the recycling but found only rinsed yogurt cartons and a clear plastic blueberry container.

"I don't see anything useful," Ag said.

"Nothing helpful here in the mail either," Betty said and stacked it neatly on the table.

"Do you know who all those people are in the photos on her refrigerator?" Ag asked.

Betty moved past the island and into the kitchen.

"Well, these with Ace are people at his school. Merit was there for a fundraiser and science fair. So, these must be his teachers and friends," Betty said.

"Right," Ag said. "This one?"

"It's hard to tell, but that's Mark Green, her golf pro," Betty said. "You saw his picture at the office."

Ag nodded.

"The other man is the course manager, Bob Tom. I've been seeing him, so he's not involved with this."

Really? Randy women. It must be in the water at the firm. Ag didn't say aloud.

"This pic is at Austin Creek Country Club. That must be Natalie. I can tell by the haircut that Merit described. She plays golf with her and these other women. Maybe that's who she was playing with at Lion's. Her online calendar didn't say who with, just that she was going there to play," Betty said.

"I've already been to Lion's. I'll head over to Austin Creek and ask around," Ag said.

"I'm going too. They know me a little. I might be able to help," Betty said.

"Would it do any good to say no?" Ag asked.

"Absolutely not. I'm in a horn-tossing mood," Betty said.

∞

Ag and Betty made their way to the pro shop at ACCC.

"No sense beating around the bush. Merit spent a lot of time here with Mark Green. You know her penchant for younger men," Betty said.

"Let's start with Green, then," Ag said.

"Ag, this is Joe. He knows Mark and Merit," Betty said.

"Howdy," he said to the tall, thin man at the counter of the pro shop with Joe on his name plate.

Ag explained the situation.

"I'm so sorry to hear that. Merit is a very nice lady and I can't imagine anyone wanting to hurt her," Joe said.

"We should probably talk to Bob Tom," Betty said.

"He and Mark have already left for Milwaukee."

"When did they leave?" Ag asked.

"Few hours ago."

So, Mark had had enough time to incapacitate Merit and then get out of town, Ag reflected. He knew as well as any law enforcement officer that it was the people close to victims who generally hurt them. The significant other was always an excellent direction to look to.

"So, tell me about this Mark," Ag said and leaned against the counter.

Joe looked serious. "He's a good kid. He wouldn't hurt a fly."

"What about the two of them together?" Ag asked.

"They care a lot about each other so far as I can tell," Joe said.

"Anything else I should know?" Ag asked.

"Let's get Bob Tom on the line," Joe said.

He dialed Bob Tom's mobile, but it went directly to voice mail.

"They must be on the plane," Joe said.

"Anything else you can think of?" Ag asked.

Joe shook his head.

"Can you help grease the wheels with the club's employees? I need to ask them some questions."

Joe nodded his agreement and they set off to question the rest of the staff.

Chapter Seventy-Four

Mark and Bob Tom flew into Milwaukee, Wisconsin and took Highway 43 about an hour north to The Village of Kohler, where they'd be staying during the tourney. They decided to go to the course first and check into the hotel later. Bob Tom drove them another fifteen minutes northeast to the shore of Lake Michigan, home of Whistling Straights and this year's U.S. Professional Golf Association Championship.

As the scenery flew by, Mark fidgeted with the door handle. He was so worried about Merit that he didn't take time to feel the pleasure of being in his home state.

"You're going to pull that off if you keep messing with it," Bob Tom said.

Mark put his hands in his lap, but a few miles further on was back to the door handle. Bob Tom didn't comment further.

They drove due east and pulled up to the entrance of Whistling Straights. A large metal sign bearing the face of what appeared to be a weather god was set between limestone columns and surrounded by tall grass.

Pete Dye, architect for the Kohler Company had designed the bent grass course to be reminiscent of the great old seaside links courses of the British Isles. Mark felt swept back over four hundred years to when the game was founded in Scotland.

Bob Tom drove up the long entrance to the course, which was built along two miles of uninterrupted shoreline. Lake Michigan, on their right, sparkled in the August sun, blue like the color of sapphires.

Bob Tom's research had revealed that the course had huge sandy areas, deep pot bunkers, grass-topped dunes, fescue fairways, and big rolling greens. Every hole had a view of Lake Michigan. Eight holes hugged the shoreline. Mark, Bob Tom, and Yee had been over each hole on paper a hundred times and had researched the way almost every pro for the life of the course had played it.

Mark already knew a lot about the course, having played there when he was younger. He still wondered how something so beautiful could be built on a trash dump and wondered even more how it could have been used as a dump in the first place.

As they drove toward the clubhouse, they admired a flock of Scottish Blackface Sheep grazing beside one of the fairways. Ahead, the Whistling Straits clubhouse was reminiscent of a rustic Irish country farmhouse with huge chimneys at each end of the main building constructed of chunky limestone.

The Golf Network had a crew set up by the circular driveway at the main entrance shooting establishing shots and canned spiels for the upcoming week's coverage. An announcer with a microphone stood by the entrance giving the background for the event. Mark and Bob Tom saw that it was Moustache from the Frisco tourney.

Mark had one hand fidgeting with the door handle and one playing with the cup holder. Bob Tom's eyes went from the road to Mark's agitated dance and back again..

"Damn, that man wears ugly shoes," Bob Tom said.

"What?" Mark said.

"His shoes. They are so damn ugly," Bob Tom repeated. "I bet those aren't Fairway shoes."

Mark looked at Bob Tom as if he were crazy, then started laughing as he realized that Bob Tom was intentionally being absurd. He laughed to release the tension that had him locked down so tight he could barely breath.

Moustache looked into the camera and flipped the switch on a smile as the crew counted down three, two, then showed one finger.

Moustache began, "Twenty club professionals having qualified have arrived at Whistling Straits for the PGA Championship. Many think that the club pros should be excluded or at least limited from playing in the PGA Championship. Debaters feel that the Tiger Woods and Mike Michelson's of the world are more entitled to be here, and that having the club professionals involved lowers the prestige of the event. It is argued that the club pros also take places that could be filled by more qualified players."

Moustache droned on, "Part of the discussion comes from the fact that the PGA is the most prestigious, oh shit, flubbed a line. Let's try it again."

The producer said," Be sure and mention the ten-million-dollar purse."

"Right," Moustache said.

The crew gave him another start, and he began again. "Part of the discussion comes from the fact that the PGA is the least prestigious of the four majors. The other three majors, The Masters, The British Open, and The U.S. Open are all considered more desirable trophies. But the PGA has a distinguished history as players who've won are noteworthy in golf history. Greats include Sarazen, Snead, Trevino, five times for Nicklaus, Nelson, Hogan, and Hagen. Tom Watson and Arnold Palmer are purported to have said that their greatest career regret was not having won the PGA." Moustache took a breath. They wrapped the segment and moved over to shoot in front of the grazing sheep.

Moustache posed in front of the animals, but the sheep moved around, so the camera crew had to set up again. "Let's get this damn shot and get out of this pasture," Moustache complained, pulling his collar from his neck. The crew counted down again

—three, two, one finger. The sheep began to bleat in protest of the proximity of the crew to their grazing area.

Mark watched the fanfare, tried to pretend that this was a normal tournament, that Check hadn't just died, and he wasn't playing for Merit's life. If one of those cameras swung his way, and his thoughts swung another, he was finished, and so was Merit.

He let out a shuddering breath, closed his eyes and tried to bring some normalcy into the moment. He was his normal self, Merit was in the office, working. Later, he'd see her.

Just play my game. My game.

"That's a wrap," the producer shouted to Moustache over the bleating sheep while stifling a laugh. "They can fix it in edit."

Mark winced. The pressure was on.

In more ways than one.

∞

Bob Tom followed signs and drove to the player's parking lot. Both men stretched as they unfolded from the car and went to meet Yee. They found him in the player's lounge watching the weather channel and making notes on a tablet.

After polite hellos, Yee said, "the elements are so in-your-face here, it's going to be one of the most important factors of the week. I think most of the players will play this course fairly conservatively."

Bob Tom said, "I agree. I don't see anybody going too far under par."

Mark was well aware of the air coming off the lake and the treeless terrain and how the two interacted on the course.

"Right," Yee said, "only way that will occur is if the wind doesn't blow at all for four days, and that's not going to happen. It will blow for at least one day, if not all four."

∞

Mark, Bob Tom, and Yee walked the entire course while there was still light.

Yee turned to Mark, "You can expect the course to play firm and fast because it's been dry. Your good shots will really be good, but your bad ones will be punishing. As you know, there are dunes and bunkers sprinkled throughout."

They walked up to the bluffs overlooking the lake. Bob Tom's phone rang, and he saw Betty's face on the screen. "Let me catch this," Bob Tom said and stepped to the side for privacy.

Betty's voice sounded distraught.

"Merit is missing. She's been gone for several days and her car had blood in it," Betty said.

"How terrible," Bob Tom said.

"Do you know anything about a woman from the club named Natalie? The authorities can't find her either."

"No, she's a member, but that's all I know of her."

"Mark hasn't said a word about Merit. I'm sure he doesn't know where she is. He said she's supposed to be out later in the week," Bob Tom said. Bob Tom looked over at Mark and considered calling him over but didn't.

"If you think of anything or if Mark does, please call right away," Betty said.

"I will. Take care of yourself. I can hear how upset you are," Bob Tom said.

They chatted for a moment longer then Bob Tom went over to Mark.

"What's wrong?" Mark asked.

Bob Tom mulled his answer. What good would it do for Mark to worry? Maybe Merit had just taken a trip or had an accident and would show up soon. The kid had been waiting for this day for so long and there was nothing he could do to help.

Bob Tom made his decision. He was sure he was doing the right thing.

"Just some issues at Austin Creek. Joe's handling it," Bob Tom said.

Mark gave him a strange look, then turned away.

Bob Tom pointed to each side of the course, "Dye designed the four par-three holes along here. Those two run north to south." He turned around and pointed in the other direction, "Those two run south to north. You can expect one or the other to play into the wind, and the other downwind."

Yee confirmed, "And, don't be surprised if the wind direction changes from day to day."

"It is spectacular," Bob Tom admired the course and the lake.

"Many think it's one of the five best golf courses in the world," Yee said.

They walked the entire course, about four miles around. When they came to the last hole, the disastrous eighteenth, Mark froze.

Yee and Bob Tom chatted on about the hole and walked ahead. Mark stood fixated on the spot where he'd stood so long ago. The pressure of the past and the present collided in his brain, heart and soul.

∞

A younger Mark walked up to the eighteenth hole at Whistling Straits. It was cold. A cameraman stood in front of the crowd, held back by ropes and course marshals. Pansies were blooming along the water's edge. Mark tried to focus. He saw the television crew and became nervous. He could see the camera pan down to his hands, and he was embarrassed and afraid. He looked over at Check who nodded for him to hit the ball.

Mark looked out over the fairway to a four-leaf clover shaped green five hundred yards away. It was a par four. Four shots are all he had to make. Four shots, maybe five and he'd be one over par, and he'd be happy, and Check would be happy, and the day would be over. The cameras would be gone. Just four or five shots.

He wished he hadn't left so much hanging on this last hole. He should have been five or six strokes ahead, so he could have plenty of cushion on this last hole. It wasn't called Dyeabolical for nothing.

Mark teed up the ball and steadied his driver. He decided to go for the shorter approach to the left. It would require a two-hundred-and-seventy-yard carry over sand dunes and bunkers, but distance was his best asset, and he needed to use what he had.

He waggled, looked down the fairway, went into his swing, and caught sight of movement of the television camera in his peripheral vision. He hit the ball wild. The prevailing wind blew it further, and it sunk deep into the bunker. He had lost his focus.

Mark's face turned brilliant red, and he saw the television camera zoom in for a close-up. He looked over at Check for assurance but met only cold disappointment in his eyes.

After the others had hit, the entourage of men headed down the fairway and split about two hundred yards out to their respective ball locations. Mark waited his turn, growing more nervous by the moment. He dared not look at Check again. He kept his eyes on his ball down in the bunker and tried to forget about the cameras.

When his turn arrived, he set up in the bunker with his sand wedge and tried to pop the ball out of its sandy nest. He hit it, and it moved, but he hadn't gotten under it well enough, and it hit the embankment of the bunker and rolled back down into the sand.

The crowd groaned and so did Mark. He rushed the next shot to end the embarrassment and repeated the same mistake. He was finally able to pop the ball out on the third try, but it didn't go far, and he now had four shots on the hole and he was still over two hundred yards away from the green.

Now, he was in the unenviable position of making a forced carry over Seven Mile Creek that guarded the front side of the huge green. The wind was still blowing like a gale, and the crowd and camera were even closer because they were in the narrow part of the fairway.

He pulled an iron from his bag and approached his ball; made the shot he had made a thousand times on other courses, on other days, but this time he overpowered the ball. It didn't stop short and rolled down the drop off and into the creek. Mark was beside himself. All of his concentration and focus was gone. He couldn't go on. He walked off the course.

He had choked.

"Mark, Mark," Bob Tom said.

Yee patted Mark on the back. "Hey kid."

At the touch, Mark jerked. He was jolted into present time, but for a moment didn't know where he was.

"What's going on with you?" Bob Tom asked.

"I don't want to talk about this today," Mark said.

Bob Tom and Yee looked at each other, turned, and walked quietly on toward the clubhouse with Mark between them.

Chapter Seventy-Five

Merit woke up again to the sound of dripping water. She had been in and out so many times, she didn't know if it was day or night. She moved her tied hands and felt metal. As she struggled against grogginess, she realized she was lying down.

The sweat allowed her to push the blindfold up a bit with her shoulder. She looked through the side at wire and measured the space with her head and legs. She was in a large dog kennel. There was a padlock on the wire door.

She tried to remember how she'd gotten there but couldn't. She looked for a way out but didn't see an escape route. She tried to stay awake, but the groggy feeling swept over her and she went out.

∞

When Merit awoke again, she was hanging by her arms. Had she dreamed the dog kennel? Her arms were completely numb and tingled when she tried to bring blood back into them by jumping up and down to take the pressure off.

She felt as if she were in a horrible nightmare, but she wasn't.

She could hear voices through a large metal door at the end of the room but couldn't be sure that it was live persons and not TV. The muffled interaction sounded like a soap opera in a foreign language with two voices fighting and slamming about.

She turned her head to look as far as she could behind her, but the blindfold blocked her view. What little light there was came from her left where the voices were now yelling at full volume.

The door opened, casting light across the floor and she could dimly make out a figure approaching her with a flashlight. She tried to rouse herself fully awake and made a muffled sound. Suddenly, the blindfold was snatched away.

"Natalie!" Merit screamed. "Help me! I'm hurt. Untie me. Let's get out of here."

"Stop struggling and be quiet and I'll give you some more water," Natalie said with an accent that Merit didn't recognize.

Merit slumped against the ropes and tried to speak but couldn't. Natalie tipped a bottle of water against Merit's lips, getting part of it into her mouth and part running down her chest and onto her bra. She tried to pull herself from the grogginess and think.

"It's about time you woke up," Natalie said.

Merit looked around the room through heavy eyes and saw a large space with cinder-block walls without windows. In one corner was a stack of old cardboard boxes sagging from the damp. She could see a mop bucket with a huge mop flopped over the edge and a large maintenance sink that looked like an old-fashioned washing machine with a ringer on the side.

Her cell phone vibrated from across the room. She could see her golf bag where she'd stored the phone, her purse and briefcase, the shirt she'd been wearing at Lion's, and one golf shoe.

Closer was a table with an arrangement of metal objects. Merit wasn't quite sure what it was, but what was there was shiny and new-looking.

Merit stared at her and tried to register the accent she'd never heard coming from her friend's mouth. As she revived further, she realized that this was not her friend. The person she had trusted and cared for, golfed with, partied with, and invited into her life, this person was speaking with a Russian accent and it all started to make sense.

"Natalie? Why?" Merit asked.

"Natalia, actually. You foolish girl. Silly, that's what you are. Silly and foolish," Natalie said.

Merit finally realized the full extent of her dilemma and the fact that she wasn't being rescued. Tears welled in her eyes.

"You are going to cry? After listening to your stories and drivel for weeks, now I have to put up with your silly crying," Natalie said.

Merit moved her legs and bare feet and Natalie took a step back.

"You get it now. Don't even think about kicking me."

"Help!" Merit screamed.

"Scream all you want. No one can hear you. I enjoy the screams."

Merit calmed down and willed herself to be still and think. She looked around the room again and assessed what was available to her. She looked up past the meat hook at the metal beams from which she was suspended and saw no help there. The mop bucket was too far away. She looked at Natalie, Natalia, betrayer, bitch, and vowed to kill her with her bare hands if she were to get free.

"What do you want?" Merit said.

"Don't you know? Your little friend doesn't want to play. Browno doesn't stand for anyone refusing his wishes. You were just a handy way to get your little Mark to get out there and win some cash. Browno can take credit for finding a big golf star. We knew your little Mark would fold if we had you in our hands."

"You bitch!" Maybe her bare hands weren't enough. Maybe she'd use her gun.

It's in the BMW. Some use to me there.

"You sniveling brat. You have everything and still you have to tell your friend over wine how you miss your Ace, and your Tony, and work is so hard, and your life is so tough," Natalie mocked Merit in a whiny tone.

Merit stared at her.

"You have no idea what hard work is. A hard life is something you've never seen until you've been to Russia in a cold winter without heat."

"But you're free now, you have all you could possibly want. Why are you doing this?" Merit asked.

"Haven't you figured it out? Browno is my benefactor. He helped me as a young girl. He gave me heat and beautiful clothes and brought me to America to study and learn. He's my hero, my father. His man, Petrov, takes care of me."

"Why don't you take care of yourself?" Merit asked.

"That's none of your business. I'll give you another little shot in a minute so you can sleep in the cage. We can't pull your arms out of the sockets until little Mark wins. For now, let's give him some incentive," Natalie said as she pulled her phone from her pocket.

"Browno's a murderer and a loan shark, and you're no better than he is," Merit said.

"Look who's talking while she's all tied up," Natalie said. "Now smile for the camera."

Chapter Seventy-Six

With no leads to pursue, Betty and Ag went back to ACCC to speak with the second shift of members, management and employees in the club and cafe. They were still hoping to find Merit's new friend Natalie, but no one had seen her, and club charges showed no activity for a week. The membership records showed her address and phone number. Ag alerted Chaplain and had his men checking for her, but they had not found her.

Was she kidnapped, too?

Chaplain had no missing persons reports matching Natalie's description. Ag had nothing to go on, and it was irking the hell out of him.

Ag was speaking to the restaurant hostess and Betty headed down the hall to Bob Tom's office to make a call. She passed the young man wearing the Z-Ro ball cap.

"Excuse me, young man. May I ask you a few questions?" she asked.

He looked up, surprised. Then ran for the restaurant exit.

"Ag, get him," Betty said and pointed.

Ag snagged the man near the exit and held him.

"What's the rush? Why are you running away from us?" Ag asked.

Joe came around the corner at the noise. Ag pulled the Z-Ro ball cap from the man's head and they all looked at his face.

"Who are you? You're not a member here," Joe said.

Betty saw how scared he was.

"If we let you go, will you answer our questions?" Betty asked.

Ag saw the nod and let go of his arm but stayed close by in case he tried to run again.

"My name is Betty, what is yours?"

He blurted out, "Bobby Jakes," and then looked surprised that he'd said anything at all.

"Bobby?" Joe said.

"You related to Bob Tom Jakes?" Betty asked.

"He's my father," Bobby said.

Joe's eyes widened.

"Have you seen a woman named Merit Bridges or her friend Natalie? Merit is missing, and we can't locate Natalie" Ag said.

Bobby nodded.

"When was the last time?" Betty asked gently.

"A few days ago. Your friend's been here a lot lately. I've seen both of the women together," Bobby said.

"Can you tell me," Betty said, "How it is that you know that?"

"I just do is all. I've been here watching my father. I wanted to talk to him, but I never had the nerve. I was trying to be near him."

"I see," Betty said. "Can you help us? Do you know anything that would help us find either of the women?"

"I've seen Browno Zars and some tough looking men in his SUV. The other day they took Mark somewhere in it for an hour or so, then brought him back. He didn't look very happy. He almost fainted in the parking lot."

Ag winced. "What were you doing in the parking lot?" Ag asked.

"I watch Bob Tom's parking spot so I know when he's out. I didn't want to run into him until I was ready," Bobby said.

"You're sure it was Browno Zars that day?" Ag asked.

"Yes, I've seen him many times. He vouched for me with the security guards so I could come and go. I think he was on to me.

I made up a story and lied to him, but I don't think he believed me," Bobby said.

Ag considered the information. Merit's files involving Mark's case and Browno were back at the office. He'd have to go over them again.

Ag was already racing to his car, but Betty stopped to put her hand on Bobby's arm.

"Thank you young man. I know your father very well and he's been looking for you for a long time. He will be so pleased to see you. I hope you'll let me tell him you're in town."

"I'd appreciate that," Bobby said. "Tell him I'm clean and sober. Got my one-year coin last month."

"He'll be proud to hear that," Betty said.

"I'll get his contact info and make sure we can get them together," Joe said. "Let me look at you, son."

Betty squeezed Bobby's arm.

"I hope to be seeing a lot of you. Come to dinner. Promise?" Betty said.

"I will. I promise."

Betty went out the door and Ag picked her up on the way out.

They were on the trail. They would find Merit before it was too late, she just knew it.

Anything else was unthinkable.

Chapter Seventy-Seven

Mark, Bob Tom and Yee had a pow-wow at the Whistling Straits cafe to get organized. The three planned to follow a similar schedule to the one Mark had used at Frisco, with a few modifications by Yee. He had already reserved time on the driving range and course for Mark leading up to Thursday's play.

After they wrapped it up, Bob Tom and Mark went back to Kohler Village to find their hotel, get unpacked, and find some food. Mark drove, and Bob Tom checked his phone. He'd had several calls from Joe and Betty while he was on the plane. The day was so full, he'd not had time to check his messages.

He called Betty first.

"Hi, Darlin'. Sorry I'm just getting back to you. It's been a full day," Bob Tom said.

Mark winced. He knew Betty would be worried sick about Merit and the guilt he felt about keeping the secret was palpable.

"Yes, he's here with me. I'll put us on speaker," Bob Tom said.

"I'm here with our investigator, Ag Malone," Betty said.

"Merit is missing, and we've been told that Browno Zars has been strong arming you, Mark," Ag said.

"What?" Bob Tom said.

Mark gripped the wheel. Tears streamed down his cheeks and he pulled over on the shoulder and buried his face in his hands.

"Hang on," Bob Tom said to the phone, then to Mark, "What's going on, son?"

"Browno Zars has Merit. He's holding her to make me play this tournament. He made me sign another contract that gives him control of my winnings," Mark said.

Mark took out his phone. "He's been texting me a picture of her every day to prove she's still alive." He showed Bob Tom the photos.

"Oh my," Bob Tom said.

"What. Is she all right?" Betty asked.

"She's alive, but I think she's hurt," Mark said.

"I need those photos. Sent them to me right now," Ag said.

"I'm texting you Ag's phone number," Betty said.

"Browno told me if I told anyone he'd kill her and me, too," Mark said. "He's a monster."

"You should have told the police," Betty said.

"I couldn't take the chance," Mark said.

"Do you have any idea where he might be holding her?" Ag asked.

"He has her stashed somewhere in Austin. The daily photos show her in the same place," Mark said.

"I'm receiving the photos now," Ag said.

"He has someone watching me. There was a young man at the club and now there are people all around us here. I don't know who might be spying for him," Mark said. "He has a henchman named Petrov who does his dirty work."

"The young man at the club is Bob Tom's son, Bobby," Betty said. "He's been watching Bob Tom, not you."

"Bobby?" Bob Tom said.

"Yes, he's back and wants to see you. I'll tell you all about that later. Right now, we need to find Merit," Betty said.

"We'll fly right back," Bob Tom said.

"No, he'll know something's up and could kill Merit," Mark said.

"He's right," Ag said. "You'll have to keep playing along until Chaplain and I can find him."

"He's not with her. He's here. I've seen him," Mark said. "His goon Petrov is here with him."

Then who has her?

Chapter Seventy-Eight

Ag checked his gun and went into Chaplain's office at APD. "You don't look so good," Chaplian said.

"Like looking in a mirror. You don't look like you've slept in a month," Ag said.

"At least a month," Chaplain said.

"A man named Bobby Jakes has led us to the Russian named Browno Zars," Ag said.

"So, he was involved as you thought," Chaplain said.

"Yes. He apparently took Mark Green from ACCC and threatened to kill Merit if he didn't re-sign his contract with him and play the tour for money," Ag said.

"I think I have something for you that ties this Browno thug to The Enforcer. I saw on the news that the man you found tortured to death was a tennis pro," Ag said.

"You think this Browno Zars could have killed him?" Chaplain said.

"I've got a file full of information in Merit Bridges office about Browno Zars lending money to and coercing boxers, golfers, and tennis pros. He's a Russian loan shark out of Brighton Beach who set up shop in Austin."

"What point would there be for him to kill borrowers? Dead people can't pay debts," Chaplain said.

"I think the Russian might have other motives besides being bat-shit crazy. Mark Green is being forced to play golf for him. Mark says he's seen him in Wisconsin where the tournament is being held," Ag said. "Browno's henchman Petrov is reported to be with him, so he must still have someone working for him here in Austin."

"Maybe this is the break we need. I'll get my men working on where he might be staying up there. Does he know we're onto him?" Chaplain asked.

"I don't think so. I'm afraid if we can tie The Enforcer to this Browno Zars guy, it means Merit is in more danger than ever."

"We'll get to the bottom of it," Chaplin said.

"We must be very careful. Browno must keep Merit alive as long as Mark Green is playing."

"When does the tournament end?" Chaplain asked.

"Sunday," Ag said.

"Then we have to find her fast," Chaplain said.

Chapter Seventy-Nine

Day one of the PGA Championship dawned bright red over Lake Michigan. After two days preparation in Wisconsin, Mark was ready to start play. He had an early tee time, so he was up to see the colors of dawn change to daylight.

Mark dressed in his new clothes, sporting the Fairway and Nano logos, and hooked up with Bob Tom. David Yee came by at breakfast to wish him luck and give him final bits of advice and encouragement.

Mark and Bob Tom went through the morning ritual, being superstitiously careful to do things the same way as always. Mark stretched, warmed up on the driving range, and was ready to tee off ahead of schedule. Bob Tom gave the clubs a final swipe with a polishing cloth and packed the bag just as he always did. This time, he also packed Ramjack golf balls, since they were now a sponsor.

Bob Tom also made sure that the oxygenated water supply was close at hand. Lastly, he put on his caddie vest with GREEN stenciled across his back, spit out his chewing tobacco, and picked up Mark's clubs.

Mark was playing with other golf pros from around the U.S. The big names, with the best scores, were scheduled later in the day. The camera crews would concentrate on those groups and put them on live television at primetime.

Mark and Bob Tom shook hands with fellow players and caddies respectively, and then moved onto the first hole, a par four called Outward Bound. Mark had practiced his shot in his mind a thousand times.

Mark felt a jolt of nerves.

Settle down, settle down.

But Mark knew he played for Merit's life, and he couldn't afford to get too settled. It helped so much that Bob Tom and everyone else knew about Merit. He no longer carried the burden alone.

Mark pulled his glove onto his scarred hand. He moved his attention to the game and assessed his first shot. He wanted a drive down the center of the fairway, avoiding a series of bunkers and sand dunes down the left side. He executed the tee off fairly well while controlling his opening day jitters. He favored the center of the green to avoid deep bunkers short, left, and long. He played it by the book and wound up with par and a solid start to the day.

"Good job," Bob Tom said and re-bagged Mark's putter.

"We're off," Mark said and strode across the grass to the second hole.

Mark stayed steady from hole two through nine, but had a hiccup on the tenth hole, a three-hundred-and-sixty-yard par four. His training kicked in and his focus remained constant for most of the day.

He could go for glory and use his driver, but he'd have to avoid more sand bunkers and hit into a steep hillside guarding the front of the green. Distance was his best asset, and he couldn't play it safe all week and expect to come in fourth or better. It would require a carry of at least two hundred and forty yards over a deep bunker. That would set up a wedge approach to the elevated green.

"Let me have the driver, Bob Tom," Mark said, holding out his gloved hand.

"You sure?" Bob Tom asked.

"I'm sure."

"Good call," Bob Tom bit back advice as he handed him the driver. A good caddie knew it was part of his job to put a positive note in the player's mind right before the shot.

Mark made a beautiful swing, struck the ball soundly, and sailed the ball out toward the hillside at the front of the green. It looked like it was going to land smoothly, but at the last minute a puff of wind forced a slight turn left and the ball dropped into a bunker.

"That's okay, we'll pick it up," Bob Tom said.

Mark read his face.

"It wasn't your fault. It was my call," Mark said.

He popped the ball out of the sand in one shot, but it still put him at par after a two putt. He'd hoped for a birdie to get a few strokes ahead. He had no idea how other players were faring and didn't dare lose focus to find out. Maybe par on that hole was good enough.

He found out later that it was, as others had tangled with the course here and there, and the best score of the day was sixty-eight. At the end of the day's play, Mark was in sixteenth place.

Mark and Bob Tom caught up with Yee for a first day recap and strategy meeting. All three agreed that Mark would have to take a few more chances the next day, but he was off to a solid start, and the goal was still possible to reach.

The crowd had taken notice of Mark's play, and the buzz began. Who was this kid out of Austin? Had anyone heard of him? What was going on with his hands? He had a few sponsors, where did those come from?

The media, always looking for a fresh face and a new angle, focused on his hands. Moustache called his producer at The Golf Network and told him to dig up some stuff on this kid, and to make sure and find out how his hands were damaged.

Mark left the course exhausted from the stress and physical exertion of the day. He thought of Merit.

I won't let you down.

Chapter Eighty

Ag and his crew continued to work out of Merit's conference room. Betty kept them all in coffee and iced tea and mother henned him to death. Val helped where he could, but threw up everything he ate. Betty and Val had gone through Merit's computer twice and her calendar a half dozen times. No clues to where she might be.

Chaplain had made some police resources available to him, and Ag was going through some of the information on Browno. Turned out, Browno was a slippery sucker. There'd been some sort of turf war that went down a few years before in Brighton Beach, but the Russians weren't known for being exactly loose-lipped.

Chaplain was tagging a few of his resources, but it would take a while.

Chaplain was coordinating help from the Wisconsin police, and they had Browno and Petrov under surveillance at their hotel and at the golf course, or at least as close as they could get without tipping him off. Browno and his entourage watched every move Mark made from the exhibition areas as the Wisconsin authorities watched both Mark and Browno.

The best thing they could do was grab Browno in Wisconsin and force him to tell where Merit was, but they didn't want to do anything that would get Merit killed. They had a tap on his phone which had netted them exactly nothing; Browno was probably using a burner cell to text the photos or going through Petrov in some way.

Ag went into Merit's office and sat at her desk. He opened each drawer. He'd done it a dozen times, but something was bothering him. He picked up a stack of business cards again and shuffled through it. Just regular people with regular legal probl"I scan those after she gets a large stack. We put them on the computer system then recycle all the cards," Betty said.

"Can you show me the last ones you scanned?" Ag asked.

"Sure." Betty typed in Merit's password and opened the page to contacts. She clicked a few keys and a list of the last entries came up.

One of the latest entries said, Natalie Kain, Sem'ya Holdings, etc.

"ACCC didn't have this company name on file," Ag said.

Sem'ya, Sem'ya. Where had he heard the name before?

"I've heard it, too," Betty said.

Ag leapt to his feet and kissed Betty on the cheek.

He ran to the conference room and opened the file he had given Merit on Browno. Betty followed him in with the Terrence Long closing file in her hands.

"There were a series of corporations that Browno owned with a convoluted series of sub-corps. Sem'ya was one of the sub-corps. It's a real estate investment trust," Ag said.

"It's also the company that loaned Terrence Long two hundred thousand dollars to bail out Hill Country Homestead," Betty said as she flipped through the file.

"Sem'ya Holdings is linked to Browno," Ag said.

"This Natalie Kain must have something to do with all this," Betty said.

Chapter Eighty-One

Day two of the PGA Championship was as beautiful as the first. On Mark's way to meet Bob Tom, a couple of players introduced themselves to Mark and said, "Nice game."

"Thanks," Mark said. He would normally have swooned at meeting these icons of golf, but his mind was on Merit.

Please find her.

Mark and Bob Tom ran through the morning ritual as usual. Bob Tom put his arm around Mark's shoulder to steer him away from the cameras and microphones and said, "Let's play some golf."

"Right," Mark covered the first nine without upset, and managed to avoid a repeat of the prior day's problems on the tenth hole. He didn't shy away from the driver on ten, even though that had been a problem on the prior day.

Bob Tom read his mind and already had the driver in his hand. "You can do it."

Mark made the shot running his tee ball just short of the green. He pitched to five feet and sank his birdie putt.

"Now, that's the way," Bob Tom clapped him on the shoulder.

"Thanks," Mark beamed, then was ashamed of himself. How could he be happy when Merit was in danger. Mark played from ten to thirteen with skill and determination.

Coming up on Cliff Hanger, a four hundred and four-yard par four, Mark felt confident. He'd played this hole without incident before and hadn't had any problem with it. The wind picked up just as he approached the tee, and he slowed his rhythm to see if it would die down. The change in pace threw him a little and he tried to settle as he stepped into the tee box and waggled.

He knew he needed to avoid the sand dunes on the right and stick the ball on the cliff hanger green next to Lake Michigan, but there were sand bunkers he needed to avoid short right and left.

"Settle down," he told himself. He forced himself to keep his eyes open. Every time he closed them he saw Merit, hanging off that hook. If he didn't get this shot, it could mean the end of her life.

Just play my game.

He swallowed, hard. He could see Browno, Petrov, and a couple of other goons standing behind the exhibitors rope. It was intimidating.

Mark was so nervous he struck the ball a little wide, and watched it sail out over the fairway to the right. He thought it was going to roll down the cliffhanger into the water, but it held right on the edge.

How am I going to hit that?

The crowd gasped as his ball landed. After all players had all hit their first shot, Mark split off from the group to take a closer look at his ball until his turn to make his second shot.

Mark assessed his lie on the edge of the steep bluff hanging over the great lake. He stretched his legs wide, putting one foot down the side of the embankment and one on the edge with the ball. Mark twisted body like a pretzel and whacked the ball with a seven iron out of danger and into the fairway near the green. The crowd loved it, and congratulated Mark with applause for the shot.

Mark regretted the addition of the count on the hole but was grateful the ball hadn't rolled into the lake. He putted well, and saved par. He finished the day in good form, and a birdie on ten moved him up to twelfth place.

His play secured his place in the finals. Mark had his shot at the brass ring. The next two days would determine the direction of the rest of his life.

And Merit's.

Chapter Eighty-Two

Ag and Chaplin were at the police station, running down leads on the properties that were owned by Sem'ya Holdings. Ag had Googled what Sem'ya meant. Family. He was positive that Natalie and Browno were in cahoots together. They had to find out where Merit was being held before the tournament ended. Mark had not been able to tell Ag what Browno planned to do with her once the tournament was over.

"Sem'ya holds some downtown properties and part of an office building." Chaplin said. "She could be there."

Their eyes were glued to the computer terminal.

Ag shook his head. "Too many people. But we'll check it out. There has to be something else in here."

"Keep looking," Chaplain said.

Ag was frustrated as all hell. He'd also been running down leads on Natalie Kain but was getting nowhere. He shook his head and tried to focus.

"Sem'ya's address is actually a post office box," Chaplain said.

"The background in the photos looks old. Crumbling cinderblock and old equipment. Like something half falling in," Ag said.

Chaplin swore like a sailor and kept looking.

Then Ag found what he was looking for.

∞

Merit's shoulders were going to separate, she was sure of it.

Natalie, or Natalia, arrived and gave her some water and part of a protein drink and taunted her again.

"So," Natalia said, her Russian accent tinting her words. "Your man is doing very well. Browno is pleased."

Natalia smiled. "Do you know why they call me The Enforcer?"

Merit said nothing. She wasn't going to give Natalia an inch.

Natalia stepped closer. "Because I always, always, force my will on people, and I enforce Browno's contracts."

Merit slumped, making it look like she had given up.

"Let's get a pretty picture for boyfriend Mark today."

Natalie picked up a razor and cut a small nick on Merit's forehead. The blood flowed down her left cheek and dripped small red flowers on her chest and bra.

She thought of her sweet Ace and held on. He gave her strength and resolve to find a way out of this horror.

Natalie flicked the razor again, using a little wrist action to cut Merit's shoulder. Blood trickled down her right arm like teardrops in a tattoo.

Merit screamed.

"Good one," Natalie said.

Merit gritted her teeth.

"This is just a taste. I can't wait until this whole mess is over and I get to play with you," Natalie said.

Merit wished that Natalie would get close enough in front of her so that she could kick her, but Natalie watched her like a hawk.

Natalie stood a few feet away and took a gruesome shot of Merit with the blood in living color. She typed in a few key strokes and hit SEND. She moved a bit closer and focused the camera on Merit's face, neck and shoulders.

Merit had been practicing and waiting for just such a mistake and Natalie had made it. Merit swung forward on the meat hook and wrapped her legs up and around Natalie's waist. Natalie tried to push her away, but it was too late. Merit pulled her forward with her legs while at the same time using Natalie's body as leverage. She pushed herself up and unhooked the rope from the hook. They both fell to the floor and scrambled for an advantage.

∞

"Can't you drive any faster?" Ag snarled at Chaplin. They were in a black-and-white, sirens blazing. Ag hoped they were keeping Merit at an industrial address held by a numbered company that they had tracked back to Sem'ya. It looked like it could be the age and condition of the room in the pictures.

He tapped the dashboard and gave Chaplin a meaningful look.

The traffic cleared, and Chaplin stepped on the gas. They cut the sirens two blocks away and crept around the building seeking entrance. They found a side door with a lock hanging on the hasp. Ag smiled bitterly. It was arrogance that made a criminal so sure they wouldn't get caught.

Ag squared his shoulders and entered the building with his pistol drawn. Chaplain did the same.

They crept slowly down a dark hallway pausing to listen before proceeding to the next room.

∞

Merit was weak after days of her imprisonment, but a surge of adrenalin had kicked in, racing through her. Natalie broke free and Merit kicked her in the knee. Natalie lunged at Merit and grabbed her ponytail pulling her head back and causing her to lose her balance. Merit went down.

Natalie grabbed the razor and came after Merit on the floor. Merit rolled away and got to her feet. She hit Natalie's arm causing her to drop the razor and shoved her back.

Natalie was lying on the floor, stunned, and Merit frantically looked around for a weapon. She dashed over to her belongings in the corner.

Merit grabbed her golf shoe with the spiked bottom and turned just in time to cut a big gash in Natalie's left shoulder. Blood began to run down her arm as she lunged at Merit and got inside the sweep of the shoe avoiding a second cut. Merit dropped her shoe weapon and fell backward against the wall.

Natalie pulled a seven iron from Merit's bag and swung it. The club head hit just beside Merit's ear on the cinder block wall and broke from the shaft. Merit grabbed the end of the shaft and they wrestled with the metal rod until Natalie broke free and came at Merit again with the pointed end aimed at her chest.

Merit dodged the strike and her elbow connected with Natalia's jaw and dislodged her grip, throwing her to the floor. Merit found herself next to the golf bag and pulled a driver with a huge wooden head. Merit took a swing at Natalie with the club, the air whooshing by her ears.

At the last minute, Natalia rolled over. The club hit the floor and the big head broke off the handle and rolled away.

Natalie regained ground and rammed her head into Merits torso knocking the breath out of her and causing her to drop the driver shaft. Merit fell to the floor and Natalie picked up the razor. She came at Merit with the razor out before her.

Merit rolled over and grabbed the club head from the floor. She got to her feet and just as Natalie took a swipe with the blade, Merit hit the side of Natalie's head with the wooden club. Merit heard the crack in Natalie's skull like a shot.

Merit screamed in pain as the razor cut her arm, but Natalie went down and out.

∞

Ag and Chaplin heard the rumble and crashed into the room just in time to see Merit whack Natalie in the temple with the driver head.

"Merit!" Ag rushed over to her. She collapsed in his arms. She was half naked and covered in blood. Her hair was a disaster.

"You've never looked more beautiful," Ag said.

∞

That night at the hospital, Ag and Betty alternated sitting by Merit's bedside as she slept. She was pale, had forty-four stitches total on her forehead, arm, and shoulder and was taking constant IV fluids to re-establish electrolyte balance.

"Betty," Merit said.

"I'm here, Darlin'," Betty said and took Merit's hand.

Ag came over to the bedside and joined them.

"What happened?" Merit asked.

"You're in the hospital. You don't have a concussion, but you are depleted from dehydration. All of your wounds will heal. We had a plastic surgeon do the stitches to minimize scarring," Betty said.

"It may be a while before your arms feel normal. Your doctor is keeping you here for observation and pain management," Ag said.

"Ace?" Merit asked.

"He's fine. I sent one of my guys down to guard him the minute we realized you were missing," Ag said.

Joy and Tucker explained the whole thing to him after it was over. He never knew a thing until you were safe," Betty said.

"Thank you," Merit whispered.

Merit looked around the room at all the flowers. One particularly large bouquet caught her eye.

"From Dalton," Betty said. "He's been by. He'll check back later."

"Mark?" Merit asked.

"Browno was using your capture as leverage to control him. He's safe but keeping up pretenses until Chaplain can put his plan in motion," Ag said.

"Do you remember being taken from your car?" Ag asked.

"Yes, and I was in a cage and on a meat hook. I tried not to cry."

Betty hugged her gently and Ag kissed her cheek.

"Natalie cut me several times. She was The Enforcer all along. She was proud of it," Merit said.

"Well, she won't be cutting anyone else again. She's alive, but barely," Ag said.

"She's in the critical care unit on the second floor," Betty said.

Merit shivered at the thought of Natalie being in the same hospital.

"Chaplain has pieced it all together. Do you remember that he was with me when we found you?" Ag asked.

Merit pushed herself up a bit on the pillows and looked more alert.

"Yes, I saw you both break down the door," Merit said.

"Do you remember anything else?" Ag asked.

"I remember beating the shit out of Natalie. Now, get me out of here," Merit said weakly.

They all laughed and healing began.

Chapter Eighty-Three

*S*he's free. She's free. Merit is safe! It's over!

It was the only thing Mark could think of as he sat at breakfast with Bob Tom.

Ag's words still rang in his ears. As soon as Merit was released from the hospital, she'd be on the way to Wisconsin to see him.

Mark was in a late slot, so he and Bob Tom had time for a leisurely breakfast in the privacy of Mark's room. Yee joined them for coffee toward the end of the meal.

Mark barely heard anything that was said.

She's free. I'm free!

∞

On their way to the front nine, Mark swept his gaze over the crowd.

To Mark's left, he saw a commotion involving a snarl of police uniforms and one very portly spectator, Browno Zars. Mark smiled.

Ag and Chaplin were thrilled to assist Wisconsin's finest in arresting Browno. Petrov, who had been snagged at the hotel earlier, had told the police all about Browno Zars. He'd also spilled the borscht about Natalie's handy work as The Enforcer and all of their loans and illegal collection tactics.

The puzzling question of why Browno would off the people that owed him money was solved through Petrov. Browno had each of the loans tied to something of value. Collateral for some, life insurance for others, and for the tennis pros, keeping the sponsorship money after they were gone. The borrowers were truly worth more dead than alive except for Mark.

When they clapped the handcuffs on him, Browno's protective entourage melted into the rest of the crowd as fast as burly Russians could disappear.

"I done nothin' wrong," Browno protested. "You got zip on me. I be out in no time."

Ag put his hand on the back of Browno's shoulder and directed him through the crowd and into a waiting police car. Once he'd settled Browno in his seat, Ag leaned over the door.

"I don't think so, Brownose," Ag said.

Browno's lips tightened in a grimace.

"The Enforcer is in the hospital and Petrov is talking."

Ag slammed the door. The look on Browno's face made Ag smile.

It was determined that Natalie was still unconscious and expected to stay in a coma for some time. If she woke up, she could either talk along with Petrov or go to jail with Browno. Either way, she was pronounced "tied to an ant hill with ears full of jam" by Betty.

∞

Red Thallon wrapped the coverage of The Enforcer. She had promised to hold the story until after Browno was arrested and kept her word.

After Red was told of the police's arrest of Browno and the background of Browno's dealings, she related the story of Merit's narrow escape and battle with Natalie.

She showed canned footage of Mark in Wisconsin and tied up the story with a bow by reporting how brave her friend Merit Bridges had been.

It was a good news day for KNEW 9 and for all of Austin to have The Enforcer out of commission.

∞

Bob Tom watched the skirmish around Browno's arrest.

"Mark, I'm glad she's safe" he said, "but we have a job to do."

Mark's face turned serious.

"You are still playing aren't you?" Bob Tom asked.

"I am," Mark said. "Now, I work for myself."

Bob Tom clapped him on the shoulder. "Let's play some golf." And they did.

Day three at Whistling Straits held a lot fewer golfers than the first two days, but a lot bigger spectator crowd. Mark played the front nine well again but had challenges on the back nine as the wind from Lake Michigan picked up later in the day.

On hole twelve, a short one hundred and forty-three-yard par three called Pop Up, he had some trouble. The hole played downhill to a large undulating green, and Mark drove to the left of the hole due to the strong wind carrying his ball over.

He was so glad he and Yee had practiced at the lake on working with the wind and got down the fairway without incident. He was on the green, but when it came time to putt, he misread the break and lipped out. What should have been an easy two came at even par. He had let the short little hole get the best of him.

On hole sixteen, he was able to make up for it on Endless Bite, a five hundred and sixty-nine-yard par five with the sky and Lake Michigan as a backdrop. The conservative play was to use an iron off the tee, but long yardage was Mark's greatest asset, and he needed to take the risk, so he had Bob Tom pull his driver. He needed to get to the green in two.

"Knock it on," Bob Tom said as Mark grinned at him.

This was going to be fun.

Mark hit the ball at the perfect moment in the windbreak, and the ball soared over bunkers and sand dunes to land in the fairway giving him a clear second shot to the green. He putted in two, giving him a birdie on the hole, and his self-confidence soared.

He was in the flow all afternoon. He felt comfortable with the course, and he took calculated risks where he could. He played it safe where he should, coming in at par or under on every hole for the day. He came in at seven under par with the third best score of the day, beating out most of the tour hot shots, and moving into sixth place. The crowd didn't realize what was happening score wise until the day's play had ended, but the sports channels were all over it.

The media had watched Mark move up and focused the spotlight on his play and the tidbits of history they had gleaned from his friends and family. By the end of the day, the buzz was all about Mark, and all eyes were looking forward to watching him the next day.

Moustache was standing with a microphone as Mark came off the course and pushed it in his face. "Mr. Green. Could we have a moment?"

Merit materialized, stepped up to Moustache, keeping the unbandaged side of her forehead toward the camera, and said, "Mr. Green had a great day, didn't he?"

Mark stopped his usual evasive tactics, smiled his biggest smile at Merit and said, "It felt great out there today."

Moustache continued encouraged, "The drive on hole sixteen was spectacular. What made you decide to hit the driver and go for two to the hole?"

Mark fumbled for a moment and Merit said, "Wasn't that spectacular to watch?"

Mark picked up the thread, "I knew I had to make up for the mistake I'd made earlier on the twelfth hole, and I also knew I couldn't play it safe and compete with these guys. They are such great players that I admire so much."

"Were you aware of the problems some of the pros were having on the course?"

"No." Mark said. He fumbled with his hat – trying to get his plug in for Fairway Shoes, but it looked like he was scratching his head.

"Do you think you're lucky, or can you hold on tomorrow? Coming in at the top of this crowd is quite a feat."

Mark said, "I just plan to play the best golf I can."

"How have your hands affected the way you play, Mark? Your mother tells us that you overcame a lot to be here today."

"My mother?" Mark said.

"Mrs. Green is very proud of Mark, as any mother would be," Merit said.

Mark said seriously, "I play just like everyone else. Two hands, one clubMerit laughed, and Mark followed suit. Merit took his arm and pulled him away as Moustache started another question.

"Thank you. Thank you," they kept repeating until they were out of earshot and Moustache had snagged another player.

"Good job," Merit said.

"You, too," Mark said. "Hey. You made it."

"Hey. I did."

The both grabbed on tightly to each other's hand.

∞

Mark and Merit settled into a couple of lawn chairs on the back side of the clubhouse out of sight of the crowd.

"I was worried you wouldn't make it. How do you feel?

"It still hurts, especially my shoulders, but I have muscle re-laxers and pain killers, so I'm getting by. I slept on the plane. The doctors wanted me to stay in the hospital for another day of re-hydration and wound care, but I wouldn't miss this for the world," Merit said.

"Are you sure?" Mark asked.

"Betty is taking good care of me and the stitches are healing already," Merit said.

"When I saw what they did to you in those pictures, I almost lost it," Mark said. "I'm so sorry I brought those monsters into your life."

"Let's put that in the past for now," Merit said. "Thank you for giving Ag and Chaplain time to find me."

"Anything for you," Mark said.

"Anything? Then win tomorrow," Merit said.

They hugged for a long time.

∞

Later that night, Merit, Mark, Bob Tom, Yee, Betty, and Cousin Mac all met for an early dinner to celebrate Merit's arrival and Browno's arrest. Ag and Chaplain had flown back to Austin with Browno and Petrov in tow.

Mark was elated. Merit had on a lot of tan makeup, a few bandages, and long sleeves, but all in all she looked pretty pulled together. Betty stayed near her all night except when Merit stepped out to talk to Ace, who was calling almost every hour since he'd been told what happened.

Merit and Betty followed Bob Tom's lead on the subjects of conversation. No one wanted to make Mark nervous or put any added pressure on him. They kept the conversation light, joking and chatting about trivia. In a show of support for Mark and because Merit was still on pain killers, no alcohol; iced teas or Arnold Palmers all around.

They all knew that if Mark wanted to finish in the top four, he'd have to up his game the next day. He'd need to take a few more chances. He had a shot – a long shot, but a shot.

Cousin Mac left before desert to get Mark's mother who was coming to watch Mark play the last day. Mac was to be her escort for the event. Yee cut out early to make some phone calls, and Merit announced that she had to meet with the Fairway sponsor for a drink. Mark offered to walk her over to the Hole In One Bar, and Bob Tom and Betty welcomed the time alone, and a little alcohol in private.

Mark opened the door for Merit and they fell into step on the sidewalk. It was a beautiful night. The heat from the day had dissipated and the air felt soft and inviting.

"That was great. That was the best salmon I've ever had," Merit said.

"Yeah, it was. They swim up from Lake Huron to Lake Michigan, you know," Mark said.

"I've seen some great things about this state. I didn't realize Wisconsin had so much to offer."

"It was pretty great growing up here. I just hope I don't embarrass myself in front of the home crowd tomorrow," Mark said.

"You're doing great, Mark. I'm so happy for you."

"They say the game doesn't begin until the back nine on Sunday."

"I understand, there's a lot of pressure," Merit sympathized.

"I still don't feel comfortable being interviewed either," Mark said. "But now that you're safe, I don't want to whine about a single thing."

"Bob Tom gave me the notice of the interview from The Golf Network for tomorrow. I guess we should have worked more with the video camera. I'm sorry. I'm new at this management business. A more experienced agent might have known that," Merit said.

"If I'd waited for a more experienced agent, I wouldn't be here," Mark said. "Besides, you're doing great. Look at all the money you've brought in."

"Thanks. If it makes you feel any better, you came across well on camera."

Merit knew at some point he'd have to expose himself more or lose his sponsors. That was the point of sponsorship. Plus, the more he tipped his hat and showed the logo on his bag, the more money he made. Besides, the media wasn't going to let this go much longer.

"Let's go back to the pizza theory, one bite at a time. Just play your best tomorrow, and the rest will take care of itself."

"I hope I can get a good night's sleep," Mark said.

"You will. I'll handle the sponsors and the media while you play. We brought some press packets with those new pictures we shot. Betty distributed them this afternoon. That should hold them for tonight anyway."

"Merit? What do you do when all the visualizing and little tricks don't work?"

"They usually do," she said.

"But what if they don't. What if you feel all alone and everything is just too much? What did you do while you were on the meat hook?"

"I normally don't tell people things like this, because I think everyone has to decide about these things for themselves, but since you asked. When I'm so afraid or tired that nothing in my mind will work, and I'm at the end of my ability to do anything for myself, I pretend that I'm holding the hand of the all-powerful universe."

"How do you mean?"

"I just close my fist, ask the universe to be there, and hang on until the fear passes."

Mark thought for a moment.

"I understand. Thanks," he said and kissed her cheek.

"No problem, that's why you pay me the big bucks. Speaking of, I have a drink with Baker. I better get moving."

They laughed. It felt good to Mark, just the two of them. He held her hand and walked her to the Hole In One Bar, then headed back to his hotel room, hung the DO NOT DISTURB sign, and had a good night's sleep.

***

Mr. Baker from Fairway Shoes was waiting for Merit at the Hole in One Bar. It felt good to get back to work. Emotionally, Merit knew she'd probably be in shock for a while, but she wasn't going to let Natalie or Browno or anybody else get in her way or affect her life.

Merit knew she'd grown since meeting Mark. Her career was skyrocketing, and her golf game had never been better. In fact, she was sure all those golf lessons had helped make her strong enough to beat Natalie. It had even helped her choose which club to whack her with. And knowing Browno had been arrested that afternoon had given her a feeling of power she hadn't felt in a long time.

When she entered the bar, she saw Betty and Bob Tom snuggled up in a booth with large alcoholic drinks before them. Merit should have known Betty would not let her walk back to the hotel alone after the meeting. Betty had told her they were going to make a plan to bring Bobby into their lives in Austin.

She waved at them and found Baker at a table.

Baker stood and greeted her warmly.

"Let me get you a drink," Baker said and motioned to the waiter.

"I'll have a Tito One with pomegranate juice if they have it," Merit said.

"Tito One? Drinking the new sponsor? I thought you were a wine drinker," Baker said after he'd ordered for both of them.

"Well, you know, have to spread the good will around," Merit said. "I can only have a sip. Pain killers."

"I heard you had a battle royale," Baker said.

"I did, and I won," Merit said. "Nostrovia!"

"Cheers," Baker said.

"Speaking of winning, our boy did pretty well today," Baker said.

"He did," Merit smiled. "Thanks for gambling on him first. You always had a good nose for talent."

"The fact that he's made it to the last two days is a friggin' miracle, and we both know it. But, thanks for the compliment anyway," Baker laughed.

"He makes a good rep for your shoes. If he shows anywhere near the top tomorrow, you'll have all the publicity you need to pay off your investment."

"We don't have to wait, The Golf Network and ESPN have hunted down his resume and have already called his mother and half his family," Baker said.

"Oh, no," Merit groaned.

"Oh, no? Isn't publicity what we want?" Baker asked.

"Absolutely."

I hope.

∞

Day four at Whistling dawned clear and windy.

Moustache started Sunday's lament with his first announcement. "Course officials have moved the pins to the back of the greens here at Whistling Straits, stretching the course to seven thousand five hundred and thirty-six yards and making it the longest course in major championship history."

Moustache continued, "This won't be easy. The wind is stiff, and there was no water on the course overnight, which makes it firm and hard."

Mark and Bob Tom, in Mark's room, gave each other a thumbs-up. They had prepared for just this circumstance, as his long game was the best way to compete with the major players. Luck was smiling on him, at least for now.

Mark and Bob Tom watched enough to get the rest of the weather, then turned off the set when room service arrived with breakfast. They ate in silence, then Bob Tom looked at Mark.

"Before Yee gets here, I want to tell you something, Mark," Bob Tom began. "When we first met, I didn't realize the man you are."

"Aw, thanks, Bob Tom," Mark cut him off. He was embarrassed.

"Let me finish. I just want you to know that I'd be glad to have a son like you. Win or lose today, I'm proud of you," Bob Tom said.

"Thanks. I couldn't have done it without you. I mean it," Mark said. They gave each other an awkward hug and separated when Yee rapped on the door.

Since Mark's rank had moved up to the top ten, he played late in the day with some of the biggest names in golf. As he set up at the driving range, Jaguar Malone nodded and smiled at Mark.

Mark was so star-struck, he missed his first practice drive.

Bob Tom handed him another ball and whispered in his ear, "They put their pants on just like every other man, one leg at a time." Mark calmed himself and remembered that he had a job to do. His second try was better, and after a few more balls, he was in his zone.

After the warm-up Mark checked the Leaderboard and read all the names set out to make golf history.

Mark Green? How did that name get into the group?

Mark felt himself begin to float out of his body. It was just too unreal. He twisted his feet to sink his shoes into the ground and pulled himself deep into his toes.

Just to be able to play with these amazing guys was a dream come true for Mark, but he needed at least fourth place, and that meant out-playing two or more of his idols. Any of them were talented enough to beat Mark, but he had held his own. So far.

This is no time for wonder. That can come later.

The wind was whipping through the dunes, and it was a fight from the first hole. Nothing was easy, and even the best players were slammed with the combination of stiff wind and the hard course. Mark took on the challenge.

∞

Back at ACCC, Joe and Mark's students—young and old—gathered in the cafe around the new big screen TV that had been purchased for the occasion.

"He's got a shot," Joe said.

"Yes, he can do it," one of the young girls said and pumped her fist.

∞

In Milwaukee, a doctor sat in his office in a white coat behind a desk. He watched The Golf Network on a television set in a corner console. On the shelf below the screen were plaster models of hands showing tendons, arteries, and muscles. The nameplate on the desk read: DR. ANDREW HOPKINS. A picture of him and a young Mark was on the wall.

∞

Check's poker buddies were assembled at Bomnskie's Tavern to watch. The television above the bar was tuned to The Golf Network. Mo poured Jack Daniels neat for the group, and one for himself. By mid-afternoon, the entire bar was full of locals drinking beer and alternately cheering and moaning on each of Mark's televised shots.

∞

On the course at Whistling, Merit and Betty watched Mark and Bob Tom with pride as they moved from hole to hole with the other spectators. Mark's mother held an umbrella as a shield against the sun where she stood behind the ropes next to Cousin Mac. He supported her arm each time the group moved to the next hole. She smiled at Mark after each shot, whether he did well or not, and whether he could see her or not. Cousin Mac gave Mark a thumbs-up when he caught his eye.

∞

When Mark reached hole seventeen, Moustache was beside himself with excitement, "The surprise newcomer this week is Mark Green. Green's hometown is just a short drive from Whistling, and if you'll pan the crowd, you can see his mother Margaret Green rooting for her son."

The camera caught a becoming shot of Margaret looking sweet and proud. Next to her stood Betty, and next to Betty was Merit and Mr. Baker. All beamed at Mark as he strode by to the seventeenth hole.

Bart, in The Golf Network production booth, took his turn, "That's right. Our research revealed that Mark Green's father died a few weeks ago. It seems that Green's father taught him golf when he was just a boy. His hands were burned in an accident on the family farm just a few miles from here."

Moustache continued, "Yes, and even with those scars, Green stands in a three-way tie for fourth place against Freeland, and Cameron. How did this green kid, no pun intended, get this far, Bart?"

Back in the production booth, Bart responded, "It seems that Green has been working with David Yee for the past few months, and it really shows here today. The crowd loves this kid."

Moustache picked up the thread, "Yes, it does, Bart. Green is the youngest player and lowest seed to ever place this high in the

PGA Championship. It is expected that Marcus and Valnard will take the first two spots, and the battle here is probably for positions three through five between Highway, Cameron and Green. I know Mark Green will be fighting to stay in the top four so that he can move on next year to the PGA tour, not to mention some excellent prize money, Bart."

The crowd hushed as Mark stepped up to the tee on the seventeenth hole, a two hundred and twenty-three-yard, par three called Pinched Nerve. The Nerve, an intimidating hole, had been a waterloo for both Highway and Cameron. Highway went wide close to Lake Michigan on a gust of wind, and Cameron went into a large elevated sand dune just forty yards short of the green. If Mark could make it over that same bunker, he could possibly cut a shot off the hole and pass those guys.

Moustache gave the play-by-play in hushed tones as Mark surveyed the shot, "This is Green's chance to move ahead of Highway and Cameron. There is no margin for error on this signature hole. You know Green really wants this one, Bart."

Bart replied electronically, "That's right. Mark Green, just miles from his family farm here in Wisconsin, tied up with the big boys."

Moustache continued, "It's my understanding that everyone else in contention has finished the eighteenth hole and signed their score cards. We're waiting on these last four players, Bart."

"That's correct. Freeland has dropped too far behind to catch up. That leaves Green, Highway, and Cameron on the seventeenth hole battling it out for third, fourth, and fifth place."

"Only two holes left to determine the outcome of this PGA Championship."

Mark saw the television camera swing toward him. He shifted his back to the camera and said something to Bob Tom. A course marshal hushed the crowd, and the cameraman stepped back.

Mark addressed the ball, waggled, and knocked it over the bunker and onto the green. The crowd roared, and Mark smiled at Merit, Betty and Margaret and handed his club to Bob Tom in triumph.

Mark putted in one, giving him one under par on the hole.

Moustache went wild, "That could be it. That could be the one, Bart. It all rides on hole eighteen now. If they each come in at par, Green takes it. If Cameron or Highway go under par, and Green goes par, he drops to fifth place."

Bart picked it up, "That's right, the future of these players is all in the next hole, but more so for Green. His first PGA tour hanging in the balance. If he comes in third or fourth today, the door for next year is wide open to him."

∞

Mark strode toward the eighteenth hole.

My nemesis.

Moustache was already set up doing commentary. "We're on the last hole of this tournament, named Dyeabolical. It's a par four and a full five hundred yards. This hole is fierce, and the drive calls for brute strength into the prevailing wind. The green is the shape of a four-leaf clover, and the pin placement selected by the course marshals here today makes it even tougher."

In the control booth, Bart answered, "I wouldn't want to be standing on the eighteenth tee with less than a two-shot cushion which none of these players has. It's a hard tee shot, a hard second shot, and it's not an easy green to putt."

Mark tried to stay clear of Moustache, but the camera was focused right on Mark's sweating face. Then, he saw the camera pan down to his scarred hands and the trigger was too much for him. He went back in time.

∞

Mark looked over and saw Check standing in the same place he had stood then.

A younger Mark set up at the eighteenth hole. It felt cold. A camera-man stood in front of the crowd, held back by ropes and course marshals. Pansies were blooming along the water's edge. Mark tried to focus. He could see the camera pan down to his hands, and he was embarrassed and afraid. He looked over at Check who nodded for him to hit the ball. Mark looked out over the fairway to the four- leaf clover shaped green five hundred yards away. Just one more hole and it would be over. The cameras would be gone. Just a few more shots.

He looked at Check.

He saw himself waggle. He looked down the fairway, went into his swing, and caught sight of movement of the television camera in his peripheral vision.

∞

Bob Tom nudged Mark's arm. Mark looked up. There were no pansies. It wasn't cold. Check was not there.

"You okay?" Bob Tom asked.

"Yeah, I, uh." Mark shook his head and felt the memory fade. He made a fist and grabbed onto the hand of the universe. He took a bottle of water and chugged it all.

Mark looked into the crowd at Merit and Yee, then he smiled at his mother, and turned back to Bob Tom. He looked over at Moustache and his gut started to clutch. He looked down at Moustache's shoes and smiled. Ugly shoes. He laughed, then sucked in a deep breath. His body responded and relaxed.

Mark put on his glove and Bob Tom handed him his driver. Due to the wind direction, Mark decided to go for the shorter approach to the left. It would require a two-hundred-and-seventy-yard carry over sand dunes and bunkers, but distance was his best asset, and he needed to use what he had. He visualized it in his mind. He tested the wind and compensated for it. He visualized the swing and saw the ball sail out and land on the fairway. He was ready to hit.

He looked over at the place where Check had stood so long ago and smiled in his heart.

He closed his eyes and felt his father place his hands over his on the grip.

Mark opened his eyes and stepped up to the eighteenth hole of the PGA Championship knowing it was his moment. This would define him for the rest of his life, and he knew that he had already won. He'd overcome his fear of failure, he'd acknowledged his father, thanks to Merit he'd become a damn good lover, and he'd overcome the challenge of his scarred hands. He'd done his personal best. Now, all he had to do was finish this hole and get his playing card.

He pulled back into the swing and let go. Whack!

The ball flew out over the fairway to the right and hung suspended in midair for what seemed minutes. It cleared the bunkers, then plopped on the downhill landing area and began to roll. It stopped just short of the sand dunes, smack in the middle of the fairway about two hundred yards from the green.

The crowd went wild. Merit caught his eye and gave him a wave. His entourage clapped enthusiastically as Mark headed down the fairway.

Mark used a short iron and popped his ball into position at the edge of the green. Mark had to get onto the green close enough to the hole to putt in two for par or better yet, one under in case his two opponents both made par.

Putting on this hole was terrifying. The green, with tricky undulations to negotiate, was the challenge. Mark had not been able to putt this hole in three on any of the prior days' play, and today, he desperately needed to get in the hole in two.

As the players walked to the green, Moustache and his cameraman moved near the eighteenth green in a huge bowl rimmed with grandstands. The Irish stone clubhouse loomed overhead. It was a spectacular television shot.

Moustache called the play, "The eighteenth hole is set for a great finale, Bart."

"Yes, it is, and it's anyone's game to win. Mark Green must be on pins and needles in this last putting situation. The crowd is really rooting for the kid here in his home state, but he's up against a couple of pros with vast experience under their belts."

Cameron took third place. Everyone except Mark and Highway had finished up and cleared the way leaving Mark and Highway to fight it out for fourth and fifth place. Mark needed fourth. Nothing less would get him into position for next year. It was do or die right here.

Mark's stomach clutched as he studied the lay of the green. From Mark's viewpoint, as he hunkered on bended knees, the green went up and then down to the right with a small slope just before the hole to the left. He needed to putt in the form of a half figure eight.

Highway was further out, so went first. His ball went within a foot of the cup and stopped. He groaned along with the crowd and marked his ball.

Mark knew Highway's second putt would put it in the cup moving him into fourth place. To beat him, Mark had to get in the hole in one putt, to claim his spot for next year's PGA tour. A near impossible task.

Fifth place was a miracle. It would be an honor to place fifth among these giants of golf, but Mark didn't want fifth, he wanted fourth, and he wanted his tour card. As much as anyone in the crowd would disagree, fifth was losing, fourth was a win.

Makeshift signs reading GO MARK began to pop up around the viewing area. Merit, Betty and Margaret held hands.

It all came down to one putt. Mark had worked with Yee on this situation over and over. He had improved during the last months, but he needed a miracle on this shot. He took his time. He visualized the ball going down the slope to the right, catching the hump in the green, then shifting back to the left. He felt his body move. He saw the ball go into the hole. He was ready.

Mark took his putter between his scarred hands and ignored the ache that was settling in after the long day. He adjusted his grip and moved his feet until he was in just the right spot. He pulled the club back, and gently, succinctly, and fluidly tapped the ball. It followed the slope to the right, hit the bump and began to curve back to the left, but the ball slowed and was barely moving toward the hole.

Had he tapped it too lightly? The crowd held their breath. The ball rolled to the edge of the hole and caught on the lip. The crowd groaned, and Mark stared in disbelief as the ball teetered on one thin blade of grass.

To his amazement, the grass finally gave under the weight of the ball and released it into the cup.

The crowd roared and applauded, and the commentators buzzed into their microphones.

Bob Tom grabbed Mark and squeezed.

Mark stood for a moment as the fourth-place win registered on his face and the moment became his, then jumped up and down waving the putter above his head.

Moustache was beside himself. "As far as the crowd is concerned, this game is over. Young Mark Green, coming from nowhere, has secured himself fourth place in this tournament, and a player's card on next year's PGA Tour."

Mark took his ball from the hole and held it up to the crowd, then walked over to the sidelines and gave it to Merit. He held her eyes in gratitude. Cousin Mac and Betty clapped him on the back. He kissed his mother on the cheek.

∞

Back at Austin Creek, Joe and Mark's friends and students cheered.

"He did it," Joe said proudly.

The youngsters did funky chicken dances and high fived.

∞

Dr. Hopkins, surrounded by cheering nurses and staff in white uniforms said, "Way to go, son!" through misty eyes.

∞

At Bomnskie's Tavern, Check's poker buddies cheered and lifted their glasses to the television set above the bar. The entire crowd broke out in applause and cheers, glad handing all around.

Mo called out, "Jack Daniels on the house."

∞

On the course, Mark listened to the applause. He swallowed a lump in his throat and pointed at David Yee. Yee took a small bow. Mark then pointed to Bob Tom who took his bow, then pointed back at Mark. The cheering hit a new high.

After celebration and congratulations, Mark went into the player's hut to sign his scorecard. The officials in colored jackets with badges congratulated him. So formal.

Other players shook Mark's hand and clapped him on the shoulder.

Mark emerged from the hut to find Moustache putting a microphone in his face and a dozen kids and beautiful young women asking for his autograph. Mark signed their programs, hats, and visors, then turned to Moustache.

Merit watched Mark with the fans.

He's come so far from that sweet boy new to town. He won't be lonely now.

She didn't know how she was going to tell him goodbye, but it would be okay. She smiled with pride at how far he'd come, and her role in it.

She smiled with satisfaction at herself. She'd made it through step one of the empty nest phase, changed the direction of her career, and helped some others along the way. She'd escaped death and found a new sense of herself. She was surrounded by people she loved. Life was good.

Merit pulled her attention back to Moustache and the television cameras ready to step in if needed.

"How does it feel, Mark," Moustache began in his announcer voice, "at your age to place in the top four in the PGA Championship?"

"It feels great. That last hole was a real challenge with the wind and all, but it worked out and I'm happy about it."

"Did you think Highway was going to pass you on that last one and take the fourth spot?"

"I felt pretty good coming onto eighteen, but I have to admit I was nervous. Thankfully, it worked out."

"I'll say. You'll have a spot on the PGA Tour next year. What are your plans?"

"To keep my team together. Bob Tom, my caddie and former boss," he smiled at Bob Tom. "David Yee, my coach, and Merit Bridges, my attorney and manager." Mark turned his shoulder with the Nano Mobile Phones and Tito's Vodka logos toward the camera, tipped his visor with the Fairway Golf Shoes logo, and smiled. He looked like a pro.

Merit watched with pride and touched the golf ball in her pocket.

No help needed.

Moustache moved on to interview Highway. Mark and Bob Tom headed toward the clubhouse. Merit stepped up to them and smiled. Bob Tom walked on to catch Betty and gave them a moment.

"Hey, golfboy."

"Hey, ladylawyer."

"Today, I'm Markfan. You did it."

"We did it. You, Bob Tom, Yee, all of us did it," Mark beamed.

"Yes."

"Yes, yes!" he responded.

"My favorite word," she said.

He looked into her eyes and smiled a sad smile. "I'm not going to see you tonight am I?"

"I'll be at the celebration. I wouldn't miss it," Merit said.

"But you won't be with me, will you?" Mark asked.

"Not that way," she said sadly. "We can talk about all this back in Austin. Enjoy your win, Mark."

"And back in Austin will you be with me?"

"Only with my clothes on," she said. "If you'll let me, I'll stay your attorney and manager, and I'll always be your biggest fan."

"That's not enough," Mark said.

"It's a lot, and you must have known things were changing," Merit said gently.

"I knew since Check died, but I guess I just didn't want to admit it. I need you on my side. I've still got a long way to go."

"I'm here. Remember our agreement?"

"I remember. When it ends, we stay friends."

"Right," Merit said.

"That might take me a little time," Mark said.

"Me too."

"We never did play golf," Mark touched her cheek.

"No, we didn't," she said.

Mark squeezed her hand. "Remember what I taught you."

"You, too," she smiled through misty eyes.

Merit let go of his hand. Mark walked toward the clubhouse, stopped, and turned to look back at her.

He smiled at the space where she was no longer standing.

Want a peek at Music Notes? Read on...

Chapter One

On a beautiful Texas spring day, Merit Bridges found herself in a situation she never thought she'd be - a fist fight. She wrestled against her attacker's six-foot frame and found herself overwhelmed by his strength. He grabbed her from behind with an arm around her shoulders. Merit spun free, ducked to avoid a punch to the face, and popped back up with a jab to his chin. He shook his head and steadied himself. Merit took advantage of his disorientation, grabbed him from behind in a bear hug with her legs around his waist and held his arms in place. He spun around and around until she lost her grip, detached and dropped to the ground. She hopped to her feet and swung. He blocked her jab, and punched her in the stomach. Merit lost her breath and doubled over. Her attacker laughed at the amazed look on her face.

"You hit me!" Merit said.

"You hit me," Mayor Taylor said.

Both held their red boxing gloves in the air proclaiming double victory and laughed out at the crowd of over fifty thousand. A banner above them displayed in huge red letters: TEXAS KNOCKOUT ILLITERACY!

"We're calling it a draw." Mayor Taylor said into the microphone. "Let me thank Merit Bridges, Austin attorney, fundraiser extraordinaire, and one of our favorite University of Texas Longhorns."

The crowd clapped as Merit made the Hook 'em Horns sign and joined Mayor Taylor at the microphone to address the audience. The sea of milling partiers spread from Barton Springs Road to Lady Bird Lake and covered almost every square foot of grass across the expanse known as Auditorium Shores in Austin, Texas. Attendees milled about between stages, lay on blankets in the grass, and perched in folding canvas chairs. They drank beer in recycled plastic cups and ate various types of food from barbecue sandwiches to food truck tacos to corn on the cob dripping with butter sauce.

Mayor Taylor and Merit bumped gloved fists, then she turned and spoke into the microphone.

"Thank you all for being here today and for supporting our three charities in the fifth annual music festival. Thanks to our sponsors, each of our musical performers, and the runners who participated in the 10K this morning. Last, but not least, thanks to Mayor Taylor for being our master of ceremonies and a really good sport."

The audience applauded and laughed. Television cameras zoomed in and drones snapped shots of the crowd from above. A small plane flew overhead trailing a banner proclaiming: TEXAS READS!

A second banner hung on the temporary fencing near the stage: Austin Charity Music Festival benefiting: Reading for the Blind & Dyslexic, Fresh Start for Kindergarten Readers, and Reading for the Incarcerated.

"Thank you Merit for chairing the event again this year. At last count, we've raised over one million dollars to be distributed among the three charities."

Merit stepped off the stage in her hot pink silk boxing shorts and white knee high socks. Her blonde ponytail swung from side to side as she climbed down the steps. Mayor Taylor, in black silks and 'The Old Pecan Street Cafe' t-shirt, continued to work the audience, also known as future voters. Merit kept an eye on the mayor as she entered the VIP tent to check on the next act, a five-piece rockabilly band out of East Austin called Killer Delight. She nodded at Valentine Berry Louis, her law clerk, who was also a volunteer, as he gathered the rock group in a corner and went over instructions from a clipboard.

Bo, the lead singer, looked at Merit from bottom to top. He stopped at her eyes and they held there for a brief moment until a gel neck-wrap noodle interrupted his gaze when it passed before Merit's face and broke the spell.

Ace, Merit's teenage son and only child, smiled his million-dollar smile and handed out gel neck-wraps and bottles of water from a silver Yeti cooler. Ace wore the official t-shirt for the event which showed the black bats flying out from under the Congress Avenue Bridge and turning into music notes.

"Saw the mayor kick your ass, Mom," Ace said.

"Yeah, watch your language, Peaches. Give me one of those. I'm about to boil in this heat," Merit said.

Ace playfully hit his mother on the shoulder with the wet cooling tube and laughed. She'd been a single mom for some time now and the closeness of their relationship showed in their playfulness.

Merit wrapped the gel noodle around her neck and downed half a bottle of water until it flowed over her chin and down the front of her shirt.

"Easy, Mom, you'll get sick," Ace said.

"Who's the parent here?" Merit laughed.

Ace was in town for the event from his school in Houston for dyslexic students. It was good to have him home and Merit beamed at him like the proud parent she was. Joy and Tucker, Merit's best friends in Houston, had driven Ace up for the event. It was great having a houseful of fun loving guests.

Merit had been working on the festival committee for several years and had been an advocate for literacy since she'd discovered Ace's learning disability when he was in fifth grade.

A thin young man with purple hair walked toward Merit and Ace. Purple Hair looked like every other band member in the VIP tent - baggy jeans, t-shirt, no belt. Merit's armpits prickled ever so slightly. This visceral indicator of danger or intuition alert had been with her since she was a child. At this moment, she wasn't sure if something was up or if the Texas heat was giving her a heat rash. As Purple Hair got closer she saw that his clothes were dirty and his hair needed washing.

Ag, a tall, cool drink of water, with the kind of eyelashes women spent time and money to buy, stepped between Purple Hair and Merit.

"Where's your badge?" Ag Malone asked.

"I'm with the band," Purple Hair said.

"I don't think so," Ag said.

"I just want to talk to Ms. Bridges," Purple Hair said.

"You can't be in here without a VIP badge. Security reasons. You'll have to leave." Ag said as he escorted the interloper by his elbow to the nearest exit.

Merit was glad that Albert "Ag" Malone was doing his job. Ag was her private investigator for the Law Office of Merit Bridges, and coordinating security for the VIP portion of the festival. He wore his standard maroon shirt and jeans, a uniform of sorts for him, which showed his allegiance to Texas A&M University, his alma mater. Ag was long and lean with a quiet demeanor that was mysterious and attractive.

After Ag had ejected Purple Hair, Merit signaled to Val.

"The mayor is wrapping it up. Let's get Killer Delight up on stage as soon as he's finished," Merit said.

"All set," Val said and moved the band over by the stage entry ramp. He appeared almost too thin as he adjusted his vintage Tom Selleck type shorts and cropped Liberty Lunch retro t-shirt.

The crowd caught a peek through the tent opening at Bo Harding, the lead singer, and let out a roar.

On stage, Mayor Taylor got the hint as Merit moved back up the ramp toward him. Killer Delight held at the bottom of the stairs and the crowd roared again.

"Thank you all once more for your support this year for our very worthy charities. I'll now turn the mic over to Merit Bridges," Mayor Taylor said.

Merit stepped up to the microphone and raised her hand.

"Thank you all again for being here," Merit said. "We'll end the event with a killer local band that really needs no introduction. Without further ado, here is the band you've all been waiting for, Killer Delight!"

The audience surged toward the barriers in front of the bandstand and attendees moved away from the other four stages around the lake and toward the main stage to see the lead act of the event and the hottest band in Austin.

Purple Hair tried to go against the crowd, was pushed about and fell. Several attendees helped him up and he worked his way toward the main exit on Barton Springs Road.

∞

Red Thallon stood in the center of the festival crowd with microphone in hand. Her gimme cap had the Austin9Online logo on it. She continued her interview with a young woman with a large tattooed curl of barbed wire climbing out of her blouse and wrapping around her neck.

"Are you enjoying the festival?" Red asked.

"Loving it," said the young woman.

"How many acts have you been able to watch?" Red asked.

"I've seen six so far today including Solange, Erica Badu, and the Derailers. I'm looking forward to Killer Delight," the young woman said and pointed to the main stage.

The crowd roared as Killer Delight tuned up with a familiar chord and Red had to yell into the microphone to be heard.

"Thanks for stopping to chat," Red said and turned full face to the camera. "Catch us tonight on Austin9Online and at ten on KNEW nightly news. We'll have live interviews with Bob Schneider and Kevin Price. For now, let's have a listen to Killer Delight."

The camera panned the cheering crowd and moved toward the stage settling on a close-up of Bo Harding. The tall muscular rock star was wearing denim shirt and pants plus a pair of red leather and rhinestone cowboy boots. He shook back his long dark blonde hair and struck a strong riff on his guitar. The audience went wild again, and the concert began.

∞

After Killer Delight had finished their set and the crowds had dispersed, Merit and Val sorted out the aftermath in the VIP tent and looked around for any remaining volunteers to help.

Liam Nolan, an aging, long-haired, tanned faced guitarist with a purple guitar pick in the band of his tan straw cowboy hat stood outside the flap of the VIP tent. He put out a cigarette and chugged down a bottle of water. He looked like a worn-out rock star that some people thought they recognized but weren't sure from where. The seasoned music lovers knew him, of course. He was trying to redeem himself for years of alcoholism and drug abuse by giving back at the festival. His Narcotics Anonymous sponsor constantly reminded him that the twelve steps ended with service.

"Liam, if you're up for it, let's open all the flaps and let in the roadies." Val said.

"Glad to help," Liam said.

Merit saw Bo Harding and other members of Killer Delight walk over and shake Liam's hand.

"I grew up on your music, man," Bo said. "It got me through some rough times."

"Hey, thanks," Liam said and bumped fists with Bo.

"I saw your act at Stubb's once. Great show," Bo said.

"Those were good times," Liam said.

"If you ever decide to start writing songs again, keep me in mind. I love a good lyric," Bo said.

Merit had been helping Liam sort out his business affairs and put his financial life in order again. It was a slow process. Val was assisting by chronicling Liam's portfolio of songs from years of writing. Some had sold and some were still in old dust covered suitcases and boxes in her conference room.

"Just a minute Bo. Val, do I have anything left to sell?" Liam grinned.

Merit smiled and kept sorting through leftover t-shirts with Ace.

Val laughed. Merit knew he would never answer such a question even in jest if he wanted to continue to work in the law office. Confidentiality was her first rule for her staff. Integrity was her first rule for herself.

Merit recalled that while cataloguing and organizing Liam's songs, she and Val had discovered and hummed new tunes on the list that they recognized. They were surprised again and again that Liam had authored the songs that were part of the emerging portfolio.

Liam was the real deal. How he wound up barely surviving and in NA meetings every day was a story he didn't share with many except Merit. He had finally gotten control of his life. Liam's future was in his hands, or so he thought.

Chapter Two

Liam sat at the edge of Lady Bird Lake near the statue of Stevie Ray Vaughan at four-thirty in the morning. The crowds had long cleared from the festival and the city was settled for the night. The ember from his cigarette glowed in the pre-dawn light. He looked at the skyline of Austin reflected in the dark water with his Fender Stratocaster nestled in its case at his feet.

After the festival, he'd sat in on a set with some old classic Austin musicians at the Saxon Pub before finding his way back to the lake. He ran his hands over the guitar case and thought of the horn shape that gave the axe its balance and distinctive look. It was his favorite possession and one of the few he had not pawned or sold to cover his former habit. His addiction to various drugs culminating in Fentanyl had cost him everything except his life and one remaining Strat. Fortunately, he got into recovery before he could sell his entire portfolio of music. There were huge gaps in his memory and millions of dollars lost who knew where. With no family and a loveless bed, he was lonely but increasingly hopeful. His NA sponsor and a few remaining friends, including Merit, were a big support for him and taking life one day at a time helped him to manage his life in small bLiam watched two teenagers with handheld controllers work their way down to the water's edge flying their drones over the lake and then under the bridges that crossed over the water at regular intervals.

Liam twirled a purple guitar pick between his fingers. It had a series of quarter notes on one side and L.N. on the other side. He thought of it as his business card. It was his signature gift to fans, and his talisman when he wanted a cool way to introduce himself.

He heard bits of conversation as the skinny male teens passed a joint back and forth. They laughed and played with their flying toys that looked like four legged spiders.

"Great light," said the first teen with ginger colored hair.

"Magic hour," said the other teen, sporting a mouth full of metal braces.

"Here come the cops."

"Throw the roach in the water."

Two extremely fit policemen on bicycles rode along the shoreline and spun gravel when they stopped beside the teens. Their uniforms were navy blue with shorts in lieu of long pants and they both had Blueguns tasers on their duty belts instead of a gun. Their bicycles were fitted with saddlebags holding first aid equipment.

"What are you two doing out here at this hour?" the older policeman said.

"We're capturing the light, officer," ginger teen said.

"Right," said the younger policeman sniffing the air.

"You have a license for that drone?" the older policeman said.

"No sir. I'm just taking pics for fun. No commercial use," ginger teen said.

"We don't need a license," braces teen said and giggled.

The two policemen looked at each other and appeared to make a non-verbal decision.

"Wrap it up and get on out of here." The younger policeman said.

"Yes, sir," ginger teen said.

The policemen rode on through the area, nodded at Liam, crossed over the bridge and then patrolled the other side of the lake. There was little activity, but the water's edge was never totally quiet in Austin.

Liam played the lyrics of a new song over and over in his mind. He smelled the wet earth at the edge of the water, listed the Twelve Steps in his mind, and lingered on gratitude. He felt light and unburdened now that he was finally turning his life around. He was grateful to be alive. Maybe he would write a song for Killer Delight, earn some money, and make a comeback. Possibly perform at Antone's or Guero's again. Maybe he'd meet a nice woman. Why not? Everything was possible again.

∞

Liam got up, picked up his Strat, and walked along the lake on the hike and bike trail toward home. As he dropped down under the First Street Bridge, he looked up from his dreamy state to see a Pursuer coming toward him. The Pursuer was slight in stature, but backlit by the bridge and Liam could only see an outline.

"Hey, Liam," the Pursuer said.

"Hey. Who's there?" Liam asked.

"Don't you know who I am?" the Pursuer asked.

The voice sounded familiar. The Pursuer continued toward Liam until they were close enough for Liam to recognize the face.

"What are you doing here at this hour?" Liam asked.

"Looking for you. I followed you from the Saxon Pub."

"Well you found me. What do you want? I told you I have nothing for you," Liam said.

"Don't be that way. Let me buy you a cup of coffee. I want to talk to you," the Pursuer said.

"I don't want coffee and I don't want to talk to you. Leave me alone," Liam said and turned to go.

"Don't turn your back on me again!"

The Pursuer looked around and picked up a large rock from beside the path. Liam felt movement behind him. As he turned back, he felt a strong blow between his neck and skull. He fell, dropped his guitar case, then struggled to get up.

"You, asshole," Liam said.

As Liam pushed himself up from the ground, the Pursuer grabbed the guitar case and slammed it into Liam's head. Liam fell to the ground again and the Pursuer hit him with the case over and over until the latches broke and the case flew open, sending the Strat spiraling into the water.

Liam looked up to see the Pursuer freeze, blink, and begin to shake. A hand reached down by the dying face and gathered up the case handle and rock, and put them inside the broken case. The Pursuer ran along the trees and out of the park with the case. Liam's blood spread out over the trail, pooled at the grassy edge, and finally spilled over into the dark water.

No one came to help poor Liam or see the face of his killer. Dozens of purple guitar picks lay strewn along the water's edge.

About the Author

Manning Wolfe, an author and attorney residing in Austin, Texas, writes cinematic-style, smart, fast-paced thrillers with a salting of Texas bullshit. Her award-winning series features feisty Austin attorney Merit Bridges.

Manning is a graduate of Rice University and the University of Texas School of Law. Each of her novels springs from a real-life case in her law firm. Her experience has given her a voyeur's peek into some shady characters' lives and a front row seat to watch the good people who stand against them.

Other Books in the Merit Bridges Legal thriller Series:

Dollar Signs
Music Notes

FOLLOW THE TEXAS LADY LAWYER GANG AND RECEIVE A FREE GIFT!

If you enjoyed Merit, Betty, Ag, and the whole Texas Lady Lawyer Gang, get notifications of their adventures and receive a free gift at: http://manningwolfe.com/free-cookbook/

You will also be notified of contests, drawings, and giveaways of free Kindles, Gift Cards, and Texas Lady Lawyer souvenirs.

www.manningwolfe.com

LEAVE A REVIEW

If you enjoyed this book, please leave a **REVIEW** on Amazon or Goodreads. Reviews are the lifeblood of authors and often determine whether other readers purchase books when they shop. Thank you.

9 781944 225087